THE SCENT OF
ROSA'S OIL

THE SCENT OF ROSA'S OIL

LINA SIMONI

KENSINGTON BOOKS
http://www.kensingtonbooks.com

This book is a work of fiction. All characters in this story are fictional. Any reference or resemblance to individuals either living or dead is strictly a coincidence.

KENSINGTON BOOKS are published by

Kensington Publishing Corp.
850 Third Avenue
New York, NY 10022

ISBN-13: 978-0-7582-1924-4
ISBN-10: 0-7582-1924-5

First Kensington Trade Paperback Printing: January 2008
10 9 8 7 6 5 4 3 2 1

Printed in the United States of America

To my son
To my land

CHAPTER I

Genoa, 1910

Madam C was combing Rosa's hair when a stray gust of wind forced its way into the *caruggi,* the old downtown streets, passage-ways so narrow sunlight hardly reached below the level of the rooftops. The three panes of the front window of the Luna, the brothel Madam C had owned for nineteen years, shook lightly under the wind's attack. Set deep in the labyrinth of the *caruggi,* five blocks from the harbor, halfway down Vico del Pepe, the Luna spread over three floors of an ancient building of slate and stone that had withstood wars, storms, and the furtive erosion of sea salt. Inside, on the first floor, eight feet from the window, Rosa was seated on a stool in the corner of the dimly lit parlor, her thick, curly crimson hair loose down her torso and her neck bent slightly backward. Behind her, a wide-tooth comb in hand, stood Madam C, long-boned and slender, wearing a loose robe of pale yellow silk tied softly around her waist with a sash. Her hair, raven, with only sparse, barely visible threads of gray, was gathered in two braids rolled about her ears and fastened at the top of her head with a pearl clip. Free of makeup, her eyes had no glow. She sank the comb into Rosa's curls and gently pulled down. "Ouch!" Rosa yelped.

"Be patient, Princess Rosa," said Margherita, one of the nine Luna girls. She was ensconced in an armchair at the opposite corner of the parlor, near the front door, slowly turning the pages of an oversized, leather-bound book. She lifted her eyes for a moment, sniffed the air, then shook her head and resumed her reading.

"Rosa's hair is such a jungle," Madam C said. "And the more I comb it, the more entangled it gets."

"You say that every time." Rosa giggled.

"Your curls have a life of their own," Madam C continued. "We all know what happened on that Sunday I decided to trim them."

Rosa's first and only haircut had become a legend at the Luna and one of Madam C's favorite anecdotes about Rosa's life. She'd tell that story whenever a new girl arrived, on birthdays and anniversaries, and every time someone stared at Rosa's curls in awe. Rosa was born bald, the story went, with a smooth, healthy scalp that shone like a rainbow in the sunlight, and stayed bald for two months before her hair started to grow at an amazing speed. By the time she was eight months old, Rosa had a headful of rebellious red curls. By her first birthday the curls reached below her shoulder blades. On a quiet Sunday morning, while all the Luna girls were still asleep on the second floor, Madam C sat a cheerful, smiling Rosa on one of the parlor armchairs and took a pair of large scissors out of a drawer. "Here we go, little Rosa," she chanted. "We'll make you so beautiful no one will be able to stop looking at you." And then, she cut five centimeters off a strand of Rosa's hair. At once Rosa began to scream. She screamed, and screamed, and screamed, louder than she had ever screamed before. Awakened by the shouts, several girls came running down the stairs to find Madam C standing like a statue, openmouthed, a lock of red hair in one hand, the scissors in the other. Rosa was still screaming. "You poor child,"

Esmeralda said, picking up Rosa and patting her on the shoulders.

"She looks awful," Madam C noted. "We must finish this haircut, one way or another."

"I'll hold her in my arms," Esmeralda said, noticing that Rosa had calmed down. "You go ahead."

At that, Madam C cut a second strand of hair. Rosa let out a screech so loud the girls cupped their hands over their ears and grimaced at each other.

"It took three girls to hold Rosa down," Madam C said the first time she told someone the story. "It took the strength of five girls to keep Rosa from bouncing all over," she said on a following occasion. In the third version, all nine girls were on top of Rosa while Madam C completed the haircut amidst the child's heart-wrenching screams. "We'll let this hair grow as long as it wants to," Madam C told the Luna girls when finally Rosa's hair was all even. "Obviously Rosa can feel it, like a skin." The hair stopped growing when it reached Rosa's waist. With monumental patience, Madam C had been untangling it once a week ever since.

"Almost there," Madam C said, noticing Rosa's edgy motions on the stool, then suddenly lowered the comb and scrunched her nose. She said, "What is this odor?"

"I thought I smelled something a moment ago," Margherita said, without lifting her eyes from the pages, "but I can't smell it now."

Madam C said, "Come here."

Unhurriedly, Margherita closed the book and set it gently on the floor. It was a book of poetry. Its beige parchment pages contained a collection of famous love poems Margherita had copied in her best handwriting over the years. There were twenty of Petrarca's sonnets from *Il Canzoniere*, passages of Dante's *Para-*

diso where Beatrice appeared, the poem Giacomo Leopardi had written for his Silvia, and many more.

Born into a middle-class family, Margherita had discovered poetry by accident in her late teens, on a Saturday afternoon, while she was strolling along a tree-lined street with her aunt Genia, the austere older sister of her father. At a certain point, Margherita and Aunt Genia came across a man who stood on a bench, reciting words from a booklet in the direction of a closed window. Margherita stopped and listened, moonstruck by the sounds, entranced by the rhythms of the man's voice. Shyly, when the man stopped talking, Margherita asked him what those words he had recited were, and the man explained that they were ancient love poems written by Francesco Petrarca out of love for a woman named Laura. "There's a maiden behind that closed window," he added, pointing up. "I tried everything to win her heart—presents, flowers, music. Nothing worked. Poetry is my last resort."

The following day, at the end of Mass, Margherita approached Father Marcello, the sixty-year-old priest who had administered her first Communion and assisted her during her confirmation. "Are there any books of poetry in the church library?" she asked.

Father Marcello couldn't hide his surprise. "You don't know how to read," he said. "What would you do with poetry books?"

"I'd like to be able to read them someday, Father. And write, too. Will you teach me? Please?"

Her reading lessons with Father Marcello began the next day, without her father's or Aunt Genia's knowledge, both of them convinced that the purpose of Margherita's daily church visits was to pray. It wasn't long before Margherita, a fast and disciplined learner, thirsty for the sounds of the poems, was able to sit in the church library and read. She had Father Marcello point out to her the books of poetry and devoured them with the passion of a scholar. The meaning of the verses she read, however, was obscure. "I'll be glad to help you with the interpretation," Father Marcello told her, "as long as you help me play a special game." To explain the game, Father Marcello grazed her neck and breasts with his fingers several times.

Aunt Genia walked into the library one day while Father Marcello had Margherita on his lap and his hands under her skirt. The poetry books were open on the table in front of them, and Father Marcello was reading verses aloud while Margherita, still as a statue, stared at the written words with empty eyes. Without a word, Aunt Genia grabbed Margherita by the collar and took her home. "Get out of my house!" yelled Margherita's father once Aunt Genia had explained the situation to him. "Seducing a priest? Our family is disgraced!"

It would take Margherita years to rid herself of the memories of the priest and her unforgiving father. Her love for poetry remained, together with another heritage of her church days: in the peace of the centuries-old library, breathing the pungent perfumes of incense and burning candles, she had learned to associate a man's touch and display of pleasure with the words of illustrious poets. She could never undo that association. At the Luna, before undressing, she read twelve lines of poetry to her clients. The only place where she could read or write poetry was the brothel. Some of the Luna clients avoided her; others were bewitched. Those who were bewitched loved her routine: she kept incense and candles burning in her room; she had the man lie on the bed fully clothed and with his eyes closed; she sat on the floor, by the bed, her leather-bound book open to a chosen page. Then she read, and as she slowly whispered the twelfth line, she ran a soft hand over the man's mouth.

That afternoon in the parlor Margherita had been choosing the poetry she would read later on, during that night's celebration. She stood up and walked toward Madam C, realizing only then that she had smelled an unusual fragrance herself, all day long, in various rooms of the Luna. Meanwhile, a second Luna girl, Stella, appeared at the top of the stairs, her only clothing a shiny blue petticoat. She came down in lazy steps, dragging her feet. "Someone woke up," Rosa said, glancing at Stella from the stool.

"Barely," Stella yawned as she reached the parlor and headed for the counter at the north wall. She poured anisette in a stemmed glass, then dipped her lips in the liquor and grazed them with the tip of her tongue.

"Don't you two smell a strange odor in this room?" Madam C asked.

Margherita shrugged. "Maybe."

"It must be the wind," Stella said, setting her elbows on the counter and her chin on her cupped hands. The wind had been blowing since dawn, steadily with sudden gusts, as it often does along the coast of Liguria, enraging the sea and coating the streets with dampness. It was a southwesterly wind, the *libeccio*.

"The *libeccio* smells like wet paper," Madam C said, shaking her head. "This odor reminds me of apples."

Stella spoke in the grave voice she reserved for her worst omens. "When the *libeccio* blows, bad things happen."

Madam C shook her head again. "You and your superstitions."

"Scoff all you want," Stella said. "That's the way it is."

By the window, Margherita pushed aside the flowered curtain that hid the parlor from the street. "The *libeccio* blows for three days," she said, looking outside, "and drives everyone crazy."

"This hair is driving me crazy," Madam C said, pulling down the comb stuck in Rosa's hair.

"Ouch!" Rosa yelped again.

"Don't complain, Princess Rosa," Margherita said with a smile. "It's your big day. I can't believe you're sixteen!"

"Does that mean you're going to treat me like a woman?"

Rosa asked, straightening her neck and stretching her legs to touch the floor.

Madam C slapped her softly on the head. "No."

Smoothly, Rosa stood up and twirled around, making a pinwheel of her topaz-colored pleated skirt of gabardine. "Look at me. Do I look like a child?"

Rosa had looked nothing like a child for the past eight months. At the onset of fall, as the haze of summer had faded, letting in clearer and crisper air, her breasts had sprouted in a hurry, putting to test her corsets; her torso had taken the shape of an hourglass; her facial features had softened; and her slate-blue eyes had turned aquamarine. Everyone had caught sight of Rosa's changes: Madam C, the Luna girls, and the men and women in the street, who had begun to take notice of Rosa when she walked by. No one had ever spoken of those changes on any occasion. As for Rosa, it was common belief at the Luna that she had only vague notions of her body. They had explained to her when she was little that what men and women did at the Luna was a game, like the one the Romero kids played with three cards out in the street, except that at the Luna the girls were much smarter than the boys and the boys always lost their bets. No one had ever revised that explanation.

"No," Margherita said. "You don't look like a child today."

"Well, then," Rosa said, "let me do it."

Madam C looked at her with hard eyes. "We went over this already, and the answer is no."

With a pout, Rosa sat back on the stool.

"There goes that smell again," Madam C said, sniffing around. She placed her nose on Rosa's hair. "Is that you, Rosa?"

Hands on her hips, Rosa said, "Maybe."

Stella came over from the counter, and she and Margherita sniffed Rosa's hair three times. "I think it *is* Rosa," Stella said after a moment. "How did you get this smell on you?"

"I'll tell you if you let me do it," Rosa said, looking Stella in the eyes.

Margherita rolled her eyes to the ceiling. "How did she get so stubborn?"

Rosa shrugged.

"She didn't take after her mother," said Madam C. "Angela was a sweetheart."

"Then she must have taken after her father," Stella stated with a half smile.

Pursing her lips, Madam C gave Stella a stare. "Who has the guest list for tonight?" she asked.

"I bet her father was a sailor," Margherita said with dreamy eyes, "who fought storms and sharks and giant whales, and that's why she's so stubborn."

Stella pushed up Rosa's chin with her index finger. "No way. With this delicate profile, I bet Rosa's father was a prince. Well, a marquis at least. British."

"A British marquis? Don't get your hopes high, girl," said a laughing Maddalena, the latest addition to the Luna, walking in from the street with a rectangular cardboard box kept closed by a ribbon of pink organzine. "With that shine on your skin and that crazy hair of yours, you have Gypsy blood, like me." Turning to Madam C, she added, "And there's a man outside, who wants to come in."

"Not today," Madam C said, reaching for a piece of paper with the words *Closed for Private Party* written on it. "Hang this on the door, Maddalena, and send him away." She stood still in the middle of the parlor. "This odor . . ."

"He was a British marquis," Stella said. "I know it."

"Let's drop the topic, please," Madam C ordered in a dry voice. "Get the rest of the girls down here." She clapped her hands. "Let's go."

Stella didn't move. "It's not a good day for Rosa's birthday party."

Everybody said, "Why?"

"It's Friday," Stella explained, "and last night I had a bad dream."

"Enough of this witch talk!" Madam C snapped, raising her voice.

Rosa stood up and bowed. "We're having the party, and my father was a British marquis who sailed around the world and then joined the Gypsies. Happy?"

She had spoken jokingly, but with a tinge of sadness in her eyes. The discussions about her father were not forbidden in that house, though they were normally carried out upstairs, in the girls' rooms and the corridor, and never when Madam C was in sight. But on that day of mid-April, between the bewitching howls of the *libeccio* and the excitement for the upcoming party, the tongues of the Luna girls were restless.

"What you call witch talk," Stella said, "is mere precaution. Dreams come for a reason. And in my dream there were dead goats and a house on fire."

"What does that mean?" Rosa asked.

"Goats represent prosperity," Stella explained. "And a house is a place where people come together. A house on fire is a sign of hatred."

"I don't hate anybody," Rosa said with a smile. She turned to Madam C. "But if you keep hurting me with that comb . . ."

Madam C dipped her fingers in Rosa's hair and fluffed it twice. "All done, dear. And don't you worry about Stella's goats. You'll have a prosperous life, and we all love you to pieces."

"Any last minute birthday wishes?" Margherita asked.

Rosa shook her head, wishing quietly and with all her heart that Angela were there, to help her with the party and be the one to comb and fluff her hair. "How can you love so much someone you've never met?" she had asked Maddalena earlier that day.

"Love is strange, dear," Maddalena had replied. "The elders

in my family used to say it's a Gypsy spirit that wanders endlessly about the earth touching people's hearts as it passes by. True or not, it's a fact that love can play major tricks with your head. But you shouldn't worry about loving Angela, because we all know that she loved you madly before you were born."

"Sometimes I can feel her next to me," Rosa had added. "I talk to her as if she were in the room."

"Maybe she *is* in the room with you," Maddalena had whispered. "We don't really know what happens to people after they die."

Rosa had nodded. She never told Maddalena or anyone else inside or outside the Luna that at night she often dreamed of being in a warm darkness inside Angela's womb, feeling her movements and hearing the sound of her voice. And then she started kicking and elbowing her way out of the darkness, until she felt heat on her face and saw a ray of sunshine. To Rosa, the story of Angela's life and of how she had given birth to her child was like a fairy tale. She was certain she didn't have all the details. Madam C had told her portions of the story, and in the rooms of the Luna, over the years, Rosa had overheard other bits and pieces. In any case, for whatever reason, Rosa had grown up feeling that her mother was always by her side.

There had been no heat or sunshine on the day Rosa was born. It was 1894, a gray and cold spring day, rare in that region of Italy known for its temperate climate and clear, sunny skies. Madam C and her girls had waited on the second floor of the Luna, in the hallway outside the corner bedroom, for Angela to give birth with the help of a midwife. They heard the moans and the screams, the midwife's orders to push and not to push, and then the loudest scream of all followed by the squeaks of the newborn. A moment later, the midwife came out of the bedroom, holding the little bundle that would be Rosa. It wasn't a happy event, by any means. Angela died three days later because of an infection that spread fast and uncontrolled through her abused body. Like Madam C, she had been a prostitute most of her adult life and had no family or friends other than Madam C and the girls who worked at the Luna. So was it that Madam C, who was not fond of children and had sworn many times she wouldn't raise one, nevertheless found herself a mother. She did the best she could under the circumstances: she named the child after Angela's favorite color; for Rosa, she set aside a room at the Luna on the first floor, in the back, behind the kitchen, as far away as possible from the parlor and the rooms where the girls worked with the clients; she devoted a significant portion of her free time to play with Rosa; and every evening she sat by Rosa's bed and sang her to sleep. She owed it to Angela, and, to paraphrase her, there was nothing else to say.

Angela and Madam C went back a long time. They had been born one year apart in the same shabby building on Vico Caprettari, Angela the only child of a single mother, Madam C, Clotilde in those days, the only daughter in a family of seven: her mother, her father, Clotilde, and four loud boys. She was the youngest child. Vico Caprettari was a *caruggio* few people knew beyond those who had family there and those who called it home. It was dark, narrow, and impregnated with the smells of seaweed, garbage, and *minestrone*. It was a world apart, with tall buildings stuck to each other to mark its boundaries, ensuring that the world of the neighboring streets would not seep over.

Clotilde's family lived in three rooms on the seventh floor, with stairs so steep and narrow Clotilde's father, a tall, strong man with shoulders much wider than his waist, had to climb sideways, and the younger children had to climb on all fours or they wouldn't reach the steps. Angela and her mother had one room on the first floor, darker than a manhole. As a child, Angela used to hang out with Clotilde and her siblings in the dirty street, chasing pigeons. None of them went to school. One after the other, as soon as they were strong enough to lift, the boys went to work with their father in one of the warehouses by the docks; the girls were not educated, period. Angela's mother was a seamstress, and she had done that for so long in that dark room on the first floor that her eyes were failing. When Angela was old enough to find her way around the maze of the *caruggi*, about seven, she made pickups and deliveries of clothes, sheets, and bedspreads for her mother. The rest of the time, she sat quietly next to her and watched those swift hands push the needle in and out of hems and buttonholes. At eight, Angela did her first repair all by herself: a white linen sheet, thin and torn in the middle, where someone's body had been lying at night for years. As she mended, she thought she would meet this person someday, certainly a fat woman, and she would tell her to her face, "I know what you did to that sheet with your big behind."

Meanwhile, on the seventh floor, Clotilde and her mother worked around the clock to keep their men fed and clean. They scrubbed, cooked, washed, ironed, and made beds. With all their chores, Angela and Clotilde had little time to spend together, but when they managed to do so, it was the best part of their day. Sometimes Clotilde helped Angela deliver the mended pieces; sometimes Angela accompanied Clotilde to the fountain to wash clothes. They always talked about their dreams: Angela, of the store she'd open in Via Luccoli some day, where beautiful rich ladies would have their Sunday dresses made to measure; Clotilde, of the trip she'd take on the back of a white horse on her eighteenth birthday, up and down the hills, to see the world.

Clotilde's father had his own ideas about Angela and her mother and voiced them often and openly in front of his family at dinnertime. Who was that Angela, anyway, he'd mumble, dipping his bread in pasta sauce, who lived in that hole down below, and what kind of family was that without a man to give it respectability? And who knows who Angela's father was to begin with, possibly a drunken sailor, but there was no point asking that question, was there, because no one knew the answer, not even Angela's mother, who these days, with those tiny crossed eyes, looked more and more like a mole. Plus, who knew what was going on in that dark room when Angela was out, he'd continue, and in any case, even if nothing happened any more, surely those two females were no good for Clotilde, the daughter of a warehouse shift leader, respected by all and strong like a mountain. Clotilde's heart sank when her father spoke of Angela that way, but she was careful not to show her tears, which she pushed hard down her throat, as she knew better than to contradict her father, especially after he had stopped at Lorenzo's, the neighborhood bar, on the way home. Her mother had talked back to him one evening, over a bowl of soup that wasn't warm enough, and the little blue scar across her lip was there to remind everyone who was in charge.

A father's words, no matter how silly or mean, do make an impression on a daughter, so eventually the talk about Angela and her mother convinced Clotilde that she deserved better friends than the daughter of an unknown drunken sailor. Unconsciously, she began to avoid Angela in her outings, until the girls became estranged. So estranged, in fact, that years went by without Angela and Clotilde exchanging words. It took Clotilde a long time to realize that Angela no longer lived downstairs.

Clotilde's family fell apart suddenly when Clotilde was sixteen. Her mother died of consumption, and her father began spending more time at Lorenzo's than at the warehouse, until he could hardly stand up and finally got himself fired. He walked out of Vico Caprettari one morning, cursing his fate, and never came back. Clotilde was left alone with her brothers, who hardly talked to her at all. When they did, it was only to give her orders for a meal or ask for clean clothes. Her routine became more strenuous, as there was now one woman to take care of four men instead of two women to take care of five; her mother's absence made the routine unbearable. The two of them had talked, laughed, joked. The days went by before Clotilde knew it. Now her days felt longer than seasons. When finally night fell, Clotilde prayed to God to take her so she could be with her mother again and have a laugh once in a while. There was never a reason to laugh now that she was all alone. And she wished that Angela were still living on the first floor, so she'd have someone to talk to, not just her four brothers who ordered her around like a mule.

On a sunny spring day that made even the darkest of the *caruggi* come alive, Clotilde went to the Sottoripa market to buy fruit. On the way back, she crossed paths with a beautiful, elegant, tall woman with long wavy cinnamon hair falling on her shoulders beneath a beige satin-brimmed hat. Her dress, a perfect match to the hat in color and material, glimmered under the sunlight and fit her body like a glove. Clotilde stopped walking and stared at the woman as she passed by. In front of Clotilde, the woman stopped and smiled. "You don't recognize me, do you? I can't blame you. I've changed." It was then that Clotilde realized that the elegant woman was Angela. "You haven't changed," Angela continued. "I've thought of you many times."

Clotilde spoke with a thread of voice. "I've thought of you, too. What happened?"

"Come along," Angela said, taking Clotilde's hand. "I'll tell you everything."

They went to Angela's home, a spacious two-room apartment on the top floor of a white and gray building, with high vaulted ceilings and a tall window off the sitting room overlooking the port. The contrast to the dark room on Vico Caprettari couldn't have been starker. "This is it," Angela said. "My private palace. Bright and airy, for a change." She opened the window, and Clotilde stood by it a few moments, blinded by the brilliance of the sea, inhaling the sharp, familiar odors of salt and weeds, lost in the multitude of sounds that rose in waves from the docks. "It's beautiful here," she said, taking a seat next to Angela on a worn-out couch. Angela nodded, then explained that the reason she could afford the place was that she had found a way to make good money with little effort, and she had done that for a couple of years now, since her mother had gone blind and moved in with her sister in the Lerici countryside. "And what about you?" she asked.

Clotilde summarized her life in two sentences, then inquired about the way to make good money with little effort, asking if there was a chance that she could do that, too. As Angela went on explaining, Clotilde understood what the way was and told Angela she was happy to have met her that day but now she had to go, and, no, she wasn't interested in that way at all. True, she added, it was a bad life to be serving her brothers day and night, but at least she wouldn't be going to hell after her death, which would be coming soon, as she couldn't keep living like this much longer.

"It's not as bad as you think," Angela replied. "And you don't go to hell for this. You go to hell if you do things that hurt other people. I make men happy." She paused and cocked her head. "For a fee." She stared at Clotilde. "What's wrong with that?"

Clotilde was out of arguments against the way.

"Come with me tonight," Angela said. "You don't have to do anything. Just watch me. Then decide. Can't make a decision without knowing, can you?"

Clotilde couldn't find an argument against that, either.

"Look at my clothes," Angela said, showing Clotilde to her closet. "I buy the cloth at the market and then I cut and sew. For myself. Which is so much better than that silly idea I had of opening a store and making dresses for other people. I'll make you a dress—what am I saying—three dresses of your favorite colors. For tonight," she said, rummaging in the closet, "you can borrow this." It was a dress of pale yellow muslin, with little glass beads along the hem and the neckline.

"Me?" Clotilde said, pointing a finger at herself. "Wearing that dress? I couldn't. Look at me. My hair is wild, my hands are rough."

"We have time," Angela insisted, hanging the dress back in the closet. "Come with me." It took them a few hours of scrubbing, drying, and styling. Then Clotilde wore the yellow dress and a pair of shoes with heels and a golden buckle she had seen before only in her dreams. Angela pinned a yellow cloth flower to her hair, dabbed some powder on her cheekbones, and took her downstairs, so she could see herself in the windows of the furniture store across the street. "I guess you won't be going horseback riding on the hills any time soon," Angela said with a naughty smile as Clotilde stared at the image of a woman she didn't know. She stood still a moment, then turned around and shook her head to make her black hair bounce. Hands on her waist, she took two steps back, then two steps forward, and bowed at her reflection in the dusty glass. Angela laughed. "You're on your way to heaven, darling. Forget hell."

That night they went to a bar by the port, the Stella Maris, a pickup place for prostitutes who worked illegally out of the brothels. Angela was one of them. By then, she had already experienced most of the dangers of that life: adventurers without scruples, drunks, perverts prone to violence and rough games, and, last but not least, the hostility of the brothels' owners, who hated the "strays," as they called them, for taking away their business by charging less than the brothels did. Still, Angela entered the crowded bar with her head high, proud of her shiny pink dress and the fresh rose she wore on her heart, below the neckline. Clotilde walked behind her in a daze, staring at the men drinking and smoking cigars, intoxicated by sounds and odors she had never heard or smelled before. They sat at a table, and three sailors who were standing by the counter joined them at once. One of them bought a round of drinks. A second sailor ran a hand across Angela's breasts, and Angela chuckled, then told the sailor that would cost him and did he have any money or was he a bum. Then the third sailor grazed Clotilde's neck with his fingers, and Clotilde felt a long wave of heat filling her cheeks and going to the tip of her nose. Angela noticed at once her friend's big, fearful eyes and told the sailor not to touch her, as she was not what he thought she was. The sailor laughed and asked, "What is she doing here if she's not a whore?"

"They are not all like him," Angela said after the sailors had left the table. "I meet gentlemen sometimes, who know how to treat a lady." Clotilde stared at Angela a while, wondering where those gentlemen were, as she would have liked to be treated like a lady right there and then. Two of the three sailors came back shortly with a roll of banknotes. Angela counted the money carefully before nodding a yes and standing up. "Come along," she told Clotilde. She paused, then spoke softly in Clotilde's ear. "Unless you want to stay here by yourself."

At that, Clotilde stood up fast, and they all went back to Angela's place, which was only two blocks away. Clotilde sat outside the apartment, on the stairs, while inside Angela took care of the sailors, and that was the part of the evening Clotilde liked the least, sitting all by herself on the musty floor, and thank God she was still wearing the yellow dress, so she could look at it and feel less alone.

The sailors left in a hurry a half hour later. From the open doorway, Angela waved for Clotilde to come in. She showed her the money, stacked in a pile on the small table next to the wood stove. "One of these is for you," she said, taking a banknote and handing it over.

Clotilde shook her head.

"You helped me," Angela insisted.

So Clotilde took the banknote, hoping her mother would be busy that night up in heaven and wouldn't have time to look down and notice.

They went back to the bar ten minutes later and returned home shortly with more sailors. Again, Angela handed Clotilde a banknote after the sailors left. "I'm tired," Angela said, yawning. "Let's go to sleep."

It was then that Clotilde realized that she had left home many hours earlier to go to the market and had not returned. She hadn't made dinner for her brothers, or washed the floors, or ironed clothes. For sure her brothers would beat her if she showed up. Her stomach shrank for a moment. She looked out the window at the dark shadows of the sea, then gazed about the room and saw Angela snuggling under the covers and falling asleep. "Good night," she whispered, then understood with clarity that she would never go back to Vico Caprettari, because home for her was where she was now, in Angela's apartment, with the yellow dress, the banknotes, and the musky smell of the sailors.

The following morning, Clotilde awoke in a thick daze. From across the room, Angela lifted her eyes from her needlework. "Good morning, my friend," she blurted out in a joyful voice. Clotilde yawned and stretched before coming to a seated position. "So," Angela asked, "have you decided?"

"What?" Clotilde asked in a raspy voice.

"If you want to be in business with me."

Clotilde bent her neck forward, as if to hide her face. She thought of her brothers. As much as she tried to visualize their faces, all she could come up with was a blur. Then she thought of her mother, and her gentle, loving face came to her in full clarity. She grimaced and let out a long, deep sigh.

"It's only a job," Angela said, forcing a white thread through the eye of a needle.

"I could find a different job," Clotilde argued. "I could be a waitress. Or a maid."

"And work for someone who will treat you as badly as your brothers did? Making little or no money for the rest of your life? Believe me, being poor is no fun. No fun at all." She paused. "Wouldn't you rather work for yourself? Be independent? When you do what I do there's no one in the whole world who can tell you when to work, or where, or how. It's you who decide." She flipped the cloth over. "You're the boss."

Clotilde leaned back, raising her head to look at the ceiling. She remained silent a while, eyes fixed on a dormant fly, as Angela rhythmically hemmed the white cloth.

"I never thought of men that way," Clotilde said after a moment. "Actually, I never thought of men at all. All I ever did was try not to think about the men in my life."

"You don't think about these men, either," Angela clarified. "You use them. That's all."

The fly woke up and flew away. "I like being the boss," Clotilde stated.

Angela's eyes lit up. "Very well, partner," she chirped. "You won't regret it, I promise."

Over the next week, Clotilde spent time learning the trade. She began by watching, for which Angela charged her clients more. Then she became involved in the foreplay, and Angela's prices doubled because of that. "I'm ready," Clotilde told Angela one afternoon, as they were talking about the evening plans. Angela gave her a smile.

That night, Clotilde's first client, a tall, bearded helmsman with the belly of a whale and a sour odor of cheap alcohol and sweat, laid on her his fantastic weight. As he pounded her into the thin mattress set on the floor of Angela's sitting room, Clotilde heard her bones squeak and cry out in pain. With her eyes closed, she dreamed of her ride on the hills on the white horse and of the sweet smells of grass and flowers.

From the bedroom, separated by the sitting room by only a curtain, Angela heard every one of Clotilde's stifled moans, intermixed with the roars of the helmsman's pleasure. In the morning, she found Clotilde at the open window, elbows on the sill, staring at the sea. "It's a beautiful day," Angela said.

Clotilde nodded without turning around.

"When businesses grow," Angela said softly after a moment, "so do their offices. We need a larger place."

Clotilde nodded in silence a second time.

Angela joined Clotilde at the window. "The first time is the hardest," she murmured. "It gets easier as the nights go by."

"I hope you're right," Clotilde sobbed, laying her head on Angela's shoulder.

"I am, darling," Angela said. "I am."

The search for their new apartment began without delay. They looked first at the neighboring buildings, then as far away as the Stazione Principe and the western edge of the harbor— to no avail. Their reputation preceded them, so the owners of respectable buildings turned them down. The other buildings, the shabby ones with dirty lobbies, dark rooms, and shady tenants, which were common in the *caruggi* that bordered the port area, were something, both girls agreed, they wouldn't settle for, as such places reminded them of the building they had been born in and vowed to leave behind. It took them two months to find an appropriate accommodation. At the onset of spring, through the intercession of one of their clients to whom they had to promise three months of free service once a week, Angela and Clotilde moved into a four-room apartment on the third floor of an elegant historic building halfway up Via San Lorenzo, out of the *caruggi*. Their arrival rocked the neighborhood:

"What are those two doing in our building?"

"I thought prostitutes lived only in brothels."

"The value of our property will go down, I can assure you."

"Let's call a lawyer. There must be a way to evict them."

"Maybe now that they are here, they'll find an honest way to make a living."

"Don't count on that. Once a whore, always a whore."

"Did you see how they dress? As if it were *carnevale*."

"What am I going to tell my children?"

"What a scandal. One block down from the cathedral."

Heads high, Angela and Clotilde ignored the gossip. They nodded greetings to their new neighbors, who pretended not to see them when they walked by; and they always had a smile for Miss Benassi, the first-floor spinster who led the neighbors' march against their presence and kept a vigilant eye on the men of Via San Lorenzo to see if any succumbed to temptation. "I'm watching you," Miss Benassi said one day as Angela and Clotilde walked by her door, "and all the people who go up the stairs. You leave our husbands alone! They deserve better company than yours."

"Our husbands?" Clotilde said. "I didn't think you had one, Miss Benassi, but I must be mistaken."

Despite the hostility, Angela's and Clotilde's business blossomed like never before. They became known as "the queens" because of the beautiful dresses they wore, their regal demeanor when they walked in the streets, and the special treatments they gave clients who booked them regularly and for long shifts. By then, Clotilde had become an expert in the art of pleasuring men, surpassing Angela in creativity, audacity, and sense of humor. Her thoughts about hell and her mother looking down at her and dying all over again at the sight of her daughter in the arms of all those strangers had disappeared. She had a life of her own, being paid by men instead of doing things for them for free. "I'm proud of that," she told Angela one day, "and if I am proud, surely my mother is, too."

The brothels' owners didn't like their success one bit. Neither did the neighbors, who called the police on them at every occasion: a loud noise coming from the apartment, too much garbage left in the street, questionable individuals walking up the stairs. The policeman in charge of that block, however, was one of the queens' clients, so no one ever managed to catch Angela and Clotilde in the act. One morning, Pietro Valdasco, the owner of the Ancora, one of the largest brothels in town, exasperated by the competition, showed up with two men at the queens' place and turned it upside down. "It's only the beginning!" he screamed, as Angela and Clotilde sat terrified on the kitchen floor. "It'd be much safer for you," he hissed in their ears, "if you left town."

Given that their business was completely illegal, Angela and Clotilde couldn't press charges or even report the threat to the police. They mentioned it, though, to their policeman friend, who told his buddies at the bocce run, who told their brothers, cousins, and coworkers. At every telling, the story was inflated. By the time it reached the port and found its way inside the sailors' bars, it had become a tale of great violence, with blood gushing from wounds and broken bones. Everyone at the Stella Maris was appalled.

"What kind of person would threaten two such beautiful ladies?" the owner cried out.

"I wouldn't want anything to do with this Pietro Valdasco," a sailor said, "today or ever."

A second sailor joined in. "A business that uses such despicable practices should be closed."

As a result, Pietro Valdasco lost clients and spent many hours cursing himself for what he had done. Later that month, he waited for Angela and Clotilde in the street, holding a bouquet of spring flowers. "I apologize," he told them when they came out of the building, "for what I did to you. I must have been crazy that day. Why don't you work for me? I'll treat you like the queens you are."

"Thank you," Angela said, not taking the flowers, "but we don't work for criminals."

"And so you know," Clotilde added, "there's no criminal or threat on earth that could convince us to leave this town."

Two weeks later, in a café, the queens ran into Ildebrando Balbi—Signor Balbi, for short—the five-foot-tall, bald owner of the Carena, a newer brothel located on Piazza delle Oche. "I'd be honored to have you two join the Carena," he told them as he gallantly bowed, then made them an offer that sounded good to Angela and Clotilde for more than one reason: it included a guaranteed salary, something neither of them had ever seen; Signor Balbi was a polite, straightforward man who had never in his life threatened anybody; they were sick of the looks of contempt the neighbors gave them at every occasion; despite the apology and the flowers, they were scared of Pietro Valdasco and his men; they had been scammed by dishonest clients more than once, so by this time they clearly understood that it was easier and safer to work in a brothel than out in the bars at the mercy of adventurers and sailors. "I'm so glad you decided to work here," Signor Balbi said the first time the queens set foot in the Carena. "With you two on board, we'll make mincemeat of the other brothels."

They worked at the Carena for eight years, without incident, and, as Signor Balbi had predicted, they boosted his business by bringing in a steady stream of new clients. Then, with the help of a close friend, Clotilde took over the Luna, a rundown, unsuccessful brothel, managed at the time by a drunkard and owned by a merchant up to his ears in gambling debts. Immediately, the Luna underwent a facelift. After a thorough scrub, the *graniglia* floors were polished, the musty chandeliers replaced, and the walls freshened with a new coat of white-wash. The front of the building also came to life when the marble door frame was restored and the entrance kept beautiful with a wreath of fresh flowers. On the day of the Luna's grand reopening, Clotilde spoke to Angela and the eight girls she had hired. "From now on," she said, "everyone will call me Madam C."

The transition from protected paid employee to business owner didn't come easily in an area of town that boasted more brothels than churches and at a time when the bustling activity of the port and the large number of transients and foreigners that populated it brought along thefts, riots, and a variety of serious criminal endeavors. During the first week of business alone two Abyssinian men shattered one of the Luna's first-floor windows and broke in at four in the morning; there was a fist-fight in the parlor; and one of the girls came down the stairs one night screaming bloody murder and showing everyone the knife cut she had on her belly. Madam C and Angela dealt with the situation with their grits. They threw the Abyssinians out of the Luna with kitchen knives pointed at the men's throats; they settled the fistfight with a few blows of their own; and they delivered the man who had scratched the girl's belly to the police. "You come back," Madam C growled at him with an icy glare, "and your balls will hang in my parlor as a trophy." Soon the message spread that no one, local or foreigner, should mess with Madam C. Thereafter the incidents became rare, then only memories, and within a short eight months from its grand opening the Luna was a profitable enterprise. Angela helped all along. Three years later, one week after her thirty-third birthday, she took Madam C aside. "I will no longer be with the Luna clients," she said with a serene smile.

Madam C frowned. "Why?"

Angela circled her hand over her belly. "Someone more important."

Madam C dropped her jaw. "Who's the father?"

Angela shrugged. "It's my baby," she whispered. "There's nothing else to say."

CHAPTER 2

"Get ready, Rosa," Madam C said. She paused. "The smell of apples is still here."

"For you," Maddalena said, handing to Rosa the cardboard box she had brought in earlier from the street.

"Tonight you'll truly look like a princess," Margherita echoed, pulling the pink ribbon on the box loose.

Stella lifted the box lid and two sheets of tissue paper. "What do you think?"

In slow motion, Rosa took out of the box a long white dress of silk and Brussels lace.

"It's from all the girls," Maddalena said, "although I did all the legwork, as usual."

"I love you all," Rosa mumbled.

"Try it on," said Madam C. "It may need adjustments, and we don't have a lot of time before the guests arrive. And you," she told the three girls, "help me with the wine. *Santo Cielo*, we'll never be ready for this party."

The preparations for Rosa's sixteenth-birthday party had been underway at the Luna for one week. Margherita, Maddalena, Stella, and the other Luna girls had been on long outings in the morning looking for the perfect dress for Rosa. Antonia, the cook, an old woman with a big mole on her cheek, had worked overtime in the kitchen for days preparing vegetable tortes, *pollo alla cacciatora*, and *stoccafisso in umido* for the thirty guests Madam C expected that night. Santina, the maid, who normally came to the Luna every other morning, had come every day that week to spruce up the first floor. In the parlor, she had scrubbed the walls to make sure the whitewash was clean, waxed the *graniglia* floor to make it shine, and washed the flowered curtains to remove the smell of smoke. Then she had cleaned every inch of Rosa's bedroom twice. "This room has still a baby smell," she told Rosa, mop in hand. "We need to scrub it off. When a girl turns sixteen, it's a new life. No more baby smell for you."

"Thank you," Rosa said, grateful for the recognition of this important milestone, "but you seem to be the only one to notice. Could you explain that to Madam C?"

"Don't worry," Santina replied. "She knows."

There was a baby smell in Rosa's room because Rosa had slept there since her very first day of life, in the same double bed of wrought iron with a thick wool mattress, batiste sheets, and a soft white bedspread filled with goose feathers. Madam C didn't believe in cribs. "Cribs are a wicked invention," she had told Angela toward the end of her pregnancy. "Their only function is to keep mothers away from their babies. A man must have invented them, so he wouldn't be bothered. Your baby will sleep in a bed with tall pillows on each side to prevent falls." The double bed had been ready for Rosa for days in the room behind the kitchen—bedspread, pillows, and all. When the midwife had handed Madam C the newborn, Madam C had rocked her in her arms for a while. Then she had placed her gently on the bedspread, between the two lines of pillows, and sat on the bed next to her, caressing her tiny, soft, bald head and her forehead marked by three wrinkles. Rosa had fallen fast asleep.

Overall, Rosa was a quiet baby, at times absorbed in her own thoughts, at times staring at the people around her with large, startled eyes, as if she wondered where she was and why. She gave everyone big smiles. The Luna inhabitants were spell-bound. Madam C, who had cried over Angela's death for seven nights, held Rosa's hands for hours and talked to her about any-thing just to see her smile. All the Luna girls took turns to bathe Rosa, sing her songs, and take her down the block to Mafalda, the wet nurse, four times a day. Puzzled by the number of differ-ent women who showed up at her house with Rosa, Mafalda, a housewife with huge breasts and two loud kids of her own, asked Madam C one day, "Who's the mother?"

"I am," Madam C said with pride. "Is Rosa eating enough?"

"She is. And she's growing fast."

"Your milk must be good."

"It's not my milk," Mafalda said. "In all my life, I've never seen a baby surrounded by so much love."

"We're love experts at the Luna." Madam C giggled. "You know that."

Soon after Rosa's birth, the schedule of the Luna underwent changes. Madam C moved the brothel's opening hour from three to four in the afternoon, so there'd be time for Rosa to be brought back from Mafalda's house and across the parlor while there were no clients lingering there. At the same time, the girls, who never got up in the morning before ten, now began to wake up at eight, ready to cuddle Rosa, wash her diapers, and take her out for a stroll in the *passeggino*. It was as if they had two faces, that of ruthless businesswomen who kicked men out of the bedrooms the moment their time was over, and that of un-selfish, tender creatures devoted to the well-being of Angela's daughter. The positive effects of the activities around Rosa spilled visibly into people's lives: Rosa was calm and sociable; Madam C was relieved, as she didn't bear the responsibility of raising Rosa all by herself; and for the girls, the time they spent with Rosa was a soothing break from their stressful work with the clients. They were happier than the prostitutes in other brothels. It wasn't uncommon in those days to see men who had hopped from one brothel to the next for years become Madam C's steady clients, fascinated by the relaxed, upbeat atmosphere they found at the Luna. They couldn't have imagined, not even in their wildest dreams, that the reason for all that good humor was a child.

When Rosa began to crawl and experiment with climbing stairs, Madam C stated a few new rules for the girls. "The second floor is out. I'll fire you on the spot," she said in a tone that left no room for discussion, "if I find out that you let Rosa into your rooms. And after four in the afternoon she must stay in the kitchen or in her bedroom. We'll take turns to keep her company till she's asleep."

The kitchen became Rosa's evening world for a long time. She was fascinated by all the pots and pans, which she stacked on the floor to make strange buildings; she made music banging the stove with the silverware; she poured water in and out of cups for hours. Of all the girls who were at the Luna at that time, her favorite companions for those games were Marla, who taught her how to float pierced eggs in a pot filled with warm water; Lisa, who danced around the kitchen as Rosa drummed with spoons and knives; and Esmeralda, who told her tales of monsters, witches, and magic wands. The sounds of the parlor mingled in with the sounds of Rosa's games: male voices, glasses tinkling, loud laughter. Odors seeped into the kitchen as well: strong, sweet perfumes, sweat, and the acrid smell of smoke. To Rosa, the sounds of her games and the lingering cooking odors became one with the odors and sounds of the parlor, and even many years later, when she no longer lived there, she'd still experience that strange combination of sensations whenever she'd think of the days of her childhood at the Luna. She'd also often wonder about love and loss, the two defining elements of her life, and how they had crept into her heart early, even as she drummed with the silverware and listened to Esmeralda's stories. Transience came with the territory. By the time Rosa was four, other than Madam C, there was only one girl at the Luna who had witnessed her birth and had known her real mother. Marla had left around Rosa's third birthday, Lisa and Esmeralda shortly after that. It was beyond Rosa to understand departures. Madam C explained to her that the girls who left had wanted to see the world and would return someday with beautiful presents for everyone, and new girls would soon be coming, who surely would love Rosa as much as the old ones. Rosa nodded in silence, thinking she'd give up all the presents gladly to be able to hold on to her friends, and what was the point of getting new girls when it'd be much easier to keep those who were already there.

It was shortly after Esmeralda's departure that Rosa began to daydream. Madam C had taken Rosa on morning outings since she had been able to walk. They went shopping for food together and once in a while made their *passeggiate* longer, strolling all the way to the port. They'd look at the ships coming and going, the passengers embarking and disembarking, and the longshoremen loading and unloading merchandise on the docks. To Rosa, the port was magic. She loved to watch the ships detaching slowly from the piers and tooting their sirens in the air. She asked Madam C one day how far the ships were going.

"Some go very far," Madam C explained, "to the other side of an immense sea called the ocean. The land there is called America. Others stay close by, just down the coast from here. They all have a great time speeding in the water."

"Is America the place where Marla, Lisa, and Esmeralda went to see the world?"

"Maybe."

"Can I go to America some day?"

"Sure you can," Madam C said. "After you've gotten yourself an education."

"How do I get myself an edu . . . education?" Rosa asked, having no clue what the word meant.

"By going to school, you silly girl."

Rosa looked at Madam C with cheery eyes, thinking that whatever school was, she'd get it done quickly, and then she'd hop on one of those ships, those that went very far, and she'd go find all the friends who had left her, and when she'd find them all they'd have a big chocolate cake, like the one Antonia made on Sundays.

Antonia did not live at the Luna. She came every day from noon to four to cook dinner and lunch for the following day, and she had done that for years, since before Madam C had owned the brothel. In those days, Rosa liked to spend time in the kitchen in the early afternoon, watching Antonia dice and bake, amazed at the many uses kitchen utensils had beyond drumming, construction, and floating eggs. She thought constantly of Marla, Lisa, and Esmeralda exploring mysterious lands on the other side of the ocean.

"What are you thinking about, Miss Rosa?" Antonia asked once in a while, puzzled by the faraway look in Rosa's eyes.

"The ship I'll ride to America after I've gotten myself an education."

"Who put these crazy ideas in your little head?" Antonia would laugh.

"I did," Rosa said with one of her big smiles.

"Eat something. Thin as you are, you wouldn't make it past the Gallinara Island. Forget America."

"Where is the Gallinara Island?" Rosa asked.

"Couple of hours west of here," Antonia explained. "I was born on the coast just in front of it."

"Can you take me there some day?"

"There's nothing on that island," Antonia said, "other than rocks and caverns."

As she nibbled at a piece of *focaccia*, Rosa felt relieved at the thought that maybe Marla, Lisa, and Esmeralda had stopped at the Gallinara Island instead of going all the way to America, in which case they'd be much easier to find. And they must be happy there, she thought to herself that night, with an island all to themselves and caverns where they could sleep and sit in when it rained outside. Still, it'd be fun to go all the way to America, and perhaps Marla, Lisa, and Esmeralda could go with her if they ever grew tired of sitting on the rocks of the Gallinara Island with no one else living nearby.

Rosa seemed always to pick her best friends at the Luna in threes. Marla, Lisa, and Esmeralda were her first friends; Maddalena, Margherita, and Stella would be her last. In between were Carla, Francesca, and Annaclara, her favorites at the time Rosa enrolled in school. It was 1901, and at that time there were no real schools in the *caruggi*. From Arianna, the woman who sold vegetables at the corner of Via Banchi, Madam C had heard of a certain Miss Bevilacqua, who taught children to read and write in her apartment, a four-room dwelling only three blocks from the Luna. Miss Bevilacqua was very selective, Arianna had said: she didn't take children who had no manners, showed up dirty, whose mothers were unmarried, and whose fathers were thieves or had anything to do with the illegal activities that went on in that part of town.

Madam C went to see Miss Bevilacqua one day at noon, dressed in an outfit she had bought especially for the occasion: a blue dress with tiny white polka dots, a cream-colored brimmed hat with a fresh gardenia on its side, and a cream-colored parasol with a blue hem of French lace. She looked stunning. She found Miss Bevilacqua, a thin, tall elderly woman with gray hair and a wooden stick in hand, dismissing class for the day. The class was composed of seven boys and two girls, ages seven to thirteen. Madam C introduced herself as Miss Clotilde Paraggi, governess for the young Miss Rosa, whose parents were on a business trip to South America and had entrusted the child's education to her before departing.

"I'll take good care of Miss Rosa," Miss Bevilacqua said in a humble tone, flattered that such important people had chosen her as their daughter's only teacher. And if this is the governess, she thought to herself staring at Madam C and the envelope full of banknotes she set on the desk, imagine how beautiful and elegant the mother must be. Surely, having the daughter of such important people in her home school would add to her reputation and make her business grow.

"Don't talk to Rosa about her parents, please," Madam C said with an imploring voice. "She's heartbroken, and any mention of their trip will make her cry."

"You can count on me, Miss Paraggi. My lips are sealed."

Madam C took Rosa to Miss Bevilacqua's the following day. Rosa, then seven years old, dressed like a perfect young lady, was not thrilled at all, because going to school meant the end of her morning *passeggiate* to the port. She said nothing against it, however, because she knew she had to get her education, whatever that meant, before being able to ride one of those ships and cross the ocean. Hand in hand with Madam C, Rosa stood at the door of the classroom and looked around. For the first time she was seeing a room filled with children. She stared at them with her curious eyes, intrigued by their different looks, expressions, and voices. "Come in, sweetheart," Miss Bevilacqua said with an exaggerated smile. "Children, let's all say, 'Hello, Miss Rosa.' "

Rosa was a fast learner. Miss Bevilacqua attributed her amazing progress to her good upbringing, unaware of the fact that Rosa was learning as fast as she could in order to cross the ocean. After two months in the classroom, Rosa could read and write, and had caught up with the older children and even left a few behind. She was a respectful, neat young lady, and Miss Bevilacqua couldn't stop saying good things about her to the governess when she came to pick up Miss Rosa at noon. One day, a few months later, Miss Bevilacqua gave the four children who could write best an assignment: write about your mother and father. She had remembered Madam C's request that Miss Rosa's parents not be mentioned, but concluded that after that much time had gone by, surely those wonderful parents must be back from their trip and living with their daughter. The following day Rosa showed up with two wide-ruled pages beautifully handwritten with her ink pen. Miss Bevilacqua asked the four children to read their essays aloud, beginning with Miss Rosa. Rosa stood up and read her composition with pride: "I have ten mothers and no father, but there are lots of men who come to my house to play a game. They are not very smart, so they lose all the time and pay my mothers money. My favorite mother is Madam C, but I also love Carla, Francesca, and Annaclara a lot. They tell me stories and show me their rooms, where they play the game. Madam C doesn't know. Luckily, or I would be in trouble."

The children in the classroom loved the story. As for Miss Bevilacqua, she showed the governess the essay at the end of class and asked for an explanation. Madam C looked at Rosa with sweet eyes. "You naughty girl. Making up stories again? I can't believe it." She turned to Miss Bevilacqua. "This child has the wildest imagination."

Miss Bevilacqua didn't buy it. "I'd like to meet her parents, if you don't mind. They must be back from South America by now."

Rosa looked at the two women with wondering eyes.

"I'll see what I can do," Madam C said, dragging Rosa outside.

"What was that about?" Rosa asked on the way home.

"Never mind, darling. We'll just have to find you another

school. It's May already, so we won't have to worry about it until summer ends."

"I don't want another school. I want to go on a ship to America."

"You will someday," Madam C said, caressing Rosa's hair. "It may be a while."

Rosa wasn't quite sure what had gone wrong with her essay that day. She had told the truth, which is what Madam C always said she should do at all times, but after she was finished reading, Miss Bevilacqua had snatched her paper and said, "*Dio Santo!*" And now Madam C wanted to send her to a different school. That night, in the peace of her bedroom, Rosa struggled to fall asleep. She had this funny tingling in her gut that told her that there was something strange about her life. After reading her story, she had heard the stories the three other children had written, and she had gathered from what they had read that they all had one mother and one father, who lived together in a house where no one came to play games. Then one of the girls in the class had told her during recess that for a child to be born there must be a mother and a father, who are called husband and wife, so her story of ten mothers and no father had to be fake for sure. Three days after her last day in Miss Bevilacqua's school, Madam C walked with Rosa to the port. While they watched the ships coming and going, Rosa asked, "Who's my real mother? And where's my father?"

Madam C sighed. They sat on a bench, facing the blue water. She took Rosa's hand and said, "I knew you'd ask someday. Now I'll tell you the story of how you were born." They spent a long time on that bench talking and crying. When they got up to return home, Rosa knew that she had been born on the second floor of the Luna, in the room Carla had now, that Angela was her mother, that Madam C had been Angela's friend all her life, that Angela and Madam C had played the game together for years, and that while Angela was dying Madam C had promised her that she would take care of her baby as if she were her own. "I also promised Angela I would give you an education, so come September, you're back in school, Signorina."

"What about the girls who live in our house?" Rosa asked. "Who are they?"

"Friends," Madam C whispered, "who love you very much."

"And my father?"

"Angela told me your father was a fisherman," Madam C lied, "who worked on a boat. She said he'd be back soon, certainly in time for your birth. Maybe something happened to his boat. There are storms out there, you know. He would have loved you to pieces, I'm sure."

"Have you met him?" Rosa asked.

"No," Madam C replied. "I would have liked to."

Rosa pondered a little. "So would I."

"I love you," Madam C said with soft eyes.

Rosa nodded and held on to Madam C's hand tight. "Did Angela have red hair like mine?"

"She did," Madam C lied again. "Red and wild."

That summer, Rosa's fantasies about the ships became more frequent, growing richer and longer every time. She imagined that the ships that crossed the ocean went to mysterious lands, where people talked funny languages and the towns were populated by humongous tame animals, trees with rainbow-colored leaves, and little birds with red-and-blue eyes who could talk to the fish in the water. Her father lived there, in a hut by the ocean. He was poor. All he had to eat was his catch, and that's why he hadn't come back to Genoa to see her. And then she imagined Angela with her red hair, flying over the hut like an angel and blowing her husband kisses when he was close by. She dreamed while she was at the port and also while she was at the Luna, when she sat at the kitchen table for the *colazione*, when she watched Antonia peel and dice potatoes, and when she stood by the parlor window looking outside. "She's growing," Madam C said of Rosa's long silences and dreamy eyes. "That's hard to do."

The girls did all they could to make Rosa smile. They took her along when they went shopping, lent her hats and bracelets, told her all sorts of stories about their lives. One day, while Rosa and Annaclara were buying glass beads to make a necklace, Rosa saw for the first time a casket being carried out of a building and a crowd of teary people waiting in the street. Rosa asked what was going on. "It's a funeral," explained Annaclara, who didn't believe in sparing children the truths of life. "When someone dies, they put the body in that box, a casket. The people you see around the casket must be the dead person's friends, because they are sad."

"Where are they taking the casket?" asked Rosa.

"To the cemetery," Annaclara replied, "which is a large beautiful meadow where all the dead people rest. They lie in spaces called tombs, underground, so they can smell the earth. And then their friends can visit them, so they don't feel alone."

That night, when Madam C put her to sleep, Rosa asked, "Is Angela at the cemetery? In a tomb?"

Madam C flinched. "Angela is in heaven, with the angels. And that's how you should think of her."

"But if she were in a tomb I could go visit her and make her feel less alone."

"Angela is not alone," Madam C said. "She is with you all the time. And with me. And with all the people who loved her. She can see you from up in heaven, and that's all that matters to her." She paused. "Dead people are not really dead if you keep thinking of them and loving them as if they were alive."

Rosa gave a sigh of relief. She hadn't liked the idea of Angela being locked up in a casket at all. Much better for her to be in heaven, she thought, flying free with the angels, so she could keep visiting her husband in the hut across the ocean. She moaned when Madam C kissed her on the cheek, then fell into a dreamless sleep.

When September came, Madam C enrolled Rosa in a different school. It was larger than Miss Bevilacqua's home school, with about thirty children divided into four grades based on their skills, not their ages. The school was in Salita Santa Caterina, a beautiful old, steep street that led to a large piazza with trees. To be admitted, children needed a recommendation, and Madam C obtained one from Beppe Marenco, owner of ships and warehouses and a faithful client of the Luna. Based on her reading and writing abilities, Rosa placed in third grade. She sat next to Clarissa, a girl her age, who asked her how she had learned to read. Rosa explained that she had learned at Miss Bevilacqua's school, which she had to leave because Miss Bevilacqua didn't like what she wrote.

"Now I know why you look so familiar," Clarissa said. "My older sister Lara used to go to Miss Bevilacqua's school. I saw you a few times walking down the hallway, while I was waiting for Lara with my mom."

At dinner, Clarissa told her parents that one of her classmates, who had long red hair, used to go to Miss Bevilacqua's school. At once, the parents recognized from that description the girl who had written the essay about the ten mothers. "*Santa Maria*," the father exclaimed. "Stay away from her. That girl lives in a brothel!"

By the end of the first week of school, all the kids knew that the girl with red hair had ten mothers and lived in a brothel. Most kids didn't know the meaning of the word *brothel*, so legends began to flourish: that a brothel was a place where one hid from the police, a place where homeless people could sleep on the floor if they helped with the chores, a dungeon guarded by giant spiders. One of the older boys set things straight for everyone one morning. "A brothel is where men go to spend the night with prostitutes."

"What are prostitutes?" a second boy asked in dismay.

The older boy explained. "They are women who walk around with no clothes, and if you give them money, you can poke at them with your fingers."

Clarissa said, "Is that what Rosa's ten mothers are? Prostitutes?"

That was how Rosa earned her nickname, Prostitutes' Daughter. Before the second week of school was over, all the children called her that when she walked by. "Hello, Prostitutes' Daughter."

"Prostitutes' Daughter!" they chanted. "Prostitutes' Daughter!"

Rosa didn't know the meaning of the word *prostitute*, but figured it must be something bad if the kids made fun of her that way. For the first time, she felt scared, and because she felt scared, she didn't have the courage to ask Madam C or the girls what that nickname meant. She cried often, at the Luna and in school, and when Madam C or her teacher asked her what was wrong, she said, "Nothing," and turned her face away. "She's still growing," Madam C told the girls, who were worried sick about Rosa.

The rumors about Rosa spread quickly beyond the student body. The children's parents began to talk, as did the parents' neighbors. Gossip was fueled by Miss Bevilacqua, who over the summer had told everyone she knew about Rosa and her essay, unable to get over the fact that the elegant lady she had thought a governess was in reality a Madam, who had duped her over and over with her stories.

Soon Miss Cipollina, the school's *direttrice*, got wind of Rosa's nickname and gave Rosa a note to take home. In the note, she asked that Rosa's mother (whom Miss Cipollina believed to be Madam C) come to school the following day for a consultation. As she gave Madam C the note, Rosa broke into tears. "I don't want to go to that school," she sobbed, "or to any other school. The kids make fun of me. They call me Prostitutes' Daughter."

In a fury, Madam C took the note and ripped it into shreds, then ran upstairs to the third floor. The third floor was the Luna's smallest, with only two rooms—a sitting room and a bedroom. These were Madam C's private quarters. The walls of both rooms were painted off-white and the windows had pale yellow curtains Madam C had chosen in memory of the dress Angela had given her on that long-ago night. The sitting room had a fireplace that had been out of order for years. On its marble mantel, Madam C kept mementos of her life: a hand-painted vase with a lid that had belonged to her mother, a purple scented candle that had belonged to Angela, letters from old lovers tied gently with a ribbon of white satin, stones she had picked up on the beach over the years. Santina had specific orders not to dust or touch those objects in any way. Next to the fireplace was an iron enameled tub with lion feet where Madam C took hot baths when her nerves needed calming. The second room, the bedroom, was a place once reserved for the Luna's best clients. Madam C had stopped entertaining men there the moment Rosa had begun climbing stairs.

This day, holding the pieces of Miss Cipollina's note in front of her, Madam C kneeled in front of the fireplace, which was what she did when she wanted to ask Angela for inspiration. "Angela, dear," she said, fighting back tears, "there are only two things we can do. One is to send Rosa away from the Luna, to live with a respectable family, so she won't have to worry ever again about what people say. The second is to keep her here, forget about school, and teach her to be proud of who we are. What do you say?"

Five minutes later, Madam C was back downstairs. She found Rosa in the kitchen, sobbing in Annaclara's arms. "I'm going to that school and I'm going to chop some of those kids' tongues off with an ax," Annaclara said with a wicked grin.

"You will do no such thing," Madam C stated. "Rosa? You don't have to go back to school if you don't want to. But if you decide not to, you must promise me you'll keep reading."

"I'll read anything," Rosa said, drying her tears. "Just keep me here, please."

"I'll go buy books later today," Madam C said, leaving the room. She stopped at the doorway. "And you," she told Annaclara, "take this lady out for an ice cream."

By the following morning, Rosa's tears had disappeared. "This is a new life for you," Madam C told her when she got up. She pointed to a pile of ten books. "In the afternoon you'll read, and in the morning you'll have chores and duties like everybody else around here. You'll do the shopping, you'll go to the fountain with the girls to do the wash, and you'll help Santina clean the rooms."

"Does that mean that I can go to the second floor?" Rosa asked, half naughty, half surprised.

"Only in the morning."

"And you want me to go shopping all by myself?"

"Do you think you can do it?" Madam C asked.

"I don't know," Rosa whispered.

"Angela did it when she was your age. She delivered the clothes her mother mended."

Rosa squared her shoulders. "I can do it."

"Good. Just stay on our shopping route."

Rosa brought her right hand to her temple. "*Sissignora*," she said, giving Madam C a big smile.

She settled into her new routine with ease. She woke up at eight in the morning, helped Santina for an hour with the cleaning chores, had *colazione* in the kitchen with the girls, and then went to see Madam C, who gave her a daily list of things to buy. "Got it," she'd tell Madam C as she rushed out of the Luna into the street. Her first stop was the vegetable stand, where she picked out fresh vegetables and ripe fruit; then she moved to the fishmonger cart, where she made sure the fish she bought didn't smell of the sewer; and then she was off to the bakery, her favorite stop, where she stood in line longer than necessary to smell the fresh bread and pastries before buying. She walked back to the Luna slowly, with her shopping bags full and her gait that of a proud soldier on the way home from war.

During her morning missions, Rosa discovered how much she loved to stroll in the *caruggi* alone and that she could do it without losing her way. She had followed Madam C in that maze since she had been able to walk, so that unknowingly she had built a map in her head of all the streets. Sometimes she took detours from the shopping route to go smell the spices at the Sottoripa markets, by the port, with all the ships nearby. She suspected by then that where those ships were going there were no talking birds or rainbow-colored leaves and no hut where her father lived in poverty and fished to survive. It wasn't that important, she found out. Dreams were dreams, thoughts that lasted as long as one believed in them, and if her dreams of talking birds, rainbow leaves, and a hut by the water had been undone, surely there must be something across the ocean to replace them, something that would make the trip there worthwhile. In those days, she was reading avidly the books Madam C had bought for her. They were mostly books of sea adventures, which scared her sometimes, but also taught her about navigation, stars, storms, and sailors' lives, making her longing for a sea trip even stronger. In the meantime, she felt so good inside when she could just look at the ships and smell the spices, and then walk the *caruggi* on the way home. "I'm Angela's daughter," she said to herself with her head held high.

CHAPTER 3

Over the years Madam C had put a great effort into keeping Rosa removed from the Luna's activities and out of the clients' sight. The long hours spent in the kitchen, the prohibition against visiting the second floor, and the strange sounds that came from the parlor had nonetheless fueled Rosa's curiosity early in life. Around the time she had turned five, when the second-floor prohibition was still strictly imposed, Madam C went shopping occasionally on her own in the morning, leaving Rosa behind. On those occasions, Rosa would follow Santina up the stairs, asking her questions about the various cleaning utensils and offering to help her carry them around. On the second-floor landing, Santina would turn to Rosa with severe eyes. "Thank you very much, Rosellina," she'd say, taking back whatever the girl was carrying. "Now go back downstairs before Madam C comes back and finds you up here."

Rosa nodded, but the moment Santina turned her back and began cleaning she'd run down the corridor and hide in one of the girls' rooms. At the sound of her footsteps, the girls who were awake would gather in that room and play a game that made Rosa laugh every time.

"Santina's coming," one of the girls would warn.

"Get in here, quickly," another would say, opening the door of a small closet.

Rosa would run into the closet with her breath quick in her throat.

"All clear," someone would whisper a minute later, knocking on the closet door.

They moved from room to room in stealthy steps, and the game was for Rosa to visit every room without Santina ever seeing her. Of course, Santina knew exactly where Rosa was the whole time, but kept sweeping and mopping and never said a word, figuring that as long as she pretended not to know what was going on she wouldn't be in trouble. In the rooms, the girls talked to Rosa, played with her, showed her their personal belongings, letters, objects, amulets, and jewelry. There were nine small bedrooms on the second floor, four on each side of the corridor and one at the end of it. Each bedroom was furnished in the same frugal way: a twin bed, a nightstand, a chair, a small table, and a shallow closet carved in the thickness of the old external walls. Despite the uniformity of the furniture, no two rooms looked or felt alike, with the different objects the girls had in them and the different odors. To Rosa, each room was a world apart, and in each one of them, no matter who was the inhabitant, she felt comfortable and safe, even more so than in her own room. "When I grow up," Rosa told the girls every time, "I want to have a room on the second floor, too. Just like yours."

The girls would shake their heads. "Don't you ever tell Madam C. She'll go nuts at the idea."

One of them would add, "Madam C goes nuts for lots of reasons. She'd better not find Rosa here."

Until two years later, when she would read Rosa's essay at Miss Bevilacqua's school, Madam C never found out that Rosa spent time in the morning on the second floor. The girls could see the street from the two rooms that had windows on the front, and when someone spotted Madam C turn the corner of Vico del Pepe and approach the Luna door, they shipped Rosa in a hurry to the third floor. "This girl has a clock in her head," Madam C said of the fact that she always found Rosa playing quietly on the floor of her sitting room whenever she returned from her morning walks, no matter the hour. "How does she know?"

All along, but especially after she had stopped going to school, Rosa had picked up conversations among the girls that made her wonder about the relationship between what was going on at the Luna and the Romero kids' game. Annaclara, Francesca, and Carla talked often about their clients, how stingy one was, how old another one looked, how good a third one was at playing the game. "When I'll have my room on the second floor," Rosa said one day, "I'll play the game, too. I bet no one will beat me."

"I'm sure of that," Annaclara said with a big laugh. "Meanwhile, eat some more pasta, girl. Or you'll be eight years old all your life."

"You can't stay eight years old all your life," Rosa laughed back.

"Maybe not all your life," Carla said. "But you can be eight for a long time. I was ten for six years because I never ate my meals."

"And I was six for five years because I talked too much," Francesca added, placing a hand on Rosa's mouth.

Annaclara left the Luna one week before Rosa turned eleven. Rosa didn't eat for three days. Six months later, Francesca and Carla also left. New girls came, but Rosa couldn't bond with them in the same way. She withdrew from the conversations, took longer than necessary to do the morning shopping, spent long hours again watching the ships and dreaming. "Puberty," Madam C explained to the girls who worried. "Never comes easy."

Rosa was almost twelve when Margherita arrived. "And who might this gorgeous young lady be?" Margherita said, faking awe, when Madam C introduced her to Rosa.

"I'm Rosa," Rosa replied, blushing.

"With hair like yours, you should be a princess," Margherita said, stroking Rosa's curls. "I think I'll call you Princess Rosa." She paused. "If you don't mind."

"I don't mind at all," Rosa said with the biggest smile anyone had seen in years.

Margherita looked at the books piled on the kitchen counter. "Do you like to read?"

Rosa nodded.

"Wait for me in the parlor, Princess Rosa. There's something I'd love to show you." She went upstairs and returned one minute later carrying her book of poetry. Rosa had never seen a book like that before. It was much bigger than her adventure books, with a soft leather cover and thick, sturdy pages, so unlike the pages of her books that often fell out after the second reading. They sat down next to each other and Margherita began to read, stopping every four lines to explain the meaning. Rosa was entranced, as Margherita had been years earlier listening to the man on the bench read to his love. All of Rosa's books were adventures, where heroes died chasing monsters, soldiers fought mighty enemies, and storms stranded sailors on far away islands. She had never read anything about love. "We'll read one page every day," Margherita said, amazed by Rosa's interest in such complicated words. "And when we're done reading all the poems, we'll start over. Before one month"—she pointed at the book—"you'll be able to understand all this on your own."

Between Dante's cryptic descriptions of Beatrice, Petrarca's ecstatic words about Laura, and what she heard and saw in the brothel, to Rosa love became a mix of strange ideas. Many times over the years, during her evenings in the kitchen, she had placed an ear to the parlor door and a curious eye to the keyhole. On a few occasions, she had opened the door ajar. She had heard the men's voices, the discussions about money, and what the girls whispered to the men, like "I love you so much," "You are hot tonight," "Come here, baby, and touch me all over." Whatever that was, she thought to herself, it was nowhere close to the three-card game the Romero kids played in the street. She had never heard those kids say "You're hot" or "Touch me" to the passersby. All they did was scream the same thing over and over to attract clients: "Find the queen, mister. *Dieci centesimi* to find the queen." Not once had she heard any of the Luna girls ask the men to find the queen, and when she had peeked in the parlor she had noticed that the money the men handed to Madam C was not *dieci centesimi*, but much more. Then there were the stories about a husband and wife she had heard in school, including the fact that a husband and wife needed to be together for children to be born; the descriptions of the prostitutes, women who walked around naked, she had heard at Miss Cipollina's school; and the evasive replies the girls and Madam C gave her when she occasionally asked questions about the game. For example:

Rosa: "Do you only play the game when you are in love?"

Madam C: "With this crazy sea, the fish will be bad tomorrow."

Rosa: "How many persons are you allowed to be in love with?"

Margherita: "That I don't know. What I know is that the number of questions you are allowed to ask is over the limit."

Rosa: "Does someone always have to win? Is there ever a tie?"

Madam C: "A tie is what I'll strangle you with if you don't keep quiet, Signorina."

Rosa: "How long does it take to play one game? Do you always play it with no clothes on?"

Madam C: "Remind me to buy more bedsheets tomorrow."

By her thirteenth birthday, Rosa had come up with her personal theory about love: for a man and a woman to love each other, the man had to have money and pay the woman beforehand. A man could love as many women as he wanted as long as he paid them. A woman could decide not to love a man if she was tired, like the girls and Madam C were sometimes. In any case, when women fell in love, they walked around naked. When a man married a woman, that woman became the only one the man was allowed to pay, and the woman could take money only from him. At that point, the man often wrote love poems for the woman, and the two became husband and wife. When a husband paid his wife, children were born.

Madam C had conversations with Angela in front of the fireplace all along. "I'll have to talk to Rosa one of these days. She's no longer a child, you know. She asks questions, acts in funny ways. I'm scared." The following night, she'd kneel in front of the fireplace again. "I wish so badly that Rosa could stay a child. But I'll talk to her tomorrow, I promise, as soon as she gets up." Any excuse was good for Madam C to delay the talk: that Rosa was still too young; that maybe she would figure things out on her own; that she was happy again now that Margherita was around, and who knew how she'd react if she knew the truth; that perhaps her puberty wasn't over yet, and it was unwise to give a girl shocking news while she was battling such big changes in her body. "*Non svegliare il can che dorme,*" don't wake up the sleeping dog, she told Angela one night. "It's an old saying, and old sayings always give good advice."

Stella arrived at the Luna the summer Rosa was fourteen. She had one suitcase, so heavy Rosa thought it was filled with stones. "It'll take two people to take it upstairs," Rosa said casually but with a plan.

"Then help me, girl," Stella said, winking, "and I'll show you what's inside."

In her room, Stella opened the suitcase, and Rosa stared at its contents with surprise. The only other set of objects she had seen before that looked remotely like those was at the corner of Via di Scurreria, where Mr. Razzano, the *robivecchi*, sold used merchandise lined up on an old blanket set on the ground. As if by magic, out of Stella's suitcase came dice, key holders, colored stones, sachets filled with sand, three images of the Madonna di Guadalupe, two balls made of lead, dozens of necklaces made with brown seeds, and an unspecified number of shells, crab legs, and dried fish bones. "They are my lucky charms," Stella explained. "They go with me wherever I go."

Fascinated, Rosa watched Stella spread the objects about the room.

"The shells must stay close to the window," Stella told her, "for good luck. And the sachets must stay on the floor, next to the bed feet, for them to retain their powers."

"Powers?" Rosa asked.

"They can predict the future. And don't you ever wear any of these necklaces, my dear," Stella continued, waving her index finger. "If you do, you'll never fall in love as long as you live."

Given the theory she had concocted about love, Rosa wasn't so sure that never falling in love was such a bad thing after all. Later, Stella laid out for Madam C the condition for her to work at the Luna: "I don't see clients on Friday. It would make my saliva turn sour."

The last Luna girl Rosa would befriend, Maddalena, joined the brothel four months before Rosa's sixteenth birthday. She had run away from her Gypsy family back in Macedonia and crossed Italy east to west until, for no particular reason, she had decided to stop in Genoa for a while. She read tarot cards to people and told their fortune, which turned Rosa into a customer at once. "You will fall in love," Maddalena said the first time she read the cards for Rosa, turning over the Lovers and the Ace of Cups. "And there'll be changes in your life and you'll take a long trip," she continued as the World showed up next to the Fool.

Rosa stared at Maddalena. "How did you know I want to go on a trip?" she asked.

"These cards, my child, never fail."

The first time Rosa entered Maddalena's room was also the first time Rosa saw wigs. Maddalena had six of them of different lengths and colors and kept them on small wooden stands lined up on her table. "What do you need them for?" Rosa asked, half curious, half suspicious.

"Some men like me blond, others like me black. And certain men like me different each time."

"Can they recognize you when your hair is different?"

Maddalena pondered a moment. "Some can, some can't, some don't want to. I love disguises."

Rosa stared at the wigs a while, dying to put one on her head, but couldn't find the courage to ask Maddalena if she could try them. She kept thinking of those wigs all day long, trying to imagine how she would look with different hair, black and straight, or maybe wavy blond. It had never occurred to her before that one could change hair colors, and the more she thought about that idea, the more it seemed to her an amazing magic trick. She wondered if Angela would recognize her if she had blond wavy hair instead of her usual red curls, but her doubts lasted only a short moment because something inside told her that dead people knew everything and could see past wigs, walls, and even past the buildings that lined Vico del Pepe and the streets beyond it.

She headed for Maddalena's room on one of Santina's off days, in the middle of the morning, when she knew the girls would likely be outside, either at the fountain washing clothes or walking around together for a breath of fresh air. Her plan was to try on every wig Maddalena had on the table and decide which hair color would make her look older, and that was the wig she would wear on the day Madam C would let her play the game. The door to Maddalena's room was closed. As she was about to turn the handle, Rosa heard sounds: a man moaning, the springs of the mattress squeaking in a rhythm, and the man's hard breathing as the squeaks stopped. She stood in the corridor a moment, listening to the fast beats of her heart, then ran downstairs and out of the Luna, and walked aimlessly about the *caruggi* until the port was in sight.

The following morning, Rosa helped Santina with the chores as usual, but instead of following the maid from room to room, she lingered in Maddalena's bedroom a while, lying on the bed quietly, trying to feel something different inside. She did the same thing the following day, and then again the morning after. Once, in Stella's room, she took off her clothes before lying on the bed, then bounced her body up and down, trying to reproduce the squeaking sounds. She felt nothing worthy of notice for a while. One week later, lying unclothed on Margherita's bed, smelling incense and scented candles, touching for the first time her hard nipples and softly squeezing her breasts, she felt a heat in her belly that she had never felt before. She left Margherita's room and went upstairs. "I'm ready," she told Madam C in a serious voice.

Madam C looked at her with surprise. "Ready for what?"

"To play the game."

"Nonsense," said Madam C.

"I'm not a child anymore."

"Yes, you are, dear. You have no idea."

"How do you know?" Rosa asked.

"I know everything."

"If you knew everything," said Rosa, "you would know that I'm sick of taking orders for no good reason."

"Who taught you to speak like that, Signorina? If Angela heard you, she'd die all over again."

"I'll be the one to die, if you don't let me do it."

"You'll survive, dear. I can assure you."

"How old were you and Angela when you started to play the game?"

"Much older than fifteen," Madam C said.

"I'll be sixteen in three days, you know."

"I know. I sent out the invitations for your party. And this is the end of the conversation."

Rosa was not ready yet to give up on the idea of becoming a Luna girl sometime soon, and that was what she had been brooding over that afternoon at the Luna while Madam C had untangled her hair and later while the girls were getting the parlor ready for the party. They were now counting plates and silverware, lining up wine bottles on the counter, and talking to Antonia in the kitchen to make sure the food would be warm and ready by seven. Rosa and Madam C were at that point on the third floor, in Madam C's sitting room, hemming the white dress. "Just a couple of centimeters," Madam C said. "It will make your legs look longer."

At some point there were knocks on the Luna door. "Don't they know how to read?" Maddalena mumbled, heading for the entryway. When she opened the door, she saw a neatly dressed young man with a pale complexion and a spiky hairdo that reminded her of the bristles of a horse brush.

"I have a message for Madam C," the young man stuttered, staring at Maddalena's large breasts and low neckline.

"What's the message, dear?" Maddalena asked.

"I have orders to deliver it to Madam C personally."

"Then why don't you come in," Maddalena said, pulling the young man by his tie. "We have a visitor, girls. Someone call Madam C."

"He's cute." Margherita giggled, as she ruffled the young man's spiky hair. She noticed the stains of fresh sweat under his armpits and the deathly pallor on his face. "And shy, too. My favorite type."

Madam C came down the stairs, followed closely by Rosa. "Can I help you?" she asked.

The young man spoke falteringly. "Madam, the mayor sent me to tell you that he will attend Miss Rosa's party tonight."

There was a murmur in the parlor swimming from girl to girl.

"He's coming!" Madam C said with a thready voice. "I can't believe he's coming!"

"You're blushing," Stella said, pointing at Madam C's face. "What are you, in love?"

"I've never been in love in my life," Madam C stated, regaining her composure. "He's an old friend, as you all know. And I haven't seen him in quite a while. The last time he was here was . . . five years ago, more or less." She turned to Rosa. "You were eleven. Do you remember him? When you were little he talked to you a few times."

Rosa shook her head.

"Thank you," Madam C told the young man. "Tell the mayor I'm looking forward to his visit, and so is Miss Rosa."

Rosa gave Madam C a long look.

Margherita stepped in front of the young man, who was heading quickly for the door. "Why don't you stay a little longer? You can't be busy this late in the afternoon."

He took a deep breath, gathering his strength before replying. "I *am* busy, Signora. I'm the mayor's secretary, and there's a lot going on at City Hall."

"Tell me," Margherita said, pushing up her breasts. "What may be going on at City Hall that is more important than this?"

The young man stepped back. "Haven't you heard? A famous American president is in town and tomorrow morning he has an official meeting with the mayor. We still have so much work to do."

"An American president?" Stella said. "My, my."

"What's his name?" Maddalena asked.

"Theodore Roosevelt."

"Theodore," Stella whispered, her eyes dreamy. "How lovely."

"Tell the mayor to bring him to the party," Maddalena said. "Maybe we can give the American president a taste of Italian love."

The young man opened the door. "I really need to go."

"What's your name?" Margherita yelled after him.

"Roberto. Roberto Passalacqua." He bowed. "I . . . need to go. Good-bye."

The city had been in a frenzy for a while. Theodore Roosevelt, on a trip all over Italy with his wife, had arrived in Genoa by train that morning amidst parades, musical bands, and an unusually large deployment of police. In several locations the traffic had been diverted to make space for the presidential motorcade. Deep in the *caruggi*, no one had heard a beep, as that part of town, in particular Vico del Pepe and the surrounding streets, was not on the list of Mr. and Mrs. Roosevelt's places to visit. When Rosa had heard from Roberto Passalacqua that an American president was in town, her heart had skipped a beat. "Can I meet him?" she asked Madam C in a frenzy. "To ask him questions about America?"

Madam C looked at her with loving eyes. "No, dear. You can't meet a president. You can't even get close to a president, or someone will shoot you. If you want to know about America, ask the mayor tonight. He's a man of the world. I'm sure he knows."

"What's his name?" Rosa asked.

"Cesare Cortimiglia. Are you sure you don't remember him?"

"I'm sure," Rosa said. "You never let me meet any of the men who come here."

"It's for your own good, and you know it," Madam C

pointed out. "And go wash this smell of apples off you. It's giving me a headache."

"I don't want a party with all these guests," Rosa moaned. "Why can't we just have it with the girls?"

"Nonsense. You are sixteen, and you need to meet new people. Those I invited are good friends of mine. Some of them saw you when you were born and occasionally when you were a baby, and are dying to see how grown up you are. Others never met you before, but heard of you many times. You'll see. By the end of the night, you'll have new friends."

"I already have a new friend," said Rosa.

"Who?"

"Isabel."

"Who's Isabel?" Madam C asked.

Rosa looked Madam C straight in the eyes. "With this wind, there'll be no fish tomorrow at the market."

Rosa had met Isabel two months earlier, during one of her morning walks. She had seen her shadow many times before, tucked in a dark, large booth at the corner of Vico Usodimare, blurred by a veil of vapor that often spilled out into the street. To Rosa, that shadow had always looked surreal. The booth was quite wide, half the width of the building it was in, and stuck out of the building wall about one meter, making the *caruggio* even narrower. It had a glass door with two windows on each side, like a store, so that some of its interior was visible from the street despite the darkness. On the rare occasions Rosa had glanced at the booth as she passed by, she had caught a faint sight of a mass of white, fleecy hair, dark skin, and a long black vest that made the shadow look as if she stood on a pedestal rather than on feet. Overall, Rosa was scared. There were rumors about the woman at the corner of Vico Usodimare, which Rosa had heard from the shopkeepers of Via San Luca and from Antonio Donegà, the chimney sweeper: that she sold spells to make a living, that she kidnapped little children and boiled them in big iron pots, that with one look she could turn a liter of milk into a sour mush. No one knew exactly who she was. The one thing everyone knew for sure was that she was a witch. "Stay away from her," Rosa had heard one of the shopkeepers tell her children, "or you'll grow pig's feet."

One day, as she was heading back to the Luna from the port all caught up in one of her dreams about the ocean, Rosa unconsciously slowed down near Vico Usodimare, coming to a halt for a short moment. She was startled by a gentle voice that said unhurriedly in an accent Rosa had never heard before, "Your hair reminds me of the sunsets back home. If you were my child, I would name you Tramonto."

Rosa turned toward the voice, holding her breath as she realized it could have come only from the booth. She stood there quietly, as if hypnotized. In her black vest, the witch was on the booth's threshold, smiling at Rosa through a thick vapor cloud. "I know what they say about me," she said in her strange accent. "Would you like to know where this steam comes from?"

Wide-eyed, Rosa turned around and ran as fast as she could to the end of the street. She arrived at the Luna panting and kneeled next to her bed with her head down. "Thank you, Angela," she whispered, "for helping me escape a horrible death in an iron pot full of boiling water." She took a breath. "I'm not a child anymore," she said, "but I'm sure witches own pots of all sizes."

The echo of the witch's voice lingered in Rosa's head for many days. She often wondered if she had heard that voice for real or if it had been a dream. She talked about it with her friends one afternoon.

"There are no such things as witches," Margherita said.

"That's what you think," Stella rebutted. "There are plenty of witches and wizards around us. People don't know about them, that's all."

"In any case," Maddalena said, "I'm sure that there's a perfectly reasonable explanation for the steam. People say the meanest things, Rosa. You of all people should know."

One week later, Rosa returned to Vico Usodimare. The witch was seated quietly by the booth door, on a black rocking chair. There was no steam blurring her figure that day, and Rosa noticed that her eyes were shiny black and the leathery skin of her face was crisscrossed with wrinkles. "Hello, Tramonto," the witch said when Rosa stopped in front of the booth.

"Hello," Rosa whispered. "I'd like to know about the steam."

"Come here," the witch said, standing up. "I'll show you."

Rosa moved forward very slowly, and her knees shook a little when she stepped past the booth threshold. The room in front of her was more spacious than she had imagined, with walls of bare stone and *graniglia* floors like those on the first floor of the Luna, only dirtier. There was a cot in a corner, behind the rocking chair.

"See all this?" the witch said, pointing at some strange equipment in the very back of the room. "I use it to make perfumes. It's a distillery, like the one my grandmother had at home."

Silently, Rosa stared at a wood stove much larger than the one in the Luna kitchen, a big iron box with pipes coming out of each side, a glass carafe with a pipe that looked like a pig's tail, and two marble mortars set on the floor. She thought those would be exactly the type of tools a witch would use to cast spells on people. "Perfumes?" she said. "I don't believe you. It stinks in here."

"Do you know how perfumes are made?" the witch asked.

Rosa shook her head.

"You pick flowers and plants and seeds and pieces of wood, and then you boil them. If you boil them long enough, they release oil. And then," the witch continued, pointing at the big box with the pipes, "you separate the oil from the steam and collect the oil"—she placed a hand on the carafe—"in here. Certain fruit peels you can't steam. You must press them in the mortars. When you do all this, it stinks. But a few weeks later, the stench goes away, and you can use the oils to make perfumes and massage balms. You can also mix them with melted wax and make scented candles."

"Where are the flowers and the plants?" Rosa asked with mistrust.

"In here," the witch said, pointing at a small door across from Rosa, next to the wood stove. The door opened with a squeak under the pressure of the witch's fingers.

From her position on the booth threshold, Rosa caught sight only of a deep darkness. *This is it,* she thought. *That's where the witch keeps the children. She uses the perfume story to lure us in, and then she boils us.*

"Don't be afraid," the witch whispered. "Look." She went in and returned a moment later holding a bouquet of lavender and a small cardboard box. "Hold on to this," she said, handing Rosa the lavender. "Smells good, huh? And look in here," she whispered, opening the box.

Rosa took a quick peak. There were white petals inside.

"They are orange blossoms," the witch said. "This," she added, taking a blossom in her hand, "is for you. You should put it between two sheets of paper and keep it there till it dries. It'll last forever."

They were both silent a while. Then Rosa stepped forward and walked cautiously toward the little door. Through the penumbra, she saw on the floor of the next room various flowers set in vases, a box filled with leaves and pieces of wood, and a second box filled with oranges, apples, and tangerines. As she slowly stepped in, she noticed shelves along one of the walls. On the shelves were boxes like the one that had the white petals inside, tiny glass bottles with cork stoppers and labels of different colors, and droppers like the one Madam C used to keep her eyes clear. Leaning against the opposite wall, filled to the top, were six cloth bags almost as tall as Rosa. "What are those?" Rosa asked.

Isabel pointed at a bag filled with purple flowers. "This is lavender," she said, then pointed at a second bag. "And these," she continued, taking in hand a few green leaves, "are eucalyptus leaves." She paused. "It takes a lot of them to make a tiny amount of oil."

"It's beautiful in here," said Rosa. She took a deep breath, and inhaled the strange aroma of the room. It was a combination of the stench from the booth and the perfumes of fruit and flowers.

"It still stinks a bit," the witch said, smiling.

Rosa nodded as she took a little blue bottle from the shelf. "Can I open it?"

The witch shook her head. "Not a good idea," she explained. "Then you'll truly smell a stench. These are the bottles where I keep the oils after the distillation. They must rest on these shelves for at least one month in order to lose their bad odors. If you want to smell something good, come this way."

It was then that Rosa noticed another door in the flower room. This time she followed the witch right away. It was the door to a pantry, with shelves on three walls.

"These," the witch said, pointing at the shelves, "are the bottles you should open. Go ahead."

Rosa took a bottle with a pink label, removed the cork, and brought it to her nose. She closed her eyes as she inhaled. It was a sweet and gentle odor, which lingered in her nostrils a long time.

"It's a blend of rosewood and tangerine blossoms," the witch said. She took a different bottle from the shelf. "Try this one now."

Rosa spent a long time sniffing bottles that day, while the witch reorganized the shelves and then peeled several tangerines and bright green apples.

At a certain point, the witch asked, "Would you like to help me with the distillery sometime?"

Rosa nodded.

"I'm always here," the witch said. "You can come back any time."

Rosa smiled. "You said that my hair reminds you of the sunsets back home. Where is your home?"

"Far away. In a beautiful land on the other side of the ocean."

Rosa's eyes glimmered. "You have been on the other side of the ocean?"

"I was born on the other side of the ocean," the witch said. "In a village called Manzanillo, on the eastern shore of Costa Rica."

Fascinated, Rosa stared at the witch with her large blue eyes. "Is that why you talk strange?"

"Yes. In Costa Rica people speak a different language: Spanish."

Rosa had heard the word *Spanish* before. Madam C had been upset one day over some men who had come to the Luna with no money. "Never let in Spanish sailors again," she had told the girls in an angry voice, "unless they show you the money at the door."

"Do people have money in Costa Rica?" Rosa asked.

"Sure they do," the witch said with a laugh. "It looks different from the Italian liras, but it's still money."

Rosa looked outside. "I have to go," she said, "or Madam C will get mad."

The witch nodded. "I'll see you later."

Rosa rushed to the street, then stopped and turned around. "What's your name?" she asked.

"Isabel," the witch replied.

"I'm Rosa," Rosa said before mingling with the crowd in motion.

CHAPTER 4

The visits to Isabel became the highlight of Rosa's days. Between her fascination with the distillation process and the fact that Isabel had crossed the ocean, Rosa couldn't wait to be finished with her chores to rush to Isabel's booth and ask her questions. Over a few days, she learned that Isabel was eighty years old and had learned the art of distillation as a child, watching her grandmother, Azul, back in Costa Rica. "There was a small hill behind our village," Isabel told Rosa, "where orchids grew year round, together with ferns and beautiful wildflowers. At least twice a week Azul would take me with her to the hill to pick what she needed to make oils. She had a distillery like this one"—Isabel pointed at the stove—"in a shack behind our house, next to the pigs and goats. No one ever complained about the stench, because it blended with the animals' odors. The trips to the hill were the best part of my days. It was quiet up there. The meadows had thick grass, and the palm trees were tall and wide. Azul and I would pick flowers for some time, then we would sit under a palm tree and she would tell me about the oils and their healing powers."

"Healing powers?" Rosa asked, mesmerized.

"These oils can heal all sorts of illnesses. Colds, infections, colics, fevers. Even unhappiness, melancholia, lunacy, and hallucinations. Azul used to say that the scent of these oils can make people fall in and out of love"—she snapped her fingers—"like that. You have to know how to combine them and use them. You can spread them on your skin, burn them in little glass pots, add them to your bathwater, or vaporize them and inhale them. It's an art. I can teach you, if you'd like."

"Yes!" Rosa shouted. "Teach me, please."

"It's not easy. And it takes time."

"I have time. I don't go to school."

"Why not?"

"Because people say things about me. They call me Prostitutes' Daughter."

"People are mean," Isabel nodded, "but you shouldn't listen to what they say."

"They say things about you, too—that you're a witch."

"I know," Isabel said. "But I don't listen. I do my things, as if these people weren't there."

"It's hard," Rosa sighed.

Isabel shook her head. "It's not hard if you love what you do."

"Do you love what you do?" Rosa asked.

"Very much. I take flowers and leaves, which are beautiful things, and I transform them into something even more beautiful."

"But when you steam the flowers, you kill them!" Rosa exclaimed.

"No." Isabel pointed at the bottles. "The flowers live in the scents of these oils. Oils are the hearts of the plants. They know everything about the plants they came from, their days of sun and rain, their skies, cloudy or blue. It's a miracle. And when I make the miracle happen, I feel rich, even if I'm poor. And I don't care what the people of this town think or say about me."

"Do you have any friends?" Rosa asked.

"The flowers and the leaves and the oils are my friends." Isabel smiled. "And you, Tramonto."

"I like it when you call me Tramonto."

"I used to watch sunsets with Azul from the back porch of our house," Isabel said. "The sun set behind the hill, and Azul used to tell me that the sun went to sleep inside the hill and while it slept it gave its energy to the plants and flowers, and that's why they had such beautiful colors in the morning."

"Where is Azul now?" Rosa asked.

"She's dead. We buried her in a meadow, under her favorite palm tree. I was your age when she died. I thought my whole world had ended."

"Did you cry?"

"I cried a lot," Isabel said. "But then I had to help my parents with the goats and other chores around the house, so I started crying less and less, and then I stopped. But I have thought of Azul every day."

"I do chores, too," Rosa said. "And I think of my mother every day. She died when I was born."

"Keep thinking of her. This way she'll never be alone."

"That's what Madam C told me."

"What do you have in there?" Isabel asked, pointing at a bag Rosa had brought along.

"Books," Rosa said. "I take them with me when I go to the port. I sit down somewhere and read. The books are my friends."

Isabel looked at her with surprise. "You know how to read?"

"I do."

"If I teach you what I know about oils," Isabel asked, "will you read me stories?"

"I can teach you how to read, if you want," Rosa offered.

"I'm too old for that. My eyes aren't good anymore. But you have good eyes. Will you read to me?"

"Sure. I love to read, anyway. And it's more fun to read to someone than by myself. At the Luna Margherita reads me poetry every day."

"Lesson one," Isabel said. "You must steam the flowers while they are fresh, or they'll lose their magic."

"Where do you find flowers around here?" Rosa asked. "And the wood and the petals?"

"Years ago, when I was much younger, I used to go to the hills behind Genoa to pick flowers. It's a long walk, much longer than the walk Azul and I had to take to reach our hill in Costa Rica. Then my legs got tired, so now I go down the street and hire a carriage once in a while." Isabel shook her head. "It's getting more complicated every day. The city has grown so much up there. The meadows are farther and farther away. Sometimes I buy what I need at the flower market, sometimes I find it in the streets nearby. You have no idea how many useful ingredients people discard as garbage. In the evening, when the market closes, I look behind the stalls and underneath the counters. It's not the same as picking flowers in a meadow, but you'd be surprised how much you can collect this way. Dried leaves, discarded stalks, twigs. You can make oils out of all of them, if you know how."

"What about the tall bags?" Rosa asked.

"Two sailors from Sevilla," Isabel said, "come by whenever their ship anchors in the harbor and bring me the eucalyptus leaves, which make good medicinal oils. I like their visits a lot, because I get to speak in my native language. For a few moments, it's as if I were back in Costa Rica. And"—she continued—"a woman who lives in the countryside brings me lavender once a month. The sailors from Sevilla also buy my oils and perfumes and take them on their ship. Azul and I used to sell our oils once a week at the market on the main plaza of the town up the coast from Manzanillo. It was a lot of fun, with all the other sellers and with the children and their families coming by."

"Why didn't you get a shop in Sottoripa?" Rosa asked.

"Years ago I tried," Isabel replied, "but the shopkeepers didn't want me there. They thought I would keep their customers from coming."

"They are stupid," Rosa said, angrily.

"Maybe. But I sell to the sailors from Sevilla, two Portuguese ship captains, a businessman from Tangiers, and a few rich women from Milan who send their maids here when they come to Genoa on vacation." She looked out of the booth at the narrow street. "Genoa is a strange place. I sell my perfumes all over the world, but I can't sell them to the people of this town. Anyway, I make enough money to keep buying flowers, the wood I need for the stove, and the ice blocks I need to cool down the steam."

"Your voice is sweet," Rosa said. "You don't sound like an old woman. Antonia is an old woman, and she has a deep voice that fades at the end of the sentences."

"Thank you," Isabel said. "Would you like to see one of the miracles of these oils?"

"Sure."

"Here," Isabel said, lifting the sleeve of her black vest to expose her arm. "Feel it."

Rosa placed a finger on Isabel's arm and slowly grazed her skin. "It's so soft! It feels like . . . a baby's skin."

"That's right," Isabel said. "Now smell it."

Rosa hesitated. She loved Isabel, but she always thought that she looked dirty. Her hair was all tangled, she always wore the same black vest, and the sheets on her cot looked like they hadn't been changed or washed in quite some time. Rosa had no desire to place her nose anywhere close to Isabel's skin.

"Smell it," Isabel said in a tone Rosa couldn't disobey.

So Rosa sniffed, and what she sniffed was the sweetest odor she had ever sniffed in her life, sweeter than Antonia's chocolate cakes, sweeter than Margherita's incenses, sweeter than the oils she had smelled in the pantry that first day.

Isabel noticed the surprise in Rosa's eyes. "These oils have marvelous qualities," she explained. "They produce different odors on different people. There's a perfect oil for everyone, and it's an oil that makes your skin smell like a meadow."

"How do you find your perfect oil?" Rosa asked.

"You try."

"When do you stop trying?"

"When you find your perfect oil," Isabel explained, "you'll know it. The oil will tell you."

"Can you help me find my perfect oil?"

"You'll have to find it yourself," Isabel said. "You can start with the ones in the pantry. Or you can make your own oils after you learn how."

"What's in your perfect oil?" Rosa asked.

Isabel cocked her head. "I'm not quite ready to give my secrets away."

"I'll read you all my books," Rosa implored.

Isabel smiled. "Come back tomorrow morning. You'll read me ten pages, and I'll show you how to make lavender oil."

Punctually, Rosa returned the following morning after her shopping duties. She read Isabel ten pages of a dragon story, then helped her place lavender bouquets inside the steamer. "How did you cross the ocean?" Rosa asked as they watched the mix of steam and oil fill the pipes.

"When I was twenty," Isabel began, "a foreigner and his crew arrived in Manzanillo on a small ship stranded by a storm. His name was Francesco Carravieri. He was from Genoa, he told us, where he had a successful import-export business, and he was always sailing seas and oceans in search of goods to buy. He stayed in Manzanillo one month, waiting for his ship to be repaired. He was tall, with dark, sparkling eyes and long brown hair that danced on his shoulders when he walked. I fell in love. He fell in love with me. Before the month was over, he told my father he wanted to marry me. So we married. It was a beautiful ceremony by the water. The whole village was there. After the ceremony we ate good food, danced, and lit fires on the docks. I was very happy. Help me with the ice, will you? We need to make sure the steam turns to water right away. See? The oil is lighter than the water, and that's how you separate them."

"What happened next?" Rosa asked, still wide-eyed.

"A few days after the wedding the ship was repaired, and Francesco told me we'd board and go to Genoa. I said good-bye to my family and my friends."

"Were you sad?"

"Yes, but also happy. I was so much in love I couldn't even think of being without Francesco for a moment. And I was excited about this long trip across the ocean. All along Francesco had told me how beautiful Genoa was, with its port and steep hills falling deep into the water. I couldn't wait. Before leaving, I went to the hill behind our house, to Azul's tomb, to say goodbye. Now, Rosa, put another block of ice over the serpentine. Like that. Good. Anyway, we took off. I brought with me a trunk filled with my clothes, oil bottles, and a jewelry box. The jewels in it were my parents' wedding present. They had belonged to my mother and to Azul and to Azul's mother. I looked at the jewels many times during the trip, especially when I became sad. They helped me feel better, because it was as if Azul and my mother were close to me, even though they were getting farther away as we kept sailing. From Manzanillo we sailed a long way south to the Colombian port of Cartagena, where we stopped for a few days for food and water. Then from Cartagena we crossed the ocean. I was sick most of the time, so I don't remember much other than water, water, water. Some days I felt so bad I thought I'd never see land again. By the time we arrived here, I had lost so much weight my clothes didn't fit anymore, and when I looked at myself in the mirror I thought I saw a ghost." She paused. "I'll always remember the first time I saw Genoa. It was a crisp September day, the sea was calm, and as Francesco's ship entered the port I caught sight of the hills, falling steeply toward us, and I felt like they were welcoming me home."

"And then?"

"Francesco turned out to be a monumental liar," Isabel said. "The ship was not his. It belonged to a company that had financed that expedition. The ship captain had died in the storm. Francesco was his cabin boy. He didn't own any import-export company. He didn't own anything, other than these two rooms. That's where we lived, although he was hardly ever here. He had no money. The first thing he did after we disembarked was to take my jewels out of the trunk and sell them on the black market. Then he bought liquor and got himself drunk. He told me he had put the rest of the money away. Where, he never said. When he was sober, he went out looking for jobs and occasionally worked at the docks for a few days. Most of the time, he was a thief. One night he got into a fight with one of his accomplices over the price of some stolen merchandise, and the accomplice stabbed him in the heart. I was left alone."

Rosa took Isabel's hand. "What did you do?"

Isabel sighed. "I wanted to go back to Costa Rica, but I had no money to pay for the trip. Even if I had had the money, I had no idea which ship to take. I was so afraid. And I didn't want to go back to my parents without the jewels. They had been in my family for so long. I felt terrible about having lost them. I tried to find a job. I could speak some Italian by then, because Spanish and Italian have similar words, but people heard my accent and saw my dark skin and turned me away. No one would hire me. I felt ready to die."

"But you didn't die," Rosa said.

"No, Tramonto. I didn't." She pointed at the stone wall on the east side of the booth. "One morning I saw a loose stone in this wall. I had never noticed it before, and I have no idea why I noticed it that day. I wiggled it, and the stone came off." She pulled a stone off the wall. "It's this one, see? Inside this hole there was a bundle of money. I don't know if it came from the jewels or from Francesco's burglaries. With it, I tried to buy a passage to South America on a cargo ship, thinking that from there I would find my way north to Costa Rica. No one would take me on board. They said women were bad luck, and women with dark skin were even worse luck. So I came back to these rooms and cried for a few days. Then I wondered what Azul would have done in my situation, and I figured she wouldn't be crying at all. She would build a distillery, no matter where she was, and make a living doing what she loved." She pointed at the stove and containers and pipes. "That's when I decided to use Francesco's money to build this. Some parts I bought, other parts I had made by a blacksmith down the street. I have been here ever since."

Rosa smiled a long time. "Sometimes, when I don't know what to do, I think of my mother and ask myself what she would do. Then I find the answer. It's strange, because I never even met her. But it's as if I had known her all my life."

Isabel nodded. "That's how it is when you love someone." She sat on the rocking chair. "Your turn, Tramonto. Tell me your story."

Over the next half hour, Rosa told Isabel about Angela, Madam C, the Luna, the girls, her school stories, and her dream of crossing the ocean. She arrived at the Luna late that afternoon, holding a bottle of diluted eucalyptus oil Isabel had given her as a present. "Rub some in the morning on your wrists and ear lobes," Isabel had told her. "You'll feel energy and happiness in you." Rosa placed the bottle on her nightstand, next to her books. In one of the books, she had the orange blossom Isabel had given her on the day they had met.

Over the next few weeks, Rosa learned as much as she could about the oils and the distillation process. When she didn't help Isabel steam flowers or press fruit peels in the mortars, she experimented mixing the oils that were in the pantry in search of the perfect blend for her skin. One evening, at the Luna, she asked Madam C, "Can you take me to the hills to pick flowers?"

"Where does this come from, Rosa?" Madam C said. "The hills? To pick flowers?"

"Yes. I would like that very much."

"Why?"

"I've never been anywhere," Rosa explained, "other than in these *caruggi* and at the port."

"Why the hills?"

"Could you take me there, please? For my birthday present."

Madam C looked at Rosa for a moment. "All right," she said. "For your birthday present."

One week before Rosa's sixteenth birthday, on a sunny and warm day, Madam C walked with Rosa to Piazza De Ferrari, the large round piazza that was the heart of the city. There were electric trams everywhere, some standing, some circling the piazza in slow motion. In the southwest corner, thick with the odors of hay and fresh manure, Madam C hired a carriage. "Take us to the meadows above San Nicolò," Madam C told the driver. "I'll guide you as we go."

The driver nodded and helped Rosa and Madam C to their seats. He made a screeching sound with the corner of his mouth and the horse began to walk.

"Can he go faster?" Rosa asked.

The driver overheard her. "Too much traffic, miss," he said. "Automobiles and trams make the horses all nervous. I've seen more crushed bodies in the past six months than in the twenty years I've been driving this carriage. These days, pedestrians can be thankful to make it across the street alive. I can't be careful enough. Do you know the saying? *Chi va piano va sano e va lontano*. Sit back, and enjoy the ride."

Rosa sank happily into her seat. It was her very first carriage ride. Up till then she had hardly ever left the *caruggi* or the port area and had been fearful of the traffic of the big town. But up there in her seat, next to Madam C, watching people and trams and the roofless automobiles pass by, she felt safe and important, and excited to be headed for the hills for the first time.

The carriage left downtown without incident. The road steepened, and the horse puffed and snorted as it proceeded slowly up the slope. Soon, the noise of the traffic subsided and the streets turned quiet, the silence broken only by the echo of the hooves on the pavement and the voices of occasional passersby. Rosa was bewitched by Genoa's beauty: the roads, much cleaner, wider, and brighter than the *caruggi*; the elegant buildings with no pigeons huddled on the gutters or roaming in flocks by the front doors; and the view of the port and the sea she occasionally could get when she looked behind. Madam C was also in awe, even though she had spent all her life in Genoa and been on those hills many times before. That day, a light northern breeze, *la tramontana*, was caressing the top of the hills, sweeping the sky clear of all clouds and flattening the water like a mirror. With a smile, Madam C removed her hat and set it on the seat. She said, "What a wonderful day we picked for our ride."

Rosa nodded and kept looking right and left with her curious, wondrous eyes.

At a certain point, Madam C asked the driver to make a sharp right and follow a steep path surrounded by patches of purple and pink bougainvillea. "We are almost there," she told Rosa, pointing ahead.

The carriage stopped at the end of the path, and Rosa and

Madam C continued on foot along a dirt trail that took them to an open green area set on the flank of the hill, high above the houses. In it were small meadows studded with wildflowers and areas with groves of olive trees, oleanders, orange, and lemon trees. Genoa's temperate slow-changing climate allowed those plants to grow lushly all over the hills as well as along the riviera, near the water. The perfumes of fruit and leaves blended with the scents of the sea to form a unique fragrance that—the natives liked to say—lingered inside the Genoeses' souls and mixed with their blood and bones. Those who had smelled that fragrance, the saying had it, were bound to it forever.

Gingerly, Rosa walked on grass for the first time. She smelled the clean earth and stared at the flowers sprouting from the ground. She sniffed and touched a long time, picked flowers, leaves, and petals, and all along thought of Isabel and Azul, together on the hill in Costa Rica, and understood how happy they must have been together. "Thank you," she told Madam C on the way home.

"Before we go back," Madam C said, "there's something I want to show you." She asked the carriage driver to make a detour on the way down and stop for a few minutes by the belvedere. It was a piazza on the lower part of the hill from where one could enjoy an unobstructed view of the city, the port, and the coastline. They sat on a south-facing bench and watched the scenery in brooding silence: streets and houses rolling steeply downhill to touch the shoreline, ships resting in the calm harbor waters, docks extending out into the sea like giant fingers pointing to reach the horizon. "It's amazing how different the city looks from up here," Madam C said to the stunned Rosa.

"Where is Vico del Pepe?" Rosa asked.

"Somewhere in that direction," Madam C replied, pointing down and to her left, "but it's impossible to pinpoint it from up here."

Rosa had never seen rooftops before. She had never even thought of what might be at the very top of the buildings she was used to looking at from below. She stared at the slate tiles, the hanging gardens, the water reservoirs that studded the terraces, the jumble of stairways, and the swallows darting in the sky. She squinted her eyes in the direction Madam C had pointed, and couldn't believe that down there, somewhere, were the Luna and the roads she had walked all her life. For a moment, she pretended she saw herself sitting by the port and dreaming. She whispered, "It's almost like looking at someone else's life."

"We should come back here at night," Madam C said. "Then you'd really be amazed."

"Thank you for bringing me here," Rosa said as they regained their seats in the carriage and headed for downtown.

"You're welcome, dear," Madam C nodded, unsure as to what was going on in Rosa's mind. She had seen her happy before, but never quite this way. It was an inner happiness, she thought, much more mature than the lighthearted happiness of a girl. She asked, "What are you going to do with all these leaves and flowers?"

"You can have some for your room," Rosa said, "and some for the parlor. The rest, I have to take somewhere."

"When I was a child," Madam C said after a moment, "I had this dream that on my eighteenth birthday I would ride on the hills on a white horse."

"Did you get to do it?" Rosa asked.

"No," Madam C replied with only a hint of sadness. "I'm happy you had your day picking flowers."

Rosa took the flowers to Isabel that afternoon. "Thank you," Isabel said, holding back tears. "It has been so long since I held in my hands flowers that still smell of the earth they were in. Well, let's get to work here."

"I think I found a blend of oils that my skin likes," said Rosa.

"Really?" Isabel asked. "Which oils are in it?"

"Apple blossoms, lavender, and basil."

"That's an unusual blend," Isabel said. "Let me smell it."

Rosa opened a small blue bottle and placed it under Isabel's nose.

"Interesting," Isabel commented. "I can almost smell the apples. Rub it on your skin."

Gingerly, Rosa poured a drop of oil on her fingertip, then turned her other hand palm up and rubbed the fingertip on the soft skin of her wrist. Isabel sniffed the wrist three times. "Very good," she said. "It smells a lot better on you than on its own, and that's a sign that the oil blends well with the quality of your skin. Keep rubbing it on you. If you never get tired of its odor, it means it's your perfect oil. If after a few weeks it starts annoying you, then you'll have to look for another one."

Rosa nodded. "In one week," she said, "it'll be my sixteenth birthday. There will be a party at the Luna. I'd like you to come."

Isabel shook her head. "Thank you, Tramonto, but no."

"Why?"

"I never go anywhere, other than to the market looking for flowers."

"So come to the Luna. It's my birthday."

"People don't like to be with me," Isabel said, continuing to shake her head, "and I don't like to be with people."

"You like to be with me, don't you?"

"Yes, but you're different." She paused. "Your eyes are clear."

"You're wrong," Rosa said, almost in tears. "Madam C would like you, and so would Margherita, Maddalena, and Stella. And the other Luna girls. They're nice. Maddalena is the one who told me that there must be an explanation for your steam and I should not reach conclusions about you without asking. She reads tarots. I'm sure she'd love to read your future."

"I love you, Tramonto," Isabel said, "but don't ask me to go to a party with lots of people. That's something I cannot do. But I have an idea."

"What?"

"We'll celebrate your birthday right here, right now. I have a present for you."

Carefully, Isabel pulled loose the stone that had hidden Francesco's money years earlier and took a small glass bottle out of the wall. "This," she said, "is the only bottle I have left from the batch I brought with me from Costa Rica. Azul and I made this oil. I want you to have it."

Rosa took the bottle but said, "I couldn't. You should keep it."

"Take it," Isabel insisted. "Azul would want you to have it."

"What kind of oil is it?" Rosa asked.

Isabel chuckled. "I don't know. I don't remember. And I can't tell what it is from its odor. For sure it was made from flowers and leaves we picked on the hill. Smell it," she said, opening the bottle. "See if you like it."

"I love it," Rosa said, sniffing gently a few times. "It's"—she paused—"very strong."

"It's very concentrated," Isabel warned her. "Try adding a few drops of it to your blend. See what it feels like to you."

With the care of a magician, Rosa poured three drops of Azul's oil into the bottle of her blend of lavender, basil, and apple blossoms.

"Wait a few seconds to let Azul's oil blend in," Isabel said. "Now rub it on your wrist again, and tell me if it feels different."

"It does," Rosa said after a moment. "It's more . . . I don't know how to describe it. More . . . real."

"Very good," Isabel said. "Maybe your apple blossoms, basil, and lavender needed Azul's oil to be your perfect blend. Who knows? Here, take this, too." She gave Rosa a small glass cup set on a metal tripod. "Pour a little bit of oil in this cup, then add water. One part of oil, ten parts of water. Place a lit candle under the cup. The water will boil and evaporate, taking along the scent of the oil. You can make your room smell of your perfect blend this way. But watch out. These scents have strange effects on people. Some will be entranced by it, others will hate it."

"I'll watch out, I promise. Thank you," Rosa said.

"Don't mention it, Tramonto. Happy birthday."

On the day of her birthday, around noon, when she was certain Santina had finished cleaning and wouldn't go back to her room, Rosa took out of her closet Isabel's birthday present and took it to the deserted kitchen. Quietly, she poured in the glass cup ten parts of water and one part of her blend of Azul's oil, lavender, basil, and apple blossoms, then opened Antonia's pantry and got hold of a small candle and a box of wooden matches. She took everything back to her bedroom, where she placed the tripod on her nightstand and the filled cup on the tripod. Seated on her bed, she lit the candle and placed it underneath the cup. Soon, her room smelled slightly of her oil. It was a delicate yet sharp smell, sweet and spicy at the same time, that startled even Rosa when she returned to her room an hour later. "This *is* my perfect oil," she said aloud. "I have no doubt."

Around seven in the evening, when the party was about to get started in the parlor, Madam C told Margherita, "I think we should do away with the poetry reading."

Margherita asked, "Why? Rosa asked for it."

"You know the mayor," Madam C said. "He hates poetry."

"I don't care," Rosa said, entering the parlor in her white dress.

"Don't be so selfish," Madam C said in a hard voice.

"It's her birthday," Stella said. "She's supposed to be selfish. Besides, who cares if the mayor doesn't like poetry."

"I do," Madam C insisted. "He's the guest of honor."

"If he comes to my party," Rosa said, "he'll have to listen to Margherita read poetry. He won't die."

"If I see him exhaling his last breath," Maddalena said with a naughty smile, "I'll give him mouth-to-mouth resuscitation. That he'll like."

"Come here, Rosa," Madam C said, handing Rosa a small jewelry case. "This is for you."

Rosa opened the case and saw two small gold earrings in the shape of a loop with a tiny pendant at the bottom.

"They belonged to Angela," Madam C explained. "I gave them to her many years ago as a birthday present. When she started to feel sick after your birth, she wanted me to have them. She'd be happy to know that they are with you now."

Rosa held them tight. "Thank you."

"Someone's knocking," Stella said.

Madam C headed for the door. "Let's see who our first guest is."

The first guest to arrive was Ildebrando Balbi, balder than ever. He had closed the Carena a wealthy man five years earlier and wed Mariangela, his lover of fifteen years. Ildebrando and Mariangela were followed by some of the neighborhood's shop-keepers and their families: Mafalda, the woman who had nursed Rosa for two years; five former Luna girls with their respective men; Pietro Valdasco—with whom Madam C had years earlier reconciled—in a wheelchair because of a recent stroke; Michele Merega, an older doctor who had been watching over the health of the Luna girls for nine years; Antonia, the crafter of all the food; Mr. Razzano, the *robivecchi*, with his wife; the two police-men in charge of the neighborhood; and other friends Madam C had fostered during the years.

Rosa, radiant in her white dress, with her shining red hair, was charming everyone with her happy smile. Her eyes glimmered in the light, and the guests couldn't stop complimenting her on her dress, her earrings, her hair, and, overall, her beauty. By eight-thirty, the party was in full swing. At eight-forty, the mayor arrived.

He made a slow, deliberate entrance, nodding right and left and smiling. "The mayor is here," Mafalda yelled, joining her hands as if she had seen the pope. Ildebrando Balbi started clapping. Immediately, everyone else joined in. As the mayor waved to everyone with satisfaction, Madam C, ravishing in a long, tight dress of blue silk, rushed toward him with her arms open. "Cesare, Cesare," she said, sighing. "It has been too long. Let me look at you." She stepped back. "You look gorgeous. What does that wife of yours do to you to keep you in such wonderful shape?"

"It's the memories of you, my dear," Cesare Cortimiglia said, hugging Madam C, "that keep me young."

"Still smoking, huh?" Madam C asked, pointing at the briar pipe the mayor had in hand. "I don't recall having ever seen you without it."

"This pipe is part of me," the mayor said, "like"—he raised his voice—"this brothel!"

All the Luna girls applauded.

"Come," Madam C said. "Meet Rosa."

When the mayor had entered the Luna a few moments earlier, from the opposite corner of the parlor, Rosa had examined him with curiosity, trying to remember if she had seen him before. She saw a six-foot-tall thin man dressed in an elegant dark gray suit. His salt-and-pepper curly hair and the round gold-rimmed glasses he wore halfway down his nose reminded Rosa immediately of Mr. Rabetti, a teacher at Miss Cipollina's school. She kept staring at him with fascination.

"This beautiful lady is Rosa?" the mayor said, exaggerating his surprise.

Rosa nodded shyly.

With a gallant motion, the mayor bent forward, took Rosa's hand firmly in his, and kissed it. As his lips touched Rosa's skin, his nose caught a whiff of her perfect oil. At once, without the slightest hint or premonition, his spine turned rigid, his forehead icy cold. His hairy, masculine fingers softened around Rosa's thin-boned ones, yet refused to let them go. He remained in that bent position a while, lips on Rosa's knuckles, head drowned in a thick fog. When he finally rose again and his eyes met Rosa's, he stood frozen by her, aware only of the scent lingering in his nostrils and the furious thumps of his heartbeat.

CHAPTER 5

The long-standing friendship between Cesare Cortimiglia and Madam C had started twenty-six years earlier, on the evening of his eighteenth birthday. As a present, three of his friends had taken him at night to the Carena. One of the friends, Guglielmo, was a regular client of that brothel, so Ildebrando Balbi walked up to the group the moment they stepped into the crowded lounge. "Welcome, my friend," he said to Guglielmo. "What can I do for you?"

"We need a special treatment tonight, Signor Balbi," said Guglielmo, a tall redheaded boy with a voice muddled by alcohol. "Our birthday boy," he went on, placing his arm around Cesare Cortimiglia's shoulders, "is a virgin!"

The young Cesare blushed as everyone in the room laughed and applauded.

Guglielmo bowed to Signor Balbi. "We entrust him"—he stood up—"to your girls."

Signor Balbi bowed back. "Only the best for you, my friend," he said, then gazed about the room and nodded at a tall, dark-haired girl standing in a corner. At once, the girl walked toward him, waving her hips in sinuous motion. She was Clotilde. In front of Cesare Cortimiglia, she ran two fingers over his sweaty neck, undoing the knot of his tie. When the knot was undone, she pulled the tie off him and tossed it into the middle of the room, accompanied by the other guests' claps and whistles. Cesare blushed even more. He put up no resistance as Clotilde untied his belt and pulled him by the belt's end to the opposite end of the lounge, toward a green door. The whistles and claps became louder. By the door, in a red and gold corset tighter on her body than a screw, stood Angela. As Clotilde approached, followed by the confused birthday boy, Angela pulled the door open. As soon as Clotilde and Cesare had walked past it, she waved coquettishly to the crowd, then followed the duo into the dimly lit hallway, closing the door behind her.

The two ecstatic hours Cesare Cortimiglia spent that night in the arms of Angela and Clotilde would forever alter his perception of the world and his role in it. He had undergone a revelation: there was nothing on earth, he told himself on his way out of Clotilde's room and later as he staggered along the *caruggi* in a state of deep bliss, worthier than love. At once, he became a habitué of the Carena and several other downtown brothels, which would remain his playground for twenty-one years. An importer by day in the shipping company of his father, he turned into a relentless lover by night and into the skilled and quick client that was every brothel girl's dream.

Like a sultan, he had favorites in his harem. There was Luz, the mulatto girl who had arrived on a cargo ship from the West Indies, with her full lips and cinnamon hair grazing her buttocks; Ortensia, tall, with a diaphanous skin and a birthmark across her lower back shaped like a half moon; and Matilda, with chameleon almond-shaped eyes, blue and green in the daylight, purple and hazelnut in the orange glow her Chinese lantern cast on the walls of her cubicle. She kept relics of her favorite clients in a box lined with red velvet. Of Cesare Cortimiglia, she kept a lock of hair she had cut with his consent after his third visit and a shirt button that had fallen off his clothes one night without his knowledge during his methodical undressing routine. It was a bottom-up process: shoes first, then socks, pants, underwear, tie, shirt, and undershirt. A looks-conscious man with a taste for elegant, expensive clothes, he took great care in folding and storing his apparel before making love. He placed the shoes next to one another at the foot of the bed; underwear, socks, and tie on the seat of a chair; his shirt on the back of the same chair; and for his pants, he always requested a wooden hanger with two clips to eliminate all chance that wrinkles could form while he was naked. He never lingered in bed after the fact, for he disliked his own nakedness as much as he relished fancy clothes. "Nakedness is a burden of love," he'd often say, "and not a condition a man should be in longer than necessary." So the moment the sexual act was over, he dressed swiftly in the exact opposite order he had undressed, beginning with his undershirt and ending with his shoes. The only word he uttered on the way out of his lover's room was "Good-bye."

His generosity matched his hunger for love. For the girls he saw regularly, like Luz, Ortensia, and Matilda, he often brought presents purloined from the warehouses of his father: exotic jewelry bought in Cairo, little mirrors set in engraved silver frames imported from the bazaars of Constantinople, colorful silk cuts manufactured in Bombay. He called the girls "princesses of my dreams," and they would jokingly bow to him as if he were their king. Of all his princesses, no one was closer to his heart than Clotilde, with whom he'd spent many wild nights at the Carena.

One evening, he arrived at the brothel in a very bad mood.

"What's the matter, Cesare?" Clotilde asked, as he slumped in an armchair and asked for a glass of red wine. "You're not your bubbly self tonight."

"It's my father," Cesare Cortimiglia sighed.

She sat on the armrest. "What about him?"

"He keeps annoying me. He wants me to marry and make children, so our breed won't die."

"Is that such a bad thing?" Clotilde asked.

"Getting married? No, not if one wants to. But I don't want to. I need to be free."

"Did you tell your father?"

"Sure I did. He said he's going to disown me if I continue to spend my nights in the brothels. 'I'm soiling the family name,' he says." He pondered a moment. "He's obsessed with my marriage. Talks about it every day. It's a nightmare."

"Most people have worse problems than this, you know."

"I guess," he admitted. "But he did get on my nerves tonight."

"I know exactly what you need to calm your nerves, darling," Clotilde said, unbuttoning the front of her camisole.

"I have an idea," Cesare said with a clever smile. "I'll tell my father I want to marry you. He'll have a heart attack, and I'll be free to spend the rest of my life in the brothels."

"Get over here," Clotilde said, standing up and beginning to walk.

Cesare pushed himself out of the armchair and staggered after her past the green door. "What is the meaning of life?" he asked as they walked toward her cubicle.

Clotilde laughed loudly, then cupped her hand against his testicles. "This," she said, squeezing, "is the meaning of life. But you know that already, dear."

They had a second personal conversation a few months later, over a glass of anisette in the lounge of the Carena. It was Clotilde who spoke about herself on that occasion. "I'm getting old," she said, "and I'm afraid. This"—she circled her hand about the room—"is all I know."

"Have you thought about running a brothel rather than working in one?" Cesare asked after a moment.

"And how would I do that? I can't even read or write."

"You're smart. You can learn."

"Even if I learned," Clotilde said with discouragement in her voice, "where would I find the money to take over a brothel?"

"You don't need money to take over a brothel," Cesare pointed out. "All you need is a loan."

Clotilde gave him a dejected look. "Do you think there are bankers out there who give loans to prostitutes?"

"If they had a guarantor, they would. You find a business you want, and I'll help you get it. Meanwhile, I'll find you a tutor. To become a businesswoman, you must be able to read and write."

"Why are you going through all this trouble for me?"

He took her hand. "My dear, you taught me all I know about love, and for that I'll always be grateful. It's my turn now to do something for you. But you take this seriously, the tutor and learning to read and write."

"Of course I will," Clotilde said excitedly.

Promptly, a tutor showed up at the Carena the following day and kept coming for Clotilde every morning at eight. As she had promised, Clotilde listened and practiced diligently until, two months later, she was able to read aloud without stuttering and write in black ink with fluid motions. "Congratulations," Cesare told her one night, handing her a set of papers. "Here's the loan for that Luna business you chose." Clotilde nodded quietly with grateful eyes.

"I like your new name," Cesare said when a few days later Clotilde told him she had decided to call herself Madam C. "It's exotic. I'm already turned on."

From then on, he never set foot in another brothel. He arrived at the Luna every evening around nine and spent most of the night there with Madam C, Angela, or any of the beautiful girls Madam C hired and personally trained. On the day Rosa was born, he sent Angela an immense bouquet of flowers. "He's a good man," Madam C said, as she laid the flowers on Angela's bed.

"He's the best," Angela replied with a fading voice.

Changes came into Cesare's life eleven years later. At thirty-nine, about the time his father had given up on the dream of a grand white wedding for his son, Cesare Cortimiglia met Maria Elena Cerutti, the twenty-year-old educated daughter of Enrico Cerutti, a wealthy man who had made his fortune in real estate and foreign trading. They married two months later, stunning everyone in town, most notably his peers, who had labeled Cesare Cortimiglia a confirmed bachelor, and the prostitutes, who couldn't begin to imagine life without the client of their dreams. "You scoundrel," Madam C said, slapping the white skin of his butt. "You figured out the meaning of life!"

There was a much simpler explanation for Cesare's drastic change of mindset. During a day-long business meeting with high functionaries in Rome, he had had his very first taste of political power. At the end of the day, he had boarded the train back to Genoa in a state of inner frenzy, completely fascinated by those ruthless, influential men in much the same way he had been fascinated on the night of his eighteenth birthday by the power of physical love. It was on that train that he decided he would marry soon, as he couldn't possibly rise to power as a bachelor with a double life, one as a businessman, one in the brothels.

He bid farewell to the brothels the night before the wedding with an erotic marathon at the Luna that would be talked about in the *caruggi* for years to come. There was music, dancing, and champagne *a gogo*. In his honor, Madam C made her bed with sheets of French linen, a white embroidered bedspread, and the plushest pillows she had been able to find. It was on that bed that the marathon took place, a flock of young girls coming and going, with the special participation, at certain times of the night, of the then seasoned Luz, Ortensia, and Matilda. Their good-byes lived up to the occasion. They pampered him with the most audacious erotic practices, including group sex and sex with each other. Before leaving, Luz hung around his neck a round amulet made of fish bones that women on her island gave as a wedding present to their brothers to bring about prosperity and fame; Ortensia gave him a card made of the finest parchment paper with a drawing on it of her moon-shaped birthmark; and Matilda left on the nightstand a tiny heart-shaped box filled with a lock of her hair. The last woman to savor Cesare's body, at the crack of dawn, as he lay languidly in the wet and disheveled linen sheets, was, of course, his oldest and dearest friend, Madam C. They made love like maniacs, screaming and panting without restraint, and when an hour later Cesare Cortimiglia said with a deep sigh, "I can't take this anymore. I'm exhausted," Madam C broke into unstoppable tears.

"I never thought I'd live to hear this," she sobbed, holding in hand Cesare's limp penis.

Not everything had gone without a hitch that night. Among the girls scheduled to participate in the marathon was Margherita, on her very first week working at the Luna. She had entered Madam C's room holding her big book of poetry, and as a naked Cesare stared at her from his horizontal position on the bed, she opened the book and read a passage from *Il Paradiso*:

> "'Fatto avea di la' mane e di qua sera
> tal foce, e quasi tutto era la' bianco
> quello emisperio, e l'altra parte nera,
> quando Beatrice in sul sinistro fianco . . .' "

At the sound of Margherita's voice, Cesare sat up straight. "What the hell is that?"

"Poetry," Margherita replied softly. "I read it before making love."

"Poetry?" he snapped. "Are you out of your mind?" he shouted. "I hate poetry! My teachers made me memorize it over and over in school." He cupped his hands over his ears. "I can't stand it!"

Madam C, who had heard everything from the sitting room, rushed in. "I'm so sorry, Cesare. Don't you worry, Luz is here." She turned to Margherita. "Go!"

Margherita left the room with a double dose of disappointment, for the failure of her poetry method and for having missed her only opportunity to be the lover of a man who was a legend in that part of town. Later, Madam C took Margherita aside. "Whatever got into your head?" she shouted. "Don't you know that all he wants is sex? With no preliminaries and no afterthoughts. I should have sent you away with Rosa. That way, you could have read poetry all night long."

Rosa, who was eleven years old at the time, had been shipped to Antonia's house to spend the night so she wouldn't hear the noises coming from the third floor or witness the coming and going of so many people. Madam C had told her that Antonia, who lived alone, wanted a friend over once in a while.

"Do you really live all by yourself?" Rosa had asked, surprised, as soon as she had stepped into Antonia's apartment.

"I do now," Antonia said. "I used to live with my siblings, but not anymore."

Rosa, accustomed to living at the Luna with no less than ten people, felt sorry for Antonia at once. "Why did your siblings leave you here alone?" she asked.

"Now that you are older," Antonia said in a grave voice, "I'll tell you everything about my family." She went on to tell Rosa the stories of her fifteen brothers and sisters: how some had died at a very young age, how others had run away from home and died afterward in catastrophic accidents or of terrible illnesses that had disfigured their faces. Over the course of the evening, she described the death of each sibling in great detail. The more gruesome the death, the deeper Antonia's voice became. There was Camelia, whose body parts had fallen off one by one because of the plague, and her twin sister Miranda, who had closed her eyes and stopped breathing at the sight of Camelia's crumbling body, so that everyone thought she was dead and they took her to the *lazzaretto* where they ended up burning her while she was still alive. "And you won't believe this," she said, brandishing a meat knife. "My brother Patrizio, the most handsome man I've ever seen, got the smallpox from his cow and died with ten holes in his face, each two centimeters deep."

Rosa listened to each one of those frightening stories with her mouth open, as if under a spell. As Antonia finished up the details of the last death, the thought hit Rosa that there were many dead people around, not just Angela and the person in the coffin she had seen. Later, in her temporary bedroom next to Antonia's room, she had fantasies about Angela walking around heaven with Antonia's siblings and wondered if they were getting along or even liked each other. "Angela, be nice to Antonia's siblings," she whispered as she fell asleep, "especially to Miranda, who isn't even supposed to be dead, if you know what I mean."

At the Luna, the farewell party wound down as the light of dawn peeked over the eastern promontories. Cesare Cortimiglia left the brothel in a stupor, his body numb, his ears ringing, and his head so heavy it felt as if it were filled with stones. He walked out of the *caruggi* slowly, without looking back.

His wedding was as traditional as his good-byes had been outrageous. The ceremony, celebrated in the Cathedral of San Lorenzo by the archbishop, was attended by the members of the Genoese upper class dressed for the occasion: men in their tails,

women in lavish dresses of silk and taffeta and hats embellished
with fresh flowers. A formal dinner at the Grand Hotel Isotta
followed the exchange of vows. A famous French chef cooked
the ten-course meal and had it served on silver plates garnished
with rose petals. As the bride and the groom left the dinner
scene headed for Biarritz, the celebration continued with a rare
private performance by members of the orchestra of the Carlo
Felice Theater.

Upon their return to Genoa two weeks later, Cesare and
Maria Elena Cortimiglia established themselves in a sumptuous
top-floor apartment on Via Assarotti overlooking downtown.
They soon became an important couple in the Genoese society,
partly because of the two families' social stature, partly because
of Cesare Cortimiglia's ability to maneuver himself into the
right places at the right time. Shortly, he became an active
politician representing the Liberals—a conservative party. In
1906, one month after his fortieth birthday, he was elected
mayor. His twenty-one years in the brothels were public knowledge all over town, so that many wondered how the city had
gotten stuck with a man of such predilections as its first citizen:

"Let's just hope he's done with those kinds of women."

"I hear he hasn't been near a brothel since his wedding day."

"You don't really think that men can give up that habit, do
you?"

"Time will tell. Let's wait and see."

Not only did Cesare stay away from the brothels, but, as
mayor, he did only good things for Genoa and its people, driven
by a vision for the city that struck a chord in many hearts. He
saw Genoa, at the time already in a position of prominence
among European cities, as the cultural capital of Europe. From
the very beginning of his tenure and even before, during his
election campaign, he worked in front of and behind the scenes
to improve the infrastructures of the port—the pulsing heart of

the city and what, in his opinion, gave Genoa its multicultural connotation and international stature. He brought together entrepreneurs, political leaders, and shipowners on projects to upgrade the transportation system and make access to the warehouses faster and more efficient. His second pet project was the arts. As soon as he took office, he set aside funds from the city budget to increase the number of yearly performances at the Carlo Felice Theater, reopen old theaters, and host famous musical and theatrical performances based in London and Paris. Eventually, the Genoese saw no reason to continue to discuss Cesare Cortimiglia's old life in the brothels, and the long list of his legendary paid lovers was scratched gradually from the daily gossip.

He received the invitation to Rosa's party four days before her birthday, around noon, while the city council was in session. As a city employee handed him the off-white envelope, the mayor had a hunch that the missive could be important and related to his old, libertine life rather than to his political one. One quick look at the back of the envelope was all he needed to know that his premonition had been correct. The color of the wax, a pale yellow, told him indeed that the envelope had come from the chambers of Madam C. Unhurriedly, he slipped the envelope into his pocket and forced himself to pay attention to the council's proceedings. Boring talk: street closures, traffic diversions, floral arrangements inside and outside City Hall, all in preparation for Theodore Roosevelt's visit to the town. He pursed his lips to hide a yawn, then smiled at the councilmen who debated the issues. It was past one o'clock when the council adjourned and he was able to lock himself in his office and break the seal. The contents of the letter made him frown. "I'll be damned," he said. "Rosa is already sixteen?"

The party at the Luna that night was informal. The food trays and the bottles of wine and liquor were lined up on the counter, next to plates and silverware the guests could freely use. No one was shy. Soon, the tongues loosened under the influence of the alcohol, and everyone was talking, laughing, and having a good time. The only guest who wasn't having a good time was the mayor. After his gallant kiss on Rosa's hand, he had been overcome by despair. "My dear Rosa," he had mumbled. "It's so wonderful to see you."

"Thank you," Rosa had replied. "Nice to see you, too. I heard a lot about you."

"Did you really?" the mayor had said rhetorically, trying to disguise his emotions.

Now, a half hour later, he felt as if he had been hit by a tram in motion. The scent he had inhaled off Rosa's skin was still in his nostrils, and none of the smells that lingered in the parlor— food, liquor, women's perfumes, cigarette smoke—could overtake it or diminish its power. He lit his pipe and breathed in deeply the tobacco smoke, drank glass after glass of full-bodied red wine, talked to the girls, the other guests, and Madam C, but the only thing he could think of was Rosa. From his position in the middle of the crowded parlor, he followed her moves, entranced by her shiny red hair, her fair, flawless skin, and her aquamarine eyes. He watched her as she blew the candles out on her birthday cake, cut the cake into slices, and laid the slices on the plates. All along, he felt his knees melt to the ground. She approached him a few minutes later. "Are you having a good time?" she asked.

He stared at her with the eyes of a puppy looking for love. "I remember you asleep in that big bed behind the kitchen," he said, completely at a loss as to how to conduct conversation with her. "You must have been three years old. Maybe four."

Rosa looked carefully about the room. When she was certain Madam C was nowhere close, she said, "It's still my bed. Would you like to see it?"

The bedroom smelled heavily of her perfect oil when Rosa opened the door and came in with the confused mayor. "See?" she said. "Here is my bed, like when I was four."

He smiled, standing by the bedroom door, realizing that for the first time in his entire life he had no clue as to what he should be doing. "Come in," Rosa said, closing the door behind him.

"Rosa . . ." he babbled. "I don't think . . . I should be here."

"I want to play the game with you," Rosa said. "Will you play with me?"

"Rosa, dear, what are you talking about? What game?"

"The game, you silly mayor. Like the girls play upstairs."

"Rosa," he mumbled, beginning to sweat and feel dizzy.

Without hesitation but with slow, deliberate moves, staring at Cesare's foggy eyes, Rosa unbuttoned her dress and let it fall to the floor. He held his breath as Rosa removed her petticoat, corset, and underwear. She stood naked in front of him, not even slightly embarrassed or intimidated, continuing to look into his eyes, watchful for his next move. That was the part of the game she was unclear about. She knew she had to be naked, but she didn't know what men were supposed to do with their bodies. As the mayor's breathing became faster, she wondered if she should ask him to show her the money right away or postpone all financial matters until the game was over. She observed him as he placed a hand on his belly and wrestled with something that stuck forward under his gray pants.

"I can't take this anymore," Cesare Cortimiglia sighed. That was when he began to undress, frantically, with no sense of where his clothes were falling, forgetting all about the undressing routine he had followed methodically for twenty-six years.

Rosa's eyes followed his movements like a hawk's, feeling in her belly the same heat she had felt a few days earlier lying on

Margherita's bed. The moment he tossed away his underwear, she stepped back and let out a short scream; the heat in her belly slowly disappeared. She had never seen a naked man before.

"I want you, Rosa," Cesare Cortimiglia moaned, almost in tears. He walked up to her and caressed her neck, breasts, and buttocks before pulling her into a long, furious embrace.

Mute with stupefaction, Rosa stood still the whole time, feeling his skin rub against hers and the strange thing he had in the front press against her belly and move up and down like a worm gone mad. She hardly realized that he had lifted her. They dropped on the bed, still entangled in the embrace.

"Touch me," begged the mayor, out of his mind.

Rosa thought that was fair. If he was allowed to touch her as part of the game, then she should touch him in order to have a chance to win. As he lay on his back, she placed a hand on his stomach and the other hand on his cheek. Slowly, he pushed her hand down from his stomach to his hard penis, and she instinctively grabbed it and looked at it with curiosity and only a trace of well-disguised fear. It was the strangest body part she had ever seen. In a rapture, Cesare closed his eyes and moved Rosa's hand rhythmically up and down. Suddenly he let out a howl and his belly twisted and his legs extended as Rosa felt his organ became suddenly harder and bigger and saw a white fountain come out of its tip and spray him and her and the clean batiste sheets. *What a weird game,* Rosa thought, as the mayor continued to howl.

He didn't open his eyes for over a minute. When he did, he stared at Rosa, still naked on the bed with him, still holding his now shrunk, wrinkled penis. "I love you," he said with humid eyes, then smiled at her and fell gradually and happily asleep. He had never fallen asleep after an orgasm, as he had never tossed his clothes carelessly on the floor. Months later, searching for the rationale for his odd behavior, he'd conclude that a combination of factors had come into play that night: the emotion of returning to the brothel, the strength of the orgasm, the red wine, his older age, and the scent of Rosa's oil.

Bewildered, Rosa watched him breathe regularly in his sleep. She slipped on her petticoat and dress and tiptoed out of the room, closing the door behind her. She had been gone less than ten minutes. In the parlor, Margherita was standing on a chair, holding her book of poetry and calling for everyone's attention. She saw Rosa in a corner and said, "This is for you, Princess Rosa," then she cleared her throat. Rosa walked up to her and clapped her hands, causing the guests to turn their attention to Margherita. "It's a love poem," Margherita said, "called 'A Silvia.'"

> "'Silvia, rimembri ancora
> quel tempo della tua vita mortale,
> quando belta' splendea
> negli occhi tuoi ridenti e fuggitivi,
> e tu, lieta e pensosa, il limitare
> di gioventu' salivi?
>
> "'Sonavan le quiete
> stanze, e le via dintorno,
> al tuo perpetuo canto,
> allor che all'opre femminili intenta
> sedevi, assai contenta
> di quel vago avvenir che in mente avevi.
> Era il maggio odoroso e tu solevi
> cosi' menare il giorno.
>
> "'Io gli studi leggiadri
> talor lasciando e le sudate carte,
> ove il tempo mio primo

e di me si spendea la migliore parte,
d'in su i veroni del paterno ostello
porgea gli orecchi al suon della tua voce,
ed alla man veloce che percorrea la faticosa tela.
Mirava il ciel sereno,
le vie dorate e gli orti,
e quinci il mar da lungi, e quindi il monte.
Lingua mortal non dice
quell ch'io sentivo in seno.'"

Margherita stopped reading as the guests remained silent a while longer. "I think it's enough," she said, closing the book. Everyone applauded. Rosa helped her down from the chair and kissed her on the cheek. "Thank you," she said. "That was wonderful. I don't know why, but when you read aloud, the poems sound so much more beautiful than on paper."

"You're welcome, Princess Rosa," Margherita said with a big smile. "Happy Birthday."

"Where's Cesare?" Madam C asked, looking around.

Rosa shrugged.

"Did you see him?" Madam C asked Margherita.

"No."

Madam C turned to the other girls. "Did you?"

A few girls shook their heads, others said no.

Madam C put on her angry face. "I bet he left when Margherita started to read that silly poem."

"It's not a silly poem," Rosa said. "It's beautiful."

"Maybe," Madam C mumbled, "but it sent Cesare away. I wanted him to stay a little longer. Who knows when I'll get to see him again."

"Watch out," Stella whispered in Maddalena's ear. "She's in a really bad mood now."

"What happened between her and the mayor in the past? Do you know?" Maddalena whispered back.

"Nothing," Stella replied, "other than paid sex. The gossip has it that she would have liked for something more to happen."

Soon the party crowd began to thin out. At the door, Madam C and Rosa bid the guests good-bye. When everyone was gone, Madam C gazed about the parlor. "What a mess," she sighed, pointing at the dirty dishes, glasses, ashtrays, empty bottles, and half-empty food plates. Then she yawned. "Let's clean up some. We'll do the rest tomorrow."

It was past midnight when everyone left the parlor and went to sleep. Gingerly, Rosa opened the door of her room and peeked in. The mayor was still asleep, curled up in a fetal position, his breathing calm, on his face a half smile. On tiptoes, she opened a closet and took out the pillows Madam C had lined her bed with when she had been born. Set on the floor, they made a perfect bed for the night. Still in her white dress, Rosa lay down on the pillows and fell fast asleep.

At eight-thirty in the morning the sounds of pots and pans and Santina's high-pitched voice woke her up. It took her a moment to remember why she was on the floor. When she did remember, she glanced worriedly at the mayor, who was still sleeping. He hadn't changed positions since midnight. As if nothing had happened, Rosa stepped into the kitchen and said, "Hi."

"Good morning," Santina said with a big smile. "How does it feel to be sixteen?"

"The usual," Rosa replied with a yawn.

Margherita, who was helping Santina with the dishes, noticed that Rosa was still wearing the white birthday dress. She said, "I'm glad to see you liked our present."

"Did you have a good time last night?" Madam C asked, coming in from the parlor.

"I did," Rosa said. "Thank you for the party." She approached the sink and began rinsing plates.

"Let's make sure it's all clean by this afternoon," Madam C said. "We've got business coming." She turned to Margherita. "Two Portuguese ships anchored last night. We'll have plenty of visitors by four o'clock."

Santina, Margherita, and Rosa continued to rinse and dry for a while, while Madam C in the parlor emptied ashtrays into a paper bag. Shortly after nine o'clock there were frantic knocks on the door.

"Your Portuguese sailors are in for an early treatment?" Margherita scoffed, joining Madam C in the parlor. The two of them opened the door. It was Roberto Passalacqua.

"I'm sorry to bother you so early," he said nervously. "Have you seen the mayor?"

Madam C and Margherita stared at each other with surprise. "The mayor?" Madam C said. "He was here last night."

"Where is he now?" Roberto asked.

"I have no idea," Madam C said. "Why?"

"I can't find him anywhere," the young man moaned, almost in tears. "He had a meeting with Theodore Roosevelt this morning at nine and didn't show up. I've been looking for him all over. His wife says he didn't come home last night, so I thought I'd see if he"—he stopped to take a breath—"stayed here."

Margherita shook her head.

"Believe me," Madam C said, "if he had spent the night at the Luna"—she pointed a finger at her own chest—"I would know."

"This is terrible," Roberto whined. "The American delegation is at City Hall, waiting. What am I going to do?"

The three stared at each other for a moment. Then someone coughed behind Madam C. It was Rosa. "I think . . . I know where he is," she said hesitantly.

"You do?" Madam C said.

Rosa nodded. "I'll show you."

They followed her through the parlor and the kitchen to her bedroom door. "Don't get mad at me," she said before opening the door. "It wasn't my fault. He fell asleep, and I didn't know what to do."

"What are you talking about?" Margherita asked.

Rosa opened the door with a sigh.

CHAPTER 6

It was on the lips of every man and woman in town: the mayor had ditched Theodore Roosevelt in order to spend the night in a brothel. On top of that, he had shown up at City Hall at nine forty-five in the morning, when the American delegation was leaving, in crumpled and disheveled clothes, without his glasses, hungover, and still reeking of the prostitutes' odor. The gossip didn't stop for days, fueled by the fact that a number of people had actually seen the mayor rush out of the Luna that morning:

"What a disgrace!"

"He embarrassed us in front of the whole world."

"Can you imagine? Explaining to an American president that the mayor was asleep in a brothel?"

"I told you men can't give up that habit."

"They say his wife left him."

"I wouldn't be surprised."

Maria Elena Cerutti had indeed left town two days after the incident and moved to Tuscany, where her family owned a country estate. Immediately, the city council met behind closed doors, led by the vice-mayor. Concurrently, the president of the Liberal Party called an emergency meeting. Both the city and the party asked unanimously that Cesare Cortimiglia resign and he complied. Roberto Passalacqua cleaned out his former employer's office at City Hall and brought everything to Cesare's home. He found the man seated on the floor of his living room, hands wrapped around his stomach, shirt wet from his tears. Roberto thought he looked a hundred years old.

"It's not the end of the world," Roberto said, patting Cesare's shoulder to console him. "There are other things you can do besides being mayor. And all your wife needs is time to get over this mess. She'll forgive you, I'm sure."

Cesare looked at him with spent eyes. "That's not why I'm crying."

"Then why?" Roberto asked.

Cesare sobbed, "I'm in love with Rosa."

At the Luna the atmosphere wasn't great, either. When Madam C had walked into Rosa's room and seen Cesare Cortimiglia naked and asleep, she had turned to Rosa in disbelief. "What is he doing here?" she had asked in a loud, angry voice. Her words woke up the mayor. He rubbed his eyes and stared inquisitively at Margherita, Madam C, Rosa, and Roberto, who stood around his bed and stared back at him, as stunned as he was.

"I'm s-sorry," Rosa stuttered. "I . . . played the game."

"You played the game?" Madam C screamed. "Are you insane?"

"Mayor," Roberto said in a worried tone. "Theodore Roosevelt is at City Hall waiting for you. If we get out of here in a hurry, we can still catch him. Come on," he said, shaking the mayor's arm. "We need to go!"

Without talking, Cesare sat up, pivoted to his left, and came wobbling to his feet. He gave a long look at his clothes, spread like stains all over the floor. "I'm coming," he said in a rasping voice. Slowly, he picked up his wear, got dressed, and glanced at

Roberto, Madam C, and Margherita. Then, his foggy eyes stopped for a long moment on Rosa.

"Let's go!" Roberto urged, pushing him out of the bedroom and toward the front door of the Luna. They spoke no words as they rushed out into the street.

Meanwhile the silence in Rosa's room was glacial. Margherita, Madam C, and Rosa stood by the empty bed looking at each other, still as marble statues. Suddenly, out of the corner of her eye, Madam C saw on the nightstand Cesare's briar pipe. She snatched it, then grabbed Rosa by the arm and dragged her through the kitchen and the parlor door. "What have you done, you little slut?" she screamed.

Rosa broke into tears. "I just wanted to show you I'm old enough to play the game," she said between sobs. "You're hurting me. Let me go!" Freeing herself from Madam C's hand, she ran upstairs and locked herself in Margherita's room.

"Come back down here!" Madam C shouted from the bottom of the stairs.

"Calm down," Margherita told Madam C. "Let me go up there and find out exactly what happened in that room."

By then all the Luna girls were out of their quarters. "I knew it wasn't a good day for Rosa's birthday party," Stella said once she found out the cause of the commotion. "Fire and hatred. Hatred and fire."

"Open up," Margherita said, knocking on the door of her own room.

"I don't want to see Madam C ever again," Rosa said, sobbing, on the other side of the door.

"It's just me," Margherita said softly. "We need to talk."

Still in tears, Rosa unlocked the door. "Let's have a seat," Margherita said. "Tell me. What happened last night?"

"I played the game with the mayor," Rosa explained, taking Margherita's hand. "I took off my clothes, and he took off his."

"Now," Margherita said, looking Rosa in the eyes. "Think carefully. Did he put his penis inside you?" She pointed to Rosa's vagina. "In here?"

"No. I . . . touched it. And held it in my hand. And then he fell asleep." She broke into tears again. "What's the big deal? Don't all you girls do that night after night?"

"We do, darling. We do."

In the parlor, Madam C could not calm down. "Where is she?" she kept screaming.

"In my room," Margherita said, coming down the stairs, "and very upset. Nothing happened last night, other than petting. So don't make a big deal out of it."

"Don't make a big deal?" Madam C screamed. "She seduced the mayor and had sex with him!"

"So what?" Maddalena questioned her. "We all agree that she's not a child anymore. Maybe she needed to explore."

"Why don't you get mad at him?" Stella said. "He's the one who took advantage of her."

"I will, you can be sure."

"So why are you so angry at Rosa?" Maddalena asked.

"Because!" Madam C yelled.

Rosa appeared at the top of the stairs.

"There she is," Maddalena said, walking up to her. "Come down here, Rosa. It's all right."

"It's not all right!" Madam C shouted, turning to Rosa with burning eyes. "What did you think you were doing?"

Rosa remained silent.

"I told you that the *libeccio* drives everyone crazy," Maddalena whispered in Stella's ear.

"It's not the *libeccio*, dear," Stella replied. "It's jealousy. Of the worst kind."

"What are you two whispering about?" Madam C groaned.

"Nothing," Stella said.

"Get back to your witchcraft and let me take care of my business!" Madam C screamed in a shaky voice. "And you," she ordered, looking at Rosa, "come upstairs with me. Now!"

On the third floor of the Luna, in the sitting room, Madam C swallowed a blue pill with water. It was a tranquilizer she took when her stomach felt tight, and it felt like a block of iron at that moment. Her ears were ringing, and her hands trembled like *gelatina*. The pangs of jealousy were clutching her for the first time. She had never objected to Cesare sleeping with other prostitutes, because she knew that he did that for physical pleasure; and she hadn't cared when he had announced that he was going to take a wife, because she knew that he married to boost his political career. But when she had seen the mayor asleep and naked, and then looking at Rosa with those sweet eyes, and then picking up without objection his wrinkled clothes from all over the floor, it had taken her only one second to understand that what the mayor felt for Rosa was love.

From the doorway, Rosa watched Madam C with her fists tight. "Sit down," Madam C ordered. "Do you understand what you've done?" she hissed. "You disgraced the Luna's name! The town will be talking about this for years!"

Rosa lifted her head high. "I don't have to listen to anything you say."

"I'm your mother," Madam C yelled. "You'll listen as long as I tell you to!"

"You're not my mother!" Rosa yelled back. "Angela is!"

"Angela's dead, you spoiled little brat! I'm the one who raised you!"

"I wish you were dead," Rosa said in a cold voice. "So I wouldn't have to put up with your bossy ways."

"You . . . ungrateful bastard. I'm bossy because you're rebellious."

"I'm rebellious because you're bossy."

"I swear to God," Madam C said, "I'll take my scissors and cut your hair one centimeter short!"

"You do that," Rosa screamed, "and I'll take everything that's on your fireplace and break it into a thousand pieces." She took the hand-painted vase and held it in front of her, ready to drop it. "Starting with this vase!"

"Put it back, you . . . Put it back, or I'll kill you!"

"What's your problem?" Rosa yelled, putting the vase back on the fireplace. "Are you mad because the mayor doesn't want to play with you anymore?"

Madam C grabbed Rosa by the hair and pulled down till Rosa's neck couldn't bend anymore. "I should have killed you when you were born. I should have drowned you in the harbor like a sewer rat! Get out of here! Get out!"

Rosa ran out of Madam C's sitting room and down the stairs. She dashed through the parlor where all the girls were, then through the kitchen, where Antonia watched her whiz by. "God help us," Antonia said, making the sign of the cross twice.

In her room, Rosa sat on the bed, crying. A moment later, Maddalena, Stella, and Margherita arrived. After them, entered a composed and cold-faced Madam C.

"You want to play the game?" Madam C said calmly. "Fine. From now on, you'll be with at least five men every night, like everybody who works in this brothel."

Maddalena said, "Are you out of your mind? She's a child!"

"Children don't take their clothes off in front of men three times their age," Madam C replied.

"Maybe," Stella pointed out, "if someone had explained things to her a little better, nothing would have happened last night."

"Either she works," Madam C said, "or she leaves."

Rosa stood up from the bed. "I'll leave."

Maddalena, Margherita, and Stella took her by the arms. "No way," Stella said.

"I think that we all need to calm down," Maddalena said, smiling.

"I'm calm," Madam C said. "So"—she turned to Rosa— "would you like me to help you pack or would you like to be on the roster for tonight?"

"I can pack by myself," Rosa said. "I've got better things to do than be a prostitute all my life," she added with disdain.

"Like what?" Madam C said sarcastically. "Go on a stupid trip across the ocean?"

Rosa approached Madam C till she was only a few centimeters from her face. "You," she hissed, "are stupid."

That's when Madam C lost control again. In a fury none of the girls was able to restrain, she picked up everything that belonged to Rosa—her clothes, shoes, books, and all the objects that were inside the room—and took them to the Luna door. She opened the door and tossed everything outside, in the middle of Vico del Pepe. "You, too," she grinned at Rosa. The moment the girl stepped out, Madam C slammed the door shut and turned to the Luna girls, who were standing, speechless, in the parlor. "Back to work," she said, then went swiftly upstairs.

Outside, Rosa stood by her belongings in a stupor. "What's happening, Miss Rosa?" asked Antonio Donegà, the chimney sweeper. "Changing wardrobe for the season?"

"I guess," Rosa said, breaking into tears.

"Now, now, what's going on?"

She looked at the cart where Antonio Donegà kept his cleaning tools. She asked, "Could you help me take my things a few blocks from here?"

"Sure," he said. "Anything to make a lady stop crying."

They pushed the cart to Vico Usodimare. "Here?" Antonio Donegà asked, somewhat surprised.

Nodding, Rosa took her things and said good-bye. Through her tears, she looked in the direction of Isabel's booth. The booth door was open, and Isabel was facing the back wall, working at something on the stove. "Can I live with you?" Rosa asked.

Isabel turned around. "Tramonto? What happened?"

"Can I live with you?" Rosa asked again.

"Of course," Isabel said with a large smile, her eyes failing to hide the worry that was building inside her. "But first let's dry those tears."

Slowly, Rosa walked in and dropped her belongings on the floor. She sat on Isabel's rocking chair and stayed there a long time, staring at the street without talking. Meanwhile, at the Luna, the girls had made a futile attempt to convince Madam C of her mistake. Then, worried sick about Rosa, Margherita and Stella had gone looking for her all over the neighborhood, while in Madam C's sitting room Maddalena persisted in her effort to make Madam C see reason. "She's only sixteen. She experimented. You shouldn't be reacting this way."

"I gave her the option to stay and work here," Madam C rebutted. "She chose to leave. What do you want me to do?"

"That wasn't an option," Maddalena argued, "and you know it. Don't you remember how hard you worked to keep her away from prostitution?"

"Yes, I remember. That's why I can't understand why she's so ungrateful."

"She's not ungrateful," Maddalena said. "She loves you. Let's go look for her. You and I."

"Never," Madam C said. "If she wants to live at the Luna again, she needs to come here on her own and apologize."

At two in the afternoon, Stella and Margherita ran into Antonio Donegà, who told them he had accompanied Rosa to Vico Usodimare. As soon as she heard that, Margherita remembered the conversation they had had with Rosa about the witch and the vapor. "I bet that's where she is," she told Stella. "Let's go."

They arrived at Isabel's booth as Rosa, still seated on the rocking chair, was sipping quietly from a cup filled with hot mint tea.

"Here you are," Margherita said, hugging her. "We were so concerned about you."

"I'm fine," Rosa said. "I live here now."

"It's good that you have a place to stay," Stella said, giving Isabel a look of complicity and a smile. "Do you need anything?"

Rosa shook her head.

"We'll come to see you often, don't worry," Margherita said. "Now we must go back to the Luna, to tell everybody where you are."

"Don't tell Madam C," Rosa said, breaking into tears. "I don't want her to know anything about me. Not how I am, not where I am."

Isabel's flower room became Rosa's bedroom from that day on. Rosa slept on an old mattress set directly on the floor, surrounded by flowers, fruits, bags full of leaves, and bottles of processed oils. She nourished herself on a variety of vegetable and bean soups, which were the only dishes Isabel cooked and had eaten since the day Francesco Carravieri had died. "Azul used to say that little food is the secret to a long life," she told Rosa on the evening of their first meal together, "and if the food comes from the earth, so much the better."

"Cows come from the earth too," Rosa rebutted, skeptical of the ability of soups to fill anyone's stomach.

Isabel shook her head. "There's nothing in cows that you can't find in this soup as well. Give it a try." With a ladle, she poured the soup of that evening—lentils, celery, onions, bay leaves, and other herbs Rosa didn't recognize—into a bowl for Rosa. Then she took a small glass shaker from a drawer beside the stove and sprinkled a tiny amount of a white powder in the bowl. "Go ahead."

"What did you just put in my soup?" Rosa asked with some mistrust.

Isabel repeated, "Go ahead."

Rosa stuck her nose inside the bowl and smelled a few times the brown, steaming liquid before taking the first spoonful. *Bye-bye, Antonia's food,* she said to herself as she swallowed. She was surprised by the soup's pleasant taste and aroma, and even more surprised, at the end of the meal, by the satiety of her stomach and the calmness she felt throughout her body for the first time that day.

Her thoughts later on, in the flower room, as she drifted into sleep, went back to the morning she had spent with Madam C on the hills picking flowers and to the breathtaking view of Genoa from the belvedere. That was the way she wanted to remember Madam C and what she considered in her head the end of her life at the Luna. Everything that had happened afterward—the party, the white dress, the cake, the mayor, the game, and the big fight—was a blur Rosa didn't even attempt to sort out.

She woke up much later than she would have at the Luna, and found Isabel at work steaming a batch of eucalyptus leaves. "Good morning, Tramonto," Isabel said without turning around.

"Do you ever sleep?" Rosa asked.

"No longer than three hours per night," Isabel replied. "When you are this old," she explained, "you don't want to close your eyes for too long."

"I feel like sleeping all the time," Rosa replied, "so I don't have to think about what happened."

"Whatever happened between you and Madam C," Isabel said, "is something you'll have to deal with sooner or later."

"Maybe," Rosa conceded. "Right now all I want to do is steam flowers."

Isabel hadn't asked Rosa a single question about her departure from the Luna. For that and for the warm hospitality Rosa was grateful. She decided to help Isabel with her oil business by going often to the hills to pick leaves and fresh flowers and by selling the oils and their by-products at the market. "I don't have dark skin," she told Isabel one day, "or a strange accent. And some of the shopkeepers have known me since I was a child. No one will send me away."

With discarded bricks and wood planks she found in the garbage on Piazza della Pece Greca, Rosa built a U-shaped stall in Piazza Banchi, a location she had chosen for its strategic position: it was close to the market, the port, and the stores of Via Luccoli, where the wealthy ladies shopped in the afternoon. There was a good crowd in that piazza from dawn till dinnertime. Rosa didn't have a proper license to sell goods or even to have a stall in a public piazza, but no one, shopkeepers or police, seemed to mind. Every morning, except Sundays when she went looking for flowers, Rosa set out bottles and candles on the planks and charmed the passersby in any way she could. She demonstrated for them the oils' powers by rubbing samples on their skins and encouraging everyone to smell the candles. "I bet you never smelled this before," she'd say, opening a flask of what she called Miracle Oil. It was a mix of eucalyptus, lemongrass, and pine, which she sold as a remedy for arthritis, bruises, and back pains. "Pamper yourself with a rub of Paradise Oil," she'd shout, rubbing on her own skin a concoction of lavender and geranium, "and you'll feel rejuvenated." In a corner of the stall, she always had a vaporizer going, with ten parts of water and one part of some oil a candle kept boiling hour after hour. Both men and women found the smells hard to resist even as they rushed by. The only mix Rosa wouldn't sell was her perfect oil. She had saved it from destruction when Madam C had picked up her things in her room and thrown them outside. Now she kept a flask of it next to her bed in the flower room, and every night, before falling asleep, she opened the flask and inhaled, so she could see Isabel's hill when she closed her eyes.

Soon, Rosa's business on Piazza Banchi produced an income Isabel had never dreamed of before. "What are we going to do with all this money?" she asked Rosa one day.

"Make our dreams come true," Rosa replied.

"What's your dream?" asked Isabel.

"To cross the ocean. What's yours?"

"To be buried on the hill behind my town, next to Azul and the orchids and the wildflowers."

"I'll take you there," Rosa said, "as soon as we have enough money to buy two tickets to Central America. I promise."

When the Luna girls found out that Rosa had set up a business on Piazza Banchi, they became at once her best customers and promoters. They all loved the oils and candles, for themselves and as tools to enhance their sexual practices and the mood of some of their most demanding clients. On her end, Madam C was aware that Rosa lived with Isabel and sold oils on Piazza Banchi, but she never approached Isabel's booth or Rosa's stall in any of her outings. For the first time since owning the Luna, she changed drastically her shopping itineraries so she wouldn't have to be within a hundred meters of either of those places.

If she had passed by Rosa's stall at any time of the day, she would have noticed a man with an unshaven beard and raggedy clothes seated on the ground on the opposite side of the piazza, staring at Rosa. He was Cesare Cortimiglia. Margherita caught sight of him one day. "Is he who I think he is?" she said, tugging at Maddalena's arm.

"He looks like a ghost," Maddalena exclaimed.

They approached him, and Cesare wept openly at the sight of them.

"What's the matter?" Maddalena asked.

"I love Rosa," he said, "and she doesn't even know that I exist."

Maddalena and Margherita looked at each other in disbelief. "We thought you had just taken advantage of her. We never suspected—"

"Help me," Cesare begged. "Please."

"Does she know that you are in love with her?" Maddalena asked.

"I told her," he said.

"Let me talk to her," Margherita said. "Wait here."

Rosa told Margherita exactly what she thought: "I have been trying to forget that night ever since it happened. I don't want to see him or talk to him for any reason. All I care about are these oils and making enough money to take Isabel with me across the ocean."

"Bad news," Margherita said when she returned to Cesare's observation point. "I think you really need to forget about her. Go home and wash. You stink of dead trout."

"I can't," the former mayor wept. "In all my life, I never felt this way about a woman."

Maddalena made her point clear. "She's not a woman. She's a child. She's sixteen, and you are forty-four. Don't you have anything better to do? Go see Madam C. She could use your company, believe me. She has been impossible since that night. We're all thinking of quitting, she's so mean."

Cesare shook his head. "All I want is Rosa."

Things continued unchanged for some time. Isabel worked in the distillery, Rosa sold oils and picked flowers. Cesare spent his days weeping in the piazza, the girls visited Rosa almost every morning, and at the Luna Madam C drove everyone crazy with her tantrums. Rosa was amazed at the perseverance with which Cesare stared at her from across the street. Enough weeks had passed from the night of her sixteenth birthday that she could think back on those events and wonder about them. "What's love?" she asked Isabel one night.

"I'm not sure, Tramonto," Isabel replied after a moment. "I thought I found it when I met Francesco. When I was still in Manzanillo with my family and he was courting me, I felt like melting every time he came by. My mouth and throat would dry up, and I felt butterflies in my stomach. I wanted to run up to him and I could hardly move. Obviously, he never felt the same way."

"I felt butterflies in my stomach when the mayor came into my room," Rosa said. "But when he took off his clothes I became scared. And the butterflies were no longer there."

"Love has nothing to do with taking off one's clothes," Isabel said.

"No?" Rosa asked, surprised.

"No, Tramonto. It has to do with what you feel inside. When you love someone, you can think of nothing but him, and it doesn't matter whether he's with you or far away."

"I've been wondering about what my friends do at the Luna," Rosa said. "Is that love?"

"It's a special kind of love," Isabel explained, "the kind men pay for. It has its reason to exist, and we shouldn't judge it. But it's not the love you and I are talking about."

"So the butterflies I felt in my stomach when the mayor came to my room were not love?"

"I don't think so, Tramonto. Or you would be with him by now."

"I see him every day on Piazza Banchi," Rosa said. "He stares at me, and he cries."

"What do you feel when you look at him?" Isabel asked.

Rosa thought a moment. "Pity, I guess. And sympathy at times."

Isabel smiled. "I can guarantee you, Tramonto, that it's not love you're feeling."

"Maddalena read me the cards when she arrived at the Luna," Rosa said, "and told me I would fall in love."

"Then you will. But the mayor is not the one."

"How do I know who is the one?" Rosa asked.

"When you find him, Tramonto," Isabel replied, "you'll have no doubt."

Cesare Cortimiglia, meanwhile, lived crippled by Rosa's indifference and by his own inexperience with emotional love. Accustomed to stop thinking about his lovers once his physical pleasure had been achieved, he was at a loss as to why the memories of that night with Rosa would not fade: the shiny red hair; the white dress; the liquid, aquamarine eyes; the soft texture of Rosa's skin; her nipples and belly; and that smell he could still feel in his nostrils if he closed his eyes. He had gone looking for her at the Luna the day after the incident at City Hall. Madam C, who had opened the front door, had stared at him with eyes of fire. "You son of a bitch. How dare you come here?"

In his confusion, all he could say was, "I came to see Rosa."

Madam C grew even more infuriated. "Your little slut no longer lives here," she said, slamming the door in his face.

He returned home limping like a wounded man. Alone in the apartment on Via Assarotti following the departure of his wife and his resignation as mayor, he spent the first few days crying and the nights haunted by nightmares. In one of them, Rosa drowned in a black lake under his eyes. He wanted to save her, but as soon as he took a step toward the lake, cuffs appeared around his wrists and ankles, attached to strong chains that prevented him from moving. In another dream, he and Rosa were on a transatlantic ship on the way to America. It was night, and they were strolling on the deck, admiring the beauty of the stars. Suddenly, he took her in his arms, lifted her, and dropped her overboard. He watched her fall into the dark waters, her white dress waving in the wind, and at the moment she hit the surface of the sea, he resumed his stroll on the deck in the direction of his cabin. During the nightmares he screamed and cried, waking up after every one of them drenched in cold sweat.

Roberto Passalacqua, who still called him mayor, was as faithful to him as when he had held power, visited him daily and brought him food and water. It was he who told Cesare one day that Rosa worked at the corner of Piazza Banchi and took him there the following morning, hoping that the sight of her would comfort him and soothe his pain. Too late did he realize how poor a decision he had made. When Cesare walked up to Rosa's stall and told her how much he loved her, she said, "Leave me alone," then turned away from him and went back to mixing and selling her oils.

He felt worse than when Madam C had slammed the door on him earlier that week. In his delirium, he told himself that if he spent enough time near Rosa, there would be a chance that she would accept his love and change her mind. That was when he decided he would spend his days on the piazza, staring at Rosa. He smiled most of the time, often sniffing the air, trying to take in the perfumes that came from the stall, searching for the scent he had smelled in the parlor on Rosa's hand and later in her bedroom and on her sheets. Rosa peeked at him occasionally, but overall her disinterest was clear. His desire was stronger than her indifference. When at seven in the evening Rosa closed down her stall and went home, Cesare Cortimiglia kept staring in the stall's direction as if she were still there. By then, he was hallucinating.

As is often the case in Mediterranean towns, before two weeks went by, an oddity had become a fixture of the neighborhood. Shopkeepers and passersby quit wondering and gossiping about the bearded man seated on the ground and even occasionally stopped by him with a cup of espresso or a shot of white wine. Next to the corner of the piazza where Cesare sat day after day was a bar called Grifone, which used to be the Stella Maris, the bar where Angela and Clotilde had long ago picked up sailors. The owners had changed since that time, as had the bar's name and the crowd that frequented it every day. The Grifone always closed before midnight, and the customers were mostly from the port crowd, longshoremen and coal-heavers who stopped there at the end of their shifts for a drink and to wind down. They became accustomed to the presence of the man outside and occasionally said "Hi" to him even though he never replied. He looked so bad by then, with his long beard and dirty clothes, that no one, other than the Luna girls and Rosa, ever realized that he was the former mayor. Roberto Passalacqua came by every evening to take him home. "You're not coming back here tomorrow," he'd say, pulling him up from the ground. "She doesn't care about you, isn't it obvious?" All Cesare would do was shake his head and cry. Not even Maddalena's frank suggestion that he go home and wash had been able to convince him to stop staring at Rosa.

Two months later, worried about Cesare's health and the stability of his mind, Roberto walked up to Rosa's stall. "I need your help, Miss Rosa. The mayor keeps babbling about a scent he smelled in your room at the Luna and won't quit coming here unless he smells it again. I understand that you don't wish to talk to him, and I have no idea what scent he's talking about, but if you do know what he wants, please do something. He's getting sicker every day."

"It's an oil I don't sell," Rosa said. "I don't even bring it to the stall. Sometimes I rub my wrists with it, though you can't smell it here, in the open air and with the odors of the other oils." She paused. "Some people claim it smells of apples," she added. "I think it smells of Azul."

"Azul?"

Rosa nodded.

"Whatever that is," said a perplexed Roberto, "could you please bring the oil with you tomorrow? So the mayor can smell it and perhaps make peace with his desires?"

"I'll bring a rag with some of the oil on," Rosa said. "All right?"

The following day, Rosa arrived at the stall with her merchandise and a square handkerchief of white cotton whose corner she had dipped briefly that morning in the flask filled with her perfect oil. Cesare was already on the piazza, by the Grifone, staring at Rosa's stall as usual. An hour later, Roberto arrived. "Good morning, Miss Rosa," he said.

"Here," Rosa said, handing him the handkerchief. "Take this to your mayor. He can keep it and smell it all he wants. This fragrance is stubborn. It will last a long time."

Roberto took the handkerchief and crossed the piazza. "Mayor?" he called, placing the handkerchief under Cesare's nose. "Is this the scent you have been talking about?"

As Cesare dipped his nose in the white cloth, his eyes lit with a glimmer Roberto had never seen before. He sniffed, and sniffed, and sniffed, then pressed the handkerchief against his heart. He would leave the piazza later that day, leaning on Roberto's shoulder, and spend the next two months inside his house, holding on to the handkerchief day and night.

As soon as Cesare and Roberto walked away from the Grifone, a group of longshoremen arrived and entered the bar in a single line. One of them stopped suddenly at the bar door. He was in his late twenties, tall, strong, and tanned, with deep, penetrating blue eyes.

"Come on, Renato," one of his friends said, "let's have a drink."

"In a minute," Renato replied. He stood outside the Grifone a few moments, inhaling. The sun was shining, and a breeze was blowing from the east, ruffling his wavy brown hair. He looked to his right, to his left, and behind him. He took a deeper breath, then entered the bar with a decisive gait.

"I smelled a strange odor outside," he told his friends.

"It's the smell of Genoa," one replied, laughing. "You know, fish, salt, and beautiful women."

Renato shook his head. "It was something else. Something"—he paused—"unreal."

CHAPTER 7

It was as if an earthquake had roared through his life. The scent was inside him, clung to his guts and bones. He thought of it every moment, while he drank with his friends at the Grifone, while he loaded and unloaded cotton parcels, and while he ate and slept in the apartment on Vico Cinque Lampadi he shared with Marco, a coal-heaver, and Gabriele, a sailor. He was unable to relate that smell to anything real. And yet it felt familiar, as if he had known it all his life. "I'm going crazy over this odor," he told Marco one night.

"Put cardamom, coffee beans, and mint leaves in a pot with water," Marco said. "When I lived with my mother, that's what she boiled on the stove all the time, so she wouldn't smell the stench of my sweat mixed with the coal."

"Smoke a cigar," Gabriele suggested, handing Renato a wooden box with three colorful crowns stamped on its lid. "On the Caribbean island where I bought them, they call these *perfume de los dioses*, gods' perfume."

With sad eyes, Renato said, "I can't even think of not smelling this odor anymore."

In the morning, Rosa arrived on Piazza Banchi and laid her bottles on the planks as usual. As she lit the candle for the vaporizer, she heard loud voices and rhythmic clanking sounds.

They were coming from the south side of the piazza, and when she got there, she saw across the street, at the foot of the pier named Ponte Embriaco, a crowd of men standing around a podium, cheering and clapping. A few meters away, two policemen watched. "What's the commotion?" Rosa asked a passerby.

"The longshoremen are on strike," the passerby replied.

That explanation didn't do much for Rosa, who had never heard the work *strike* before. Intrigued, she crossed the street and joined a few observers who stood at the edge of the group. On the podium was a man, passionately addressing the crowd. He was Renato.

"We need to fight for our rights," he boomed. "We can't allow the shipowners to take advantage of us." He raised his hands toward the sky. "Let's not go to work today! Let's show the owners who we are!" There was long applause, and a few longshoremen in the front row chanted and drummed on wooden barrels. "The shipowners wouldn't exist without us," Renato continued. "They need us, but they don't respect us! Let's tell them that we want a guaranteed number of working hours and higher pay. If we stick together, they'll have no choice!" Another round of applause.

Rosa was fascinated. The energy of the crowd and the charisma of the speaker kept her there a long time, forgetful of the oil bottles she had left unattended on the planks and of the reason she had even come to Piazza Banchi that day. She was unable to stop looking at the man the whole time. His eyes shone with passion when he spoke, and whenever he looked in her direction her legs grew heavy and she felt as if her heart were being transfixed by knives.

"Let's *all* go home!" Renato shouted. "If even one of us goes to work today, the owners will know we are weak." Then he screamed at the top of his lungs: "We are for real!" An ovation accompanied the word *real*, and the rhythmic drumming on the barrels resumed louder and faster as Renato left the podium and was soon lost in the crowd.

"Who is he?" Rosa asked a man standing next to her.

"Renato Corsi," the man said. "He's the longshoremen's political leader."

The strike lasted four days. Each morning, as the longshoremen gathered in front of the port entrance to voice their demands to the shipowners, Rosa watched them from across the street, occasionally venturing closer. Every moment, she looked for Renato. When he was not on the podium, she could spot him easily amidst the standing crowd, talking to his coworkers, encouraging them not to give up the fight. He was all she could think of. In the evening, when she was back at the distillery, all she wanted was for another day to begin, so she could see him again and hear his voice. The smell of her perfect oil, which used to make her see Azul's hill when she closed her eyes, now made her see Renato. Lying on her cot in the flower room, she dreamed of touching his shoulders, his muscular neck, the curve of his lips, and his wavy brown hair. She imagined herself kissing his eyes and him holding her in a tight embrace. He was in every fiber of her body, and she could no longer sleep. She tossed and turned, breaking into sudden sweats, aware of the shivers that ran down her spine, the hardness of her nipples, and the dull pain inside her belly that was so much stronger than the butterflies she had felt when she had walked in her bedroom with the mayor.

It never occurred to Rosa that the strike could end and Renato would not be at the port entrance to speak to the crowd. So on the fifth day, when she arrived on Piazza Banchi and heard no sound other than the voices of the shopkeepers, she froze by her stall in disbelief. She walked slowly to the port, which seemed to be in order as it had been five days before. "What happened to the longshoremen?" she asked.

Someone answered, "They're back to work. Seems that the shipping companies gave them what they wanted."

She stood by the port entrance a while, in the same spot where the podium had stood for four days, hearing the echo of Renato's voice and seeing his shadow everywhere. Back at the stall, she could hardly think or move as the day went by. The energy and good humor with which she usually promoted and sold her products had disappeared, and by seven o'clock in the evening she had sold only two candles and one small bottle of Paradise Oil. That night, she inhaled her perfect oil as usual, but when she closed her eyes, all she saw was a deep darkness that filled her heart with fear.

Without asking, Isabel knew that something had happened to Rosa in the past week. "Life can be tough at times," she told Rosa in the morning. "Don't be too hard on yourself, and you'll see things clearer."

"I don't know what to do," Rosa murmured.

"Remember?" Isabel said. "I ask Azul in this situation. And you asked your mother for advice before. Works every time."

"Angela," Rosa prayed as she left the booth and headed for Piazza Banchi, "I beg you, help me see Renato again. Go find him for me, wherever he is, and tell him to go to the oil stall because there's a girl with red hair there who's crazy about him."

Renato didn't go to the oil stall that day, only to the Grifone, around three in the afternoon. Rosa saw him open the bar door and walk in. "I'll be right back," she told her customers, then crossed the street. In front of the Grifone, she looked casually through the bar window and soon spotted Renato seated at the counter, engaged in a conversation with other customers. A man was busy behind the counter. Rosa knew he was Paolo Disarto, the bar owner. She stood still, listening to her heart racing. The bar, she could see clearly, was full of men, and even though the Grifone was a respectable place, Rosa knew by then that a woman who walked alone into a bar was labeled a prostitute and treated like one. All things considered, she thought it prudent to remain on the piazza, near the Grifone, and wait for Renato to come outside. When he did, she stepped close to him and said, "Hi."

Paralyzed by her emotion, Rosa had not really spoken. Her lips had moved, but her mouth had produced no sound. So Renato, who was in the company of his friends, walked away without noticing her, and she watched him turn the street corner and disappear.

That evening, as she was closing down her stall, she spotted Paolo Disarto out in the street, quietly smoking a cigarette by the bar door. She walked up to him. "I'm looking for Renato Corsi," she told him. "I know that he comes here."

"He does," Paolo Disarto said.

"Can you tell me where he lives?"

"I don't know where he lives. I know that he works at the cotton warehouse. Why do you want to know?"

Rosa pondered a moment. "It's nothing," she said, then returned to her stall.

"The girl who sells oils across the street asked about you yesterday," Paolo Disarto told Renato when he came in with three other longshoremen the following day around noon.

Renato's friends laughed. "Lots of girls are after Renato these days," one said. His name was Giacomo.

"Which girl are you talking about?" Renato asked.

"See for yourself," Paolo Disarto said, pointing to his left. "She's outside, staring through the window right now."

Giacomo patted Renato on the shoulder. "Let's go meet her," he said, pushing Renato toward the door.

The four longshoremen stepped outside. "Hello," Giacomo said, giggling and looking at Rosa. "We hear you've been looking for our friend Renato."

"I know her," the oldest of the four said. "She's a prostitute. She was raised in a brothel." He was Clarissa's father, the one who had exclaimed "*Santa Maria*" and then spread the rumors about Rosa when Clarissa had told him that her classmate with red hair had attended Miss Bevilacqua's school.

Renato looked at his friends and waved his hands in the air. "Of all women," he said, "prostitutes are the ones I'd never want to meet." He turned around and walked back inside, followed by Giacomo.

"How much to touch your hair?" Clarissa's father asked.

"And how much to kiss your breast?" echoed the fourth longshoreman.

Her cheeks aflame, Rosa stepped back in a haze till her back hit the cart of a fishmonger who was passing by. "Watch your step, miss," the fishmonger shouted. "This fish cost me an arm and a leg today!"

Isabel was pressing tangerine peels in the mortar when Rosa arrived. "Hello, Tramonto," she said. "You're early."

Standing near the stove, her back against the wall, Rosa bent her knees and slid down in slow motion. "I don't want to live anymore," she moaned as her buttocks hit the floor.

"Why?" Isabel asked.

"Because there's no reason for me to exist."

"What about our trip to Central America?"

"Maybe we should go now."

Isabel scratched her head. "Hmm, you can't go to Central America if you don't exist. So, which is which?"

"You don't understand," Rosa moaned. "My life is horrible. Everyone is mean to me." She was silent for a moment, then, "Now I know how the mayor felt when he stared at me all day long from across the street."

"I knew it!" Isabel said. "Who is he?"

"I don't want to talk about it," Rosa mumbled.

"After Francesco was killed," said Isabel, "when I thought I wanted to die, I had no one to talk to. I would have given my right arm to have a friend. You know how hard it is to make it by yourself? You, on the other hand, are so lucky. You have plenty of friends: me, the Luna girls, Madam C. So stop complaining. And if you have a problem, tell us, and we'll help you through it."

"You can scratch Madam C from the list of my friends," Rosa said with a grunt. She stood up. "I'm going to look for flowers."

It became a major hurdle for Rosa to get back to her business and smile at the customers as usual. She saw Renato again a couple of times, entering and exiting the bar with the longshoremen. Not once did he or his friends look in her direction, not from curiosity, not by mistake. Invariably, their indifference brought back the same burning shame Rosa had felt in front of the Grifone when she had heard the words of Clarissa's father. "Angela," she whispered, looking at the sky, "you know that this is not right. What should I do? What would you do if you were here, in my place?"

Maddalena and Stella came to see her one morning at the oil stand.

"You don't look good, girl," Maddalena said.

"I have a sore throat," Rosa lied.

"Add honey to your tea," Stella said, "and throw peppercorns behind your back three times."

Maddalena gave Stella a long stare. "Talk to me, Rosa. How come you're sick?"

Suddenly, as she looked at Maddalena, Rosa had an idea. "I need a favor," Rosa said when the two of them were alone. "Can I borrow one of your wigs? The black one. And some makeup, too."

"What do you have in mind?" Maddalena asked, surprised.

"I want to meet someone," Rosa explained, "but he must not know who I am."

"All right," Maddalena said after a moment. "You can come pick up the wig and the makeup before I start working tonight."

Rosa shook her head. "I don't want to go to the Luna. Could you bring everything to Isabel's booth tomorrow morning?"

"I guess I could," Maddalena said and smiled.

"What's going on, you two?" Stella asked. "You've been chattering all the time I was smelling oils."

"On the day you arrived at the Luna," Rosa said, "you told me that your bags of sand can predict the future."

"It's true," Stella confirmed. "Why?"

"I'm about to play a trick on someone." Rosa paused. "Only a disguise," she added, noticing Stella's worried face. "Can your bags of sand predict if the trick will work or fail?"

"I'm not listening to this conversation," Maddalena said, walking away.

"I'll give it a try tonight," Stella told Rosa. "Give me something small that belongs to you."

That evening, in her room on the second floor of the Luna, waiting for her next customer to arrive, Stella took the two white sachets she kept on the floor by the bed feet. She arranged them on her table, untied the raffia strings that kept them closed, and flattened them against the tabletop. They became square cotton cuts, with beach sand in the middle. One of the cotton cuts was golden on the inside, the other light blue. She took the round earring Rosa had given her earlier that day and buried it in the sand on the golden square. "*Amakasa deres*," she said, closing the sachet and tying the raffia string around its top. Then she shook it three times. When she opened the sachet again and flattened it into a square, the sand was in a perfect circle. At the center of the circle was Rosa's earring. She repeated the operation with the second sachet, reciting the words "*Moraka ubeme*." Again Rosa's earring appeared in the center of the sand circle.

"Stella said that your disguise will work," Maddalena told Rosa the following morning in Isabel's booth as she handed her the wig, a handful of pins, and a small bag of makeup, "but you'll have to make it unforgettable."

"Help me, then," Rosa said.

"This," Maddalena whispered, caressing the black wig, "is the best wig I have. The hair belonged to a rich woman from Montenegro who washed it every day with chamomile to bring out the shine and jasmine essence to perfume it. It's so lush no one will ever know it's not your own hair."

"Why did she cut it off?" Rosa asked.

Maddalena shrugged. "Rich people do the darnedest things. Now, let's put it on," she said, placing the wig on Rosa's head. She pulled and stretched for a while, then took it off. "No way," she said. "No wig will fit over your hair. It's too thick and long."

From her post next to the stove, Isabel said, "It's the hair of a goddess."

With no hesitation, Rosa walked to a shelf and took the long scissors Isabel used to cut the leaves and the stems of the flowers. She handed them to Maddalena. "Cut it."

"Are you crazy?" Maddalena said, not taking the scissors. "I heard that the last time someone tried to cut your hair you screamed like a stuck pig."

"Cut it," Rosa ordered. "I won't scream."

In silence, Isabel and Maddalena looked at each other quizzically.

"So?" Rosa insisted, forcing the scissors into Maddalena's hands.

"I'm not cutting your hair," Maddalena said firmly, dropping the scissors on the stove as if they were a hot potato.

Rosa turned to Isabel. "What about you?"

Isabel shook her head no.

Crossly, Rosa grabbed the scissors. She grumbled, "Fine. I'll do it myself."

Worriedly, Maddalena and Isabel watched Rosa as she separated a strand from the rest of her hair and set the scissor blades about it. As the blades closed in, Rosa pursed her lips. Her eyes became wet as the lifeless strand fell to the floor. "It's not that bad," she murmured through her teeth. "Really." Then she cut a second strand of hair, and two large tears slid down her cheeks.

"She's doing it!" Isabel said incredulously. "We'd better help her. She looks like she might faint."

Gently, Maddalena took the scissors from Rosa's shaking hands. "Of all the silly things you've done, Rosa, this must be the silliest. Don't move till I'm done, or it'll hurt more."

The haircut was over ten minutes later, with a pale Rosa staring at the red fluffy pile gathered on the *graniglia* floor. The hair that was left on her barely covered the nape of her neck. "Was it painful?" Maddalena asked gently as Isabel wiped the scissors clean.

Rosa looked at her through teary eyes. "Put the wig on," she said. "It should fit fine now."

The following day, Renato and Giacomo walked out of the port at the end of their shift at three in the afternoon. Giacomo said, "Drink?"

"Not today," Renato replied. "I'm tired." He waved at Giacomo, who crossed the street headed for the Grifone. Alone, Renato began to walk east along the shoreline. He had hardly taken ten steps when he noticed a beautiful young woman standing on the sidewalk. Her shiny black hair gently brushed her shoulders and her large aquamarine eyes glowed, enhanced by a light gray powder on the eyelids. He was entranced by the way her eyes changed colors. They were blue one moment, green the next. She smiled at him, and when he passed by her, she dropped a handkerchief to the ground. Immediately, Renato bent down. At the moment he picked up the handkerchief, his heart skipped a beat. It was that fragrance again, the one he had smelled outside the Grifone, and it was in the handkerchief, making his head spin and his legs weak.

"Thank you," Rosa said, taking the handkerchief from his hands.

"What's your name?" he asked in a quivery voice.

"Tramonto."

He smiled. "I never met anyone named Tramonto."

"My mother named me that," Rosa explained, "because while she was pregnant with me she liked to sit on the steps of our house and watch the sun set behind a hill. Are you all right?" she asked, seeing that Renato was pale and there were tiny sweat drops on his forehead.

"I'm fine," he said weakly. "Would you like to . . . take a walk with me?"

She smiled at him coquettishly. "I don't go places with strangers. How do I know that I can trust you?"

"I'm a nice guy." He smiled back. "Ask around."

"Let's go watch the ships," she said. "It's my favorite pastime. Do you like ships?"

"I do when I don't have to be on them."

"Have you been on a ship?" Rosa asked as they started to walk.

"A small one. When I was a boy my parents took me to some island. They thought it'd be fun."

"It wasn't?"

"Halfway to the island, we ran into a storm," Renato said, "with howling winds and big waves. I was so sick and scared, I swore to myself I would not set foot on anything that floats ever again. But I had to, three days later, to come back from the island. The sea was calm then, but I remember shaking the whole time. I couldn't stop crying, not even after I was safe on the pier."

"That's too bad," Rosa said. "I always thought that roaming the waters on a ship would be a lot of fun. I have been dreaming of it since I was a child."

"I have been dreaming of meeting someone like you since I was a child," Renato said, looking her in the eyes.

Near the access to the busy and crowded Ponte Spinola, watching the moored cargo ships, Renato and Rosa talked a long time. He told her about his job at the warehouse and about the fight he was leading against the greed of the shipowners. "Ten years ago," he said, "in nineteen hundred, there was a big strike in Genoa. I was in high school at the time. I'll always remember the clamor and the articles in the newspapers. It was almost Christmastime. I was amazed at how many people came together to fight for a common cause. I thought it was beautiful. Someday, I told myself, I was going to be part of it." He paused. "Life should be fair to everyone."

Rosa whispered, "Hasn't been fair to me so far."

"Why?"

"I can't complain too much, though," Rosa said. "I have good friends."

Renato nodded. "Friends are important. My best friend is Giacomo. We met when I first started to work at the warehouse. He's also interested in politics. We are like brothers. We both like to help people."

"I like the fact that you help people," Rosa said.

"Some of the older longshoremen," Renato explained, "worked so hard for so many years and have nothing. They deserve better treatment after giving their lives to the shipping companies. I look out for them. Sometimes they seem so tired I think they might suddenly drop dead."

"I know an older longshoreman," Rosa said, "who goes around telling lies about people and hurting them for no reason."

Renato looked at her inquisitively.

"I guess not everyone is good at heart," she said.

"True," Renato said. "But you can't worry about other people being good or bad. To me, the only thing that matters is that

I do something good for the people, especially for those who don't have the strength to stand up for their rights. It feels good. They look at me as their hero."

"I have a hero, too," Rosa said. "My mother. She was beautiful. She had long red hair. She's buried on the hill behind our house, so she can still watch the sunsets every night."

"Tell me the story of your life," Renato said.

"I was born into a family of Gypsies," Rosa recounted after a moment of reflection, "who traveled the world right and left. My parents stopped traveling shortly before I was born." Straight-faced, she continued on with a made-up story that was a mix of Isabel's, Antonia's, Margherita's, Maddalena's, and Stella's lives. "We lived not too far from Genoa, on the coast across from the Gallinara Island, in the house that had the hill behind. My father was killed in a fight, so my mother and I were left alone. My mother knew all along this would happen because she could read the future with the cards and with two sachets filled with sand. She loved to read me poetry aloud. Together, we made necklaces with brown and black beans and we sold them at the market once a week. Then my mother died, and I came to Genoa. By myself." She sighed. "I haven't been back to the house by the hill in a long time." She looked at him and smiled. "And you? Where were you born?"

"In Genoa, close to the port, in a house on Salita Santa Croce. Five years ago my parents moved to Marassi, a different part of town. I never see them, mostly because they don't want to see me. They wanted me to be a lawyer."

"Tell me about school," Rosa said. "Did you like it?"

"A lot. I guess because I like to learn things. I went to a *liceo* and then to the university for one year, studying philosophy. That's when I discovered who I really am. I read books written by the French utopists and by Friedrich Engels and Karl Marx, and many articles that talked about making people equal and giving everyone a chance. I read the *Communist Manifesto* at least ten times. I decided I had to do something to make those ideas become real. So I attended a few meetings of the Socialist Party, but was disappointed right away."

"Why?" Rosa asked, confused.

"They promoted violence as the weapon of choice for the working class, and violence is one thing I won't endorse or condone. And the party leaders were intellectual bourgeois who had no idea what it means to be part of the proletariat and be exploited. I grew tired of their long-winded, evasive speeches and made up my mind that I was going to fight within the working class, using the two weapons I believe in most: unity and strike. I quit the university, went to work at the warehouses, and joined the labor union. My parents were distraught, but the warehouses are the only place where I feel at home."

"It's good to have a place where you feel at home," Rosa said, having a hard time following the details of a speech filled with so many unfamiliar words.

"Do you have one, Tramonto?"

Rosa pondered a moment. "I do now."

"I must ask you," Renato said, "what's the perfume in your handkerchief?"

"A friend of mine gave me that perfume," Rosa said. "It's a mix of apple blossoms, lavender, basil, and a fourth ingredient my friend couldn't remember. Do you like it?"

"When I smell it," Renato said, "I feel like I'm entering paradise." He looked her in the eyes. "I smelled it once before, in front of the Grifone. Do you go there?"

Rosa shook her head. "I pass by Piazza Banchi sometimes. The wind must have brought it to you."

"There was a breeze that day," Renato said, continuing to stare into Rosa's eyes. He stopped talking, then took Rosa's face in his hands and pulled her close.

Rosa closed her eyes, her cheeks flushed by a sudden heat, not knowing if the fluttering in her heart was excitement or fear. Then Renato's lips touched hers, and she surrendered to him, savoring his soft, moist skin for a long moment. As he kept rubbing his lips against hers, she felt her whole body become light and float above the ground, as if she were riding a cloud. She had no idea of where she was and why. A flock of white and gray seagulls landed nearby, tucking in their large wings, protruding their webbed feet. Their squawking brought Rosa back to earth. She stepped back, her breathing fast, eyes open wide. "I h-ave to g-o," she stuttered.

"Wait," he said. "Where do you live? How do I find you?"

"I'll find you," she yelled, as she ran away from Renato along the pier, in the direction of the crowded street. "Tomorrow afternoon."

"I work the evening shift tomorrow," he yelled back. "I'll be off at nine."

In the morning, at the stall, all Rosa did was give people explanations. "I was tired of combing it," she'd say to the stunned customers and shopkeepers, who were used to the red waterfall of her hair. "This," she'd say pulling on the tips that barely covered the nape of her neck, "is so much easier to untangle and wash."

"What an insane thing I did," Maddalena had said after she had performed the operation.

"He must be someone very special," Isabel had commented in her usual wise way, "for you to be doing this to yourself."

"He who?" Maddalena had asked.

"No one," Rosa had said, frowning at Isabel when Maddalena couldn't see.

Caught up in her oil demonstrations and explanations about her hair, she almost missed Renato when he showed up at the Grifone at noon. She decided to test him on her disguise and waited by the bar door for him to come back outside. "Hi," she said.

He looked at her with a half smile. "Haircut?" he mumbled,

then headed for the port, mingling with the crowd of workers, sailors, and passersby.

At nine in the evening, in her disguise, her skin softened and scented by her perfect oil, Rosa arrived at the port entrance. It was dark, but she knew instinctively that he was there. It was the end of the last shift, and all the longshoremen were leaving. She felt a hand stroke her back, and her legs quivered as she turned around and saw him. He was holding a red rose. Without a word, he grabbed her around the waist and kissed her on the cheek. "I have been thinking of you all night," he whispered in her ear, "and all day long as well. This is for you." He handed her the rose.

She brought it to her face. "It smells beautiful. Thank you."

"Where would you like to go?" he asked.

Rosa pondered a moment. "There's a place I'd like to see. It's a belvedere up on the hills. I was there once during daytime and it was beautiful. I have been wondering what the view would be like at night."

"I know the place," Renato said. "Let's go." He signaled an empty carriage that was passing by.

In her seat, Rosa cuddled up next to Renato, and he held her in his arms with gentleness, breathing in the smell of her, moved by the light build of her bones. As the carriage moved along the quiet streets, enveloped in the warmth of Renato's strong body, holding the red rose against her heart, Rosa thought back on the ride she had taken months earlier with Madam C, amazed at how much her life had changed since the day the two of them had gone to the hills to pick flowers.

In the carriage, Renato and Rosa didn't move or speak, lulled by the movement of the horse and by the beauty of the starlit sky. At the belvedere, they stood at the edge of the piazza, breathless at the sight of the city at night. The glow of the streetlights rose toward the sky in a yellow smoke, and the moon cast its golden reflection on the sea.

"Whenever I'll look at this rose," Rosa said in a soft whisper, "I'll always remember this moment."

"The flower will die, but this moment never will," said Renato.

"I know how to keep flowers from dying," Rosa said.

"How?"

"You place the petals in a book, so they dry. Or you can transform the flowers into other things, things that know all about the flowers' lives."

"Tramonto," he said, taking her softly in his arms, "I have no idea what you're talking about. All I know is that you and I will never leave each other."

Gently, Rosa embraced him at the waist. They stood there a long time, staring at the interplay of darkness and light, breathing in the enchantment of the nighttime. A shiver shook Rosa's shoulders at one point.

"Feel like walking back?" Renato asked.

Rosa nodded.

They took a narrow, steep road paved with stone tiles, unwinding downhill amidst house walls hidden by ivy and bougainvillea, their steps the only audible sounds. Downtown was also quiet when they arrived. "I'll walk you home," Renato said as they crossed the street headed for the *caruggi*.

Rosa shook her head. "I'll go alone."

"Why?" he asked.

Without talking, she moved away from him.

"It's late," he argued, following her. "You can't walk around by yourself in this darkness."

"Please," she said, "I need to be alone. I'll meet you again tomorrow at nine." She blew him a kiss. "Good night," she murmured, then ran off, turned the street corner, and disappeared from Renato's view. Puzzled, he stood on the sidewalk for a moment, looking in the direction Rosa had taken. Then he ran after her, trying to spot her in the dim glow of the streetlights.

He couldn't see her, but her scent lingered, and he followed that trail through the *caruggi*, Via della Maddalena, Vico Corona di Ferro, and Via Luccoli, all the way to Piazza Soziglia, where he stopped, no longer sure of which direction to take. Rosa's scent was everywhere—to his right, to his left, and in front of him, in every portal and in every bend of the alleys. There was no one in the street. He yelled, "Tramonto!" A shutter opened on the fourth floor of a building. "Shut up!" an angry voice said. "We're trying to sleep here!"

Baffled, Renato stood still in the middle of the ancient piazza, looking helplessly at the sky. He made his way slowly to Vico Cinque Lampadi, while in Isabel's booth Rosa sat on her bed with her heart racing. Isabel peeked in from the distillery and noticed at once Rosa's peaceful expression and dreamy eyes. She turned around and tiptoed back to her rocking chair. Much later, in the flower room, as her eyelids turned heavy and her breathing slowed, Rosa began to dream of Renato's eyes, large, blue, and transparent like the sea. She saw herself standing at the edge of the eyes, as she would stand on a beach, and slowly walking in and sinking into his pupils till she disappeared.

The following day, on Piazza Banchi, Rosa felt as if she were floating on a cloud. The sky had never seemed so blue, the sounds of the piazza had never seemed so sweet, the people around her had never seemed so beautiful. In the evening, she rushed back to Isabel's booth, where she put on the black wig and some makeup. At nine sharp she was at the port entrance, where Renato was waiting for her with his loving smile.

"I ran after you last night," he said when Rosa arrived, "but I couldn't find you."

"Promise me you won't do that again," she said.

"Why are you so mysterious?" he asked.

"There are things I cannot say to you now. Please trust me."

"I trust you," he said. "I'm only worried about you."

"There's no reason for that." She paused. "I missed you," she said, kissing him on the cheek.

"I miss you every moment." He lifted her and kissed her face everywhere. "Even when I'm with you."

"I like that," Rosa said.

"Would you go with me to a special place?" he asked.

"Where?"

He pointed at the warehouses. "There." He saw the quizzical look in her eyes. "We'll be able to talk in peace. It's dark out-side"—he pointed at the sky where a few clouds were passing—"and it may rain."

She followed him, unable to resist the sweetness in his voice. Her legs shook as they held hands and walked, and all she could think of while they strolled silently along the pier was how warm the skin of his hand was and imagined the same warmth on his neck, chest, and every part of his body.

"This is where I work," he said, as they approached a ware-house, "but we can't go inside now. It's closed. There's a shack around the corner, where we keep tools we need to pack and unpack the cotton and other goods. It's by the water. I go there sometimes when I want to be alone and think. It's peaceful at this time of night." He embraced her again, and they held each other tightly as they turned the warehouse corner and crossed a yard, reaching the opposite side of the pier.

The shack was filled with empty brown cloth bags and ropes, set in various piles. It had no door, only a large opening that faced the water. The only lights outside were those of the ships resting in the basins and the intermittent glimmer of the *lanterna*, the lighthouse, standing tall at the west end of the port on a rocky promontory edging into the sea. They sat on a pile of soft bags, next to each other, looking at the calm water. The si-lence around them was deep, broken only by the occasional squeaks of the moorings and by the soft lapping of the sea against the pier.

"I brought you this," Renato said, handing Rosa a small, smooth blue stone. "I found it years ago on a beach. I was there with Giacomo. I can't even say why I liked this stone so much. After I took it home, I told Giacomo I would give it to the love of my life." Gazing at her face, he added, "It has the color of your eyes."

"I'll take it with me wherever I go," Rosa said.

"Wherever you'll go, I'll go," he murmured, kissing her. As she returned his kiss, Rosa pulled him closer until the weight of his body pushed her down into the sacks, and she felt liquid and boneless, filled only by her longing for him and by her certainty that she had found love. "I love you," he said with his lips on hers.

"I love you, too," said Rosa.

He kept repeating "I love you" as they groped for laces, buttons, and pins and their limbs entangled in long and passionate embraces. They left their clothes where they landed and made love desperately, with the ardor and intensity of those aware of being part of a miracle yet afraid the miracle won't last. As the waves kept lapping the pier, Renato guided Rosa as they discovered each other's textures, and odors, and sighs. Their bodies danced, their beings became one, with Rosa following Renato's lead unhampered by her childish awkwardness and with never a hint of regret or indecision, as if she were following a preset destiny and she had known all along exactly what would happen and how. When they left the shack later that night, the bags were soaked with their sweat and fluids, their bodies were drained of strength, and their hearts brimmed with the sensation of completely belonging to the other. They walked back to the port entrance in wobbly steps, leaning against each other, like two drunkards searching for ground for their feet.

"The scent of your skin," Renato said, "is the most maddening odor I've ever smelled."

Rosa nodded. "Someone warned me that this scent would have powers."

"This someone is right," Renato said. "I can feel the power of it. It's . . . bewitching."

"I am bewitched by your eyes," Rosa whispered. "I was the very first time I saw you, talking on the podium."

"I had no idea you had seen me before we met," Renato said.

Rosa gave Renato a clever smile. "We met because I had seen you."

Renato laughed. "I'm realizing now that you never asked me my name," he said after a moment. "Did you know it?"

Rosa nodded, then stopped walking. "You said that wherever I'll go, you'll go. Did you really mean it?"

"Yes."

"Even if I wanted to cross the ocean on a ship?"

"Why would you want to cross the ocean?" he asked. "Don't you like it here?"

"So you wouldn't go with me if I wanted to cross the ocean?"

He shook his head. "I'm afraid of floating on water. The very thought of it makes my stomach tight, and I can't breathe. Ask me anything, take me anywhere, but not on water, I beg you." He looked at her. "Come with me. I'll show you where I live. Then," he added, "maybe you can show me where *you* live."

He took her to Vico Cinque Lampadi, where they entered an old building with a wooden portal corroded by years of sea salt. A narrow stairway of smooth slate took them upstairs. On the fourth floor, Renato placed a finger on his lips as he opened the door to his apartment. "Two friends live here with me," he whispered. "They're asleep." In the darkness, they tiptoed through a living room and a small kitchen, then reached Renato's bedroom, frugally furnished with a bed, a table, a chair, and a tall bookshelf filled with volumes. "Stay here with me tonight," he said. "I don't want to be without you."

"I can't. I have to go," Rosa said, uncertain about the reliability of her disguise.

"Why?"

"Now that I know where you sleep," she said, "I'll think of you here." Before he could object, she tiptoed back to the apartment door. A moment later, she was rushing down the stairs.

"I won't let you walk away alone tonight," he said, taking the stairs after her.

"If you love me, you will," she replied as they reached the street.

"I love you, and I won't." He took her hand. "See? You're trapped."

Gently, she shook his hand off hers and, before he could realize what was happening, ran away.

He hesitated only a fraction of a moment before following her once more, but that minuscule amount of time was sufficient for Rosa to turn the street corner and disappear once more from view. He looked right and left, amazed at the speed with which she had vanished from his sight. Then he took the street Rosa had taken, determined to find her, knowing that she must still be close by. There was complete silence in the *caruggi* at that time of night, and in that silence he could hear the echo of her steps on the cobblestones. He followed that echo and the unmistakable trail of her odor. Rosa, who knew all the shortcuts and little alleys by heart, stayed clear of the lit streets, choosing the darkest and most mysterious passageways, never losing her bearings or looking back at her stalker. She hid in dark portals for a few moments, squatted behind piles of garbage, and took long detours that took her away from her destination. None of those tricks succeeded in deceiving Renato, who remained close to her until she reached Vico Usodimare. At the corner, Renato stopped in front of Isabel's booth, realizing he could no longer hear the steps' echo. He stared at the booth a moment, then, in the darkness, thought he saw shadows inside. Without exactly knowing why, he knocked on the glass door three times. Isabel opened the door in her black vest, and a waft of the distillery stench hit Renato in the face. "Yes?" she said.

Renato took a step back. "I'm looking for a girl," he mumbled. "Her name is Tramonto. Is she here?"

"Tramonto?" Isabel asked with a surprised face. "Have you been drinking, my friend?"

Renato shook his head without talking.

"The only girl in this joint is me," Isabel continued. "And I don't think I'm the one you're looking for."

"No," Renato said quietly. "Good night."

Isabel closed the booth door and turned around. Rosa, in her black wig, still breathing fast from the run, was seated below the window, on the floor. "You told him your name is Tramonto?" Isabel said with a slightly scoffing tone.

Rosa didn't reply.

"I like him," Isabel went on. "His eyes are clear like yours."

CHAPTER 8

They made love in the shack behind the warehouse every night, with an intensity that scared them and at times made them cry. Afterward, on the way to the street, Renato kept asking Rosa questions. Rosa kept being evasive. "How can I love you so much," he'd say, "and not know where to find you? I asked around, you know. No one has ever heard of a girl named Tramonto. Even Giacomo, who knows everybody in this part of town, has never heard of you or seen you anywhere. Where do you go at night when you leave me?"

"Why can't you just take me for who I am?"

"Who are you?" Renato asked.

Rosa cocked her head. "The girl with black hair who loves you and waits for you at the port every night."

In those days, when she was in Isabel's booth, Rosa spoke less than usual. She sat in corners in long silences, fidgeting with the blue stone, tangled up in thoughts she couldn't chase off her mind. "Are you going to tell me what's going on?" Isabel asked, half curious, half concerned about Rosa's long absences at night. One morning, Rosa told Isabel everything: the comment of Clarissa's father, the reason for the disguise, and how much she was in love with Renato. "But he's not in love with me," she explained. "He's in love with a Gypsy girl named Tramonto, who has black hair and a mother buried on a hill. What should I do?"

"Lies never solve anything," Isabel said. "They make trouble."

"That's easy for you to say," Rosa mumbled. "Every time I tell the truth, bad things happen."

"I don't believe you," Isabel said.

"You should. I told the truth about my life in an essay at school, and I was labeled a prostitute. I told Madam C the truth about what happened with the mayor, and she threw me out of the Luna. I'm done with the truth. Forever."

"I'll give you my advice anyway," Isabel said. "Tell him everything. If he truly loves you, he'll understand why you used a disguise and he'll love Rosa as much as he loves Tramonto now. And if he won't understand, then you'll know his love is not real."

"I'm afraid of losing him if I speak," Rosa sighed, squeezing tightly the blue stone in her hand. "I can't even breathe without him."

"He may find out on his own," Isabel pointed out. "Then it'll all be so much harder to explain."

"Guess what," Rosa said after a moment of silence. "He's afraid of going on boats."

"Really?" Isabel asked.

"From the first moment I saw him," Rosa said, "I had this vision of me and him on a ship, crossing the ocean. Now I know it'll never happen." She smiled. "Of all men, why did I have to fall in love with one who's afraid of the water?"

"You don't pick whom you love." Isabel smiled back. "And when you love, you adjust your dreams. But most important, when you love, you don't lie."

Rosa nodded. "I'll try."

At the oil stall that day Rosa was edgy and moody. She almost passed out when she saw Renato and Giacomo come out of the Grifone and cross the piazza, headed in her direction. "I liked you better with your hair long," Giacomo said.

Rosa shrugged.

Giacomo inspected the oil bottles while Renato stood back and examined Rosa up and down. "I want to buy one of your oils," Giacomo said at a certain point. "It's my mother's birthday, and she told me she would like one that can soften the skin of her arms."

"The best oil I have to soften the skin is this," Rosa whispered, afraid that Renato would recognize her voice. She handed Giacomo a bottle. As he examined it, she cleared her throat then spoke again in a timbre much lower than normal. "It's sandalwood and laurel, diluted with sunflower oil."

"I'll take it," Giacomo said, handing Rosa money.

"What's your name?" Renato asked. Giacomo gave him a look.

"Rosa."

"Why were you looking for me?" Renato continued.

"I wasn't," Rosa replied. She turned to Giacomo. "Here's your change," she mumbled in her deep voice. In her confusion, she dropped a coin; at once, Renato bent down, picked it up, and handed it back it to her. She froze, realizing that their motions were an exact replica of those they had performed at the time she had dropped her handkerchief in front of the port entrance. Renato froze, too, and they exchanged an uneasy glance.

"Do you know a girl named Tramonto?" Renato asked.

"Tramonto? What kind of name is that?" Rosa murmured back.

"She wears an unusual perfume. I thought she may have bought it here."

Rosa shook her head. "I sell perfumes to a lot of people."

"I bet," Renato said, "but you may remember her. She's striking. Shiny black hair. Blue eyes." He looked closely at Rosa. "Much like yours."

Rosa cleared her throat. "Like I said," she mumbled, handing the fallen coin to Giacomo, "I see many people every day." She turned away from Renato and Giacomo. "I have other customers. Good-bye."

Renato's questions to Tramonto about her home and whereabouts continued insistently for several more days, until they became more infrequent and finally ceased. In the shack by the water, glowing in the rays of the lighthouse, all they'd talk about after making love were their dreams of spending the rest of their lives together. "We'll have a house with a hill behind it," Renato said once, "and we'll watch the sunsets with our children."

Rosa nodded. "I like that." She paused. "When we'll have our house and our children, would you consider going on a boat?" she asked. "Just for a short ride. I'll hold your hand."

"Tramonto, the thought makes me shiver. I'll do anything for you, I swear. But I *must* keep my feet on land."

Rosa spoke softly. "Sometimes, when you're afraid of something as a child and then you grow up, your fears go away. When I was a child, I used to be afraid of old women. I thought they were witches. I'm no longer afraid."

"It's different," Renato argued. "Did an old woman actually make you feel sick or hurt you in any way?"

"No." Rosa admitted. "But maybe, after all these years, you won't feel as bad anymore."

Renato smiled at her. "I doubt it. I see ships and boats every day. I know how I feel."

"Won't you even try?"

Renato laughed out loud. "Do you ever give up?"

Rosa laughed back. "Never."

He bowed his head. "If it's so important to you, I promise I'll try. Maybe I could try on a boat moored in the harbor, where there are no waves. You'll have to hold me tight."

"Thank you," Rosa said, thinking of all her childhood

dreams about crossing the ocean. They had never seemed so far. She looked at the sea, longing for the very brief moment she and Renato would spend together on the deck of a moored ship, knowing she'd have to make that moment count for a lifetime. She closed her eyes and thought back on her kitchen games, Antonia's stories about the Gallinara Island, the *passeggiate* to the port, the images of her father in the hut across the ocean. "I love you," she said, cuddling tightly against Renato.

"I love you, too," he whispered. They remained silent a while, eyes fixed on the water.

"Genoa is so beautiful," Renato said at a certain point. "I become more attached to it every day. Its hills, its waters, its people. The markets, the *caruggi,* the port. There's no other place like it. I can't imagine being anywhere else."

Rosa took a deep breath "I love Genoa, too," she said, "but I always thought I'd like to see the world, especially the world on the other side of the ocean. I can't explain why or what I expect to find, but I've thought about that for as long as I can remember."

"So I'm the one ruining your dream."

She looked at him fondly. "No," she said, taking his hand in hers. "My biggest dream is you. And if it's important to you that we stay here, we'll stay."

"It'd be hard for me to leave the longshoremen, their battles, their hopes. They are what gives meaning to my life. And now there's also you." He kissed her on the cheek. "And our house, and our children."

Rosa nodded. "One boy, one girl."

He smiled. "That sounds fair."

"Did you tell him who you are?" Isabel would ask every night, when Rosa returned to the distillery with her black wig in hand and her eyes shining with dreams.

"I'll tell him tomorrow," she'd reply.

"I'm worried," Isabel said one evening.

"Why?"

"I couldn't separate the pine oil from the steam today," she whispered. "I tried twice. Azul used to say that when the oil didn't want to leave the water, it was a sign that nature was angry at us for some reason."

"What did we do to anger nature?" Rosa asked.

"I don't know." Isabel paused. "Tell the truth, Tramonto. Before it's too late."

In the morning, the longshoremen's strike resumed, more intense than ever. There was a large demonstration in front of the port entrance, with people holding signs and shouting slogans. The population of the neighborhood and a number of university students had joined in with the longshoremen, so that the number of demonstrators had doubled, prompting the presence of more police. Renato was often on the podium, inflaming the hearts of the crowd with his powerful speeches. Without her wig, Rosa watched him from across the street. In the early evening, as the demonstration wound down, Tramonto showed up at the podium, looking for Renato. "Come with me," he said when they found each other. "Giacomo wants to meet you."

"Hi," Giacomo said, vigorously shaking Rosa's hand. "I'm glad finally to meet the girl who stole Renato's heart."

"Nice to meet you," Rosa murmured, blushing.

Giacomo looked at her with a curious smile. He gazed deliberately up and down her body, occasionally squinting his eyes. Rosa swallowed twice, then turned the other way. *I'm busted*, she thought.

Then the circus arrived. They took over the road with ten long, colorful horse-drawn caravans with dancers and tumblers performing on the roofs and bowing every now and then to the passersby. The caravans were preceded by a marching band of drums, timpani, and trumpets, and followed by elephants, zebras, ostriches, and monkeys and by a line of contortionists, sword-swallowers, fire-eaters, jugglers, and clowns. They paraded through the streets of downtown and all along the shoreline with a loud clamor of shouts and music, raising the warm applause of the crowds everywhere. "I've never been to a circus," Rosa said, fascinated, once the caravans had passed by.

"I'll take you," Renato told her.

With a soft voice that didn't sound like his at all, Giacomo said, "I'm going with you." One moment earlier he had fallen hopelessly in love. The girl he had spotted on the roof of the third caravan was a dancer, wearing a white and blue leotard and a shiny diadem on her head. She had long black hair that shone even in the evening's fading light, pearly skin, and long thin bones that gave her the ethereal look that had instantly captured Giacomo's heart. She had danced up and down the caravan's roof gracefully, following the rhythm of the drums, smiling right and left, and seemingly never tiring. That night Giacomo couldn't sleep. He knocked on Renato's door at three in the morning, looking like a sick man and rambling incessantly about the girl.

The circus raised its tents slightly west of Piazza Banchi, in a vacant area two hundred meters from the water. A large red and black sign at the entrance advertised two shows a day, one in the afternoon, one at night. The day after the circus's arrival, Rosa, Renato, and Giacomo went to the night show, scheduled for eight o'clock. They arrived at the circus around seven-thirty, Rosa still wearing her disguise. "I'll meet you inside," Giacomo said, pointing at the big tent. "There's someone I must find."

Giacomo never saw the show. He found the dancer behind a caravan, seated on a chair at the edge of a canopy kept upright by two poles in the front and by the caravan on the back side. She was alone and in street clothes. "You're not dancing tonight?" he asked.

"I hurt my foot," she said in a childish voice.

Giacomo kneeled by her and, without talking, lifted her long skirt and began kissing her knees and legs, all the way down to her bare feet. She didn't move, or object, or speak.

When Giacomo laid his head on her lap and kissed her belly, she got up, took his hand, and guided him to the caravan door and then inside.

"Looks like you found your girl," Renato said, pleased, when Giacomo met him and Rosa at the end of the show. He had noticed at once his friend's relaxed attitude and smile. "You no longer look like a madman. Maybe we'll be able to sleep tonight."

Giacomo returned to the caravan every night while the eight o'clock show was ongoing and he and the girl were certain they could be alone. They never asked each other questions and, indeed, hardly spoke. The only information they had exchanged, after making love the first time, were Giacomo's occupation and their respective names. Hers was Camila Besic. Giacomo guessed she must have been fifteen. They made love furiously, with the desperation of those who are aware of the end being near. The circus was scheduled to leave town after two weeks, and throughout those two weeks Camila exaggerated the pain in her foot to make sure no one would ask her to perform, day or night.

"Don't go," Giacomo told Camila on the eve of the circus's departure. "Stay in Genoa with me." It was almost the end of the show. They were both naked on her bed inside the caravan, their bodies entangled and still sweating from their lovemaking.

"It's late," Camila whispered with a hint of worry in her eyes. "You need to go."

He stood up and began to put on his clothes. "Take your things," he told her, "and leave this circus now."

He was buttoning his pants when the caravan door unexpectedly opened and a man walked in. He was gigantic, with muscles bulging in his arms and legs, a shaven head, one earring, and a mean pair of eyes. He was a sword-swallower and also Camila's father. Since her birth he had been very protective of his daughter and recently he had been seriously worried about her foot that, strangely, refused to heal. When he saw a half-dressed stranger in the room and Camila naked on the bed, it took him only a second to figure out what had been happening all that time. "I knew it," he shouted. "I knew that your foot injury was a lie!" He turned to Giacomo. "I'll kill you." He grinned, grabbing a kitchen knife. "And I'll chop your body into a million pieces!"

In a stupor, Giacomo darted away from the bed, trying to reach the door. The sword-swallower grabbed him by the neck, dragged him back across the room, and threw him on the bed, where Camila was curled in a corner, shaking. "You'll die right here," he said, "where you committed your sin!" He lifted the knife and lowered it, aiming for Giacomo's heart. Giacomo managed to roll away slightly, so the knife landed in his left shoulder. Camila screamed.

Bleeding, blinded by the pain, Giacomo wrestled with the man to get hold of the knife's handle. The more they wrestled, the more the knife sank into his flesh. At a certain point the pain became so unbearable that Giacomo, in desperation, with a power he never suspected he had, kicked his assailant in the groin, forcing him to take two steps back and lose his balance. That was enough for Giacomo to run out the door, still holding the bloody knife. Quickly, the sword-swallower recovered his balance and ran after him. He managed to grab Giacomo outside, a couple of meters away from the caravan, in plain sight of all the performers, who were returning to their homes at the end of the night show. There were shouts and moans as the performers made a circle around the two men, who were by then wrestling on the ground. "Let them fight," said an old man dressed like a magician, waving away those who were trying to separate the rivals. "When two men wrestle with such anger, only God is allowed to intervene."

The size of the sword-swallower was imposing. He had Giacomo on his back and towered over him, his knees firmly planted on Giacomo's legs. At the same time, he had taken possession of the knife, pushing it again toward Giacomo's heart. Giacomo held on to the man's wrist in an attempt to push the blade away. "You'll rot in hell," the man shouted, "for violating Camila's innocence and pure soul!"

As the blood from his shoulder wound spread to his chest and face, Giacomo realized that his strength was about to leave him. He closed his eyes and dug the fingers of his right hand into the ground, trying to hold on to life. That was when he felt the stone. He took it and slammed it on the other man's head three times. The sword-swallower screamed and let go of the knife. Giacomo grabbed it and turned the blade around. When he hit the sword-swallower's head with the stone for the fourth time, his combatant fell on the blade, emitting only a short sigh. There were cries coming from the crowd. "He killed him!" someone shouted. "The stranger killed Manari!"

In a daze, Giacomo stood up and, wobbling, headed as fast as he could for the nearby street. "Let's get him!" someone screamed. "Don't let him get away!"

Giacomo's advantage was that he knew the town. He was bleeding copiously and crying from the pain when he reached the *caruggi* and vanished into the friendly darkness of those streets. He staggered his way east, leaning against the ancient walls, until his legs gave way and he sat down behind a pile of broken furniture at the end of an alley so dark and narrow it was practically invisible from the street. *What a stupid place to die*, he thought as he tore his shirt and held it against the blood that flowed out of his shoulder. It was a pointless effort, and Giacomo realized it. With his eyes closed, he could hear the sounds of the circus people running about, looking for the man who had killed Manari. "He can't be far," one shouted. "He was bleeding like a pig."

"We'll find him," another voice said. "Half go this way. The rest with me."

In that dark labyrinth, the circus people soon lost their bearings. They realized they were walking in circles: in the darkness they couldn't tell one *caruggio* from another and couldn't remember which ones they had already checked out. Defeated, they returned to the circus and did two things: they called the police, and they interrogated Camila about her suitor. Pressed by her people, particularly by the old man in the magician suit, who was the head of the circus and her baptismal godfather, Camila had no choice but to reveal the only two things she knew about the suitor: his name, first and last, and that he worked at the cotton warehouse.

Giacomo, meanwhile, was still in the alley, barely breathing. In his fading consciousness, he was aware that the circus people were no longer there. So when he thought he heard steps approaching, he gathered all the strength he had left and kicked repeatedly a piece of wood that hung from the pile of broken furniture he was hiding behind.

It was past midnight. Rosa was on the way back to the distillery from making love at the shack with Renato. As usual, she had taken the long way home, because even though Renato had stopped following her or asking her questions about her whereabouts, she took precautions so she wouldn't lead him straight to Isabel's in case he changed his mind. She was only two short blocks away from Isabel's booth when she heard strange sounds. She stopped, surprised. Usually, at that time of night there were hardly any sounds in the streets, and the only ones she heard occasionally were those of the stray cats pawing through the garbage. For a moment, she thought she had dreamed the sound. Then she heard it again and when she realized it was coming from the alley, she took a few steps in that direction, stopping halfway in. She noticed the pile of broken furniture and saw a few pieces of wood shaking. Her first thought was of rats, and she decided to leave. But then, out of curiosity, she asked, "Who's there?"

Practically unconscious, Giacomo moaned.

Rosa heard him and looked gingerly behind the pile. She couldn't believe her eyes. Giacomo's shirt was soaked in blood, his face was pale, and his eyes were wide open and fixed on the sky. She bent down and took his hand. "Giacomo! Giacomo! What happened to you?" When she realized he couldn't answer, she ran out of the alley to Vico Usodimare, where she knocked frantically on Isabel's door. "Come help me!" she said. "Giacomo is dying!"

Isabel, who had no idea who Giacomo was, followed Rosa to the alley and to the furniture pile. When she saw Giacomo, she took a step back and her hands began to shake.

"Don't be afraid. He's a friend," Rosa said. "A friend of Renato's. What do we do?"

"I'm not sure," Isabel replied faintly.

"Shall I call the police?"

Isabel shook her head. "It seems to me that this man is hiding from someone."

"Can we take him inside?" Rosa asked.

"He's too heavy," Isabel replied. "You and I won't be able to move him."

"Stay here," Rosa said, then, before Isabel could object, ran out of the alley. She arrived on Vico Cinque Lampadi short of breath and banged her fists on the door of Renato's apartment. Marco came to the door. "I must see Renato," she said in an agitated voice.

"Who is it?" Renato's voice asked from inside.

"It's me," Rosa shouted. "Giacomo's in trouble!"

At once, Renato rushed to the door, freezing in his tracks the moment he laid eyes on Rosa. "What?" he blurted.

In an instant, Rosa realized her mistake. She opened her eyes wide as she fingered the short strands of her red hair. "I . . ." Her words died in her throat. With guilty eyes, she kept feeling her hair tips and staring at the stunned Renato. "I'll . . . I'll explain," she finally stuttered. "Now come with me. We must rush!"

He took Rosa by the arm. "Your black hair . . . was a wig? Why?"

"You don't understand," Rosa shouted. "Giacomo is in an alley, unconscious and bleeding. Hurry up. He needs you!"

He didn't budge. "I want to know why."

"Because you thought I was a prostitute," Rosa shouted louder, "and I'm not!" She grabbed him by the arm. "If you don't go with me now, Giacomo may die!" She pulled him out of the apartment. "Let's go!"

By the time Rosa and Renato arrived, Isabel had placed rags under Giacomo's head and was blotting his wound and singing to him in Spanish. Renato took a long look at her and at Giacomo lying on the ground. "What happened?" he asked.

"I don't know," Rosa said. "I found him here."

"Giacomo," Renato called, "can you hear me?"

"He can't hear you," Isabel said. "Let's take him inside." She turned to Renato. "We can use an empty eucalyptus bag as a stretcher. I'll be able to do something for him back at the distillery."

"Eucalyptus bag? Distillery?" asked the astonished Renato.

"Please," Rosa said. "Do as she says."

With an effort they got the unconscious Giacomo onto one of Isabel's eucalyptus bags and then slid the bag up the street to Isabel's booth. Inside, they set the wounded man on Rosa's bed in the flower room, and Rosa placed fresh rags over his shoulder, which was bleeding even more copiously than before. Renato watched with astonishment as Isabel made a poultice of leaves and petals and placed it gently on the open wound. Then she rubbed Giacomo's temples with two different oils. "Let's pray," she said.

"I should go find a doctor," Renato said.

Isabel made the sign of the cross on her. "Don't go," she said. "There's nothing a doctor can do that these leaves and oils can't do as well. His wound is clean. All we can do now is sit and wait."

The night passed slowly, with Giacomo unconscious though breathing regularly and Rosa, Renato, and Isabel seated quietly by his side. Renato turned to Isabel at a certain point and mimicked sarcastically: "The only girl in this joint is me?"

Isabel smiled at him. "She wasn't ready."

He turned to Rosa. "Are you ready now?"

She nodded.

He said, "I can't believe you went through all this trouble to hide your identity from me."

"I was afraid of losing you."

"Do you have so little faith in me?"

"No." Her eyes clouded. "I have no faith in myself."

"Why?"

"It's a long story. It has to do with the people who raised me. And with things that happened while I was growing up."

"I want to know everything."

She nodded and dried her tears. "I'll tell you everything."

He asked, "Do you love me? Or was it all a joke?"

She caressed his cheek with a shaky hand. "I love you more than anything in the world."

He asked, "You're not going to lie to me again, are you?"

She shook her head. "I only lied about my name."

He raised his voice a little. "You're not going to lie to me again, are you?"

"No."

"How do I know you're telling the truth now?"

She swallowed twice. "What do I have to do to prove to you that I'm not lying?"

He kept silent a moment. "Look me in the eyes," he finally

said, "and tell me one more time that you'll always tell the truth to me, no matter how difficult, no matter how painful."

"I promise," she whispered. "I'll always tell the truth, no matter how difficult, no matter how painful."

"Good," he said, taking her in his arms. She laid her head on his shoulder and began to sob. He kept holding her. "I love your red hair."

"Did you know?" Rosa asked after a moment.

"That's not important," he replied.

She whispered, "It's important to me."

He kissed her on the hair and cheeks. "The only things that matter are that you and I are together and Giacomo is safe." He paused then spoke with emotion. "I look at you in your red hair and I'm falling in love with you all over again."

Rosa gave him one of her radiant smiles.

"Try to sleep a little," he said.

She nodded, cuddled up against him, and closed her eyes.

The following day, a report of the murder of the sword-swallower was on the front page of the late edition of the newspaper, together with the name of the killer—Giacomo Gattamelata. The circus was offering a reward of one thousand liras for his capture and one of five hundred liras for information on his whereabouts. The article contained interviews with the circus people, who described the victim as a talented performer and a good father and the killer as a libertine with no scruples who had forced an innocent girl to sin in secret for a long time. Everyone in town was talking about it. Renato read the newspaper and then heard the gossip when he briefly left the distillery in the early afternoon to buy food:

"I can't believe how vicious the murder was."

"They say he smashed the guy's head open with a stone and then stabbed him in the heart three times."

"I always say that the circus people bring trouble."

"I hope they get him. Then the circus will leave town."

Renato returned to the distillery with the news. "I know what happened," he said, then told the whole story to Isabel and Rosa.

Meanwhile, Giacomo's breathing had stabilized, and the blood from his wound had stopped flowing, though he remained unconscious, moaning softly on occasion. When he slowly woke up, around four in the afternoon, his first thought as he looked about the flower room was that heaven was a very strange place. Then he saw Isabel, and his body twitched with fear. "This is no heaven," he murmured. "I was sent straight to hell."

"You're not in hell," Rosa said. "This is Isabel's home."

"And by some miracle you're alive," Renato added, wiping Giacomo's forehead with a towel.

"Camila . . ." Giacomo whispered. "Don't let her leave."

The explanations took everyone some time, during which Giacomo couldn't stop staring at Rosa. "She's the girl with the black hair?" he asked with disbelief.

Renato nodded. "She's also the one who saved your life. You're wanted," he continued, "and the circus put out a reward for your capture. You must stay here, and don't even think of leaving."

Giacomo's eyes lit up. "The circus is still in town?"

"Yes," Rosa said. "All the circus people are looking for you, and not in a friendly way."

"The reward they're offering, I heard in the street, is a thousand liras for you dead or alive," Renato said. "In this part of town there are people who would kill their own mother for much less than a thousand liras."

"Go find Camila, please," Giacomo begged, "and bring her here."

Renato stopped to think a moment. "Your first and last names are in the paper. How did anyone know who you are?

The police didn't know. So the only explanation is that the circus people knew. How?"

"The only person in the circus who knows my name is Camila," Giacomo said sadly.

"She turned you in, and you want me to go look for her?" Renato asked in disbelief.

"If I don't see her again," Giacomo said, closing his eyes, "I may as well stop breathing."

Rosa turned to Isabel. "Didn't you tell me one day that your oils can make people snap out of love?"

"That was Azul's claim," Isabel said. "I have no idea if she was right."

Renato looked at the two of them. "Giacomo is twice as stubborn as I am. Believe me, no oil will make him change his mind."

"Then we'll have to find this girl," Rosa said. She took Renato's hand. "I know how it feels when you can't live without somebody."

"Do you really think that any one of us could get close to her after what happened?" Renato asked.

"Not you," Rosa said. "I, on the other hand, may be able to find her."

Rosa and Renato returned to the circus that very same day. "We're closed," said the man seated by the entrance. "There are no performances today because we are mourning Manari." He pointed to a sign—*The performances will resume tomorrow at the usual times.*

"The circus is not leaving?" Renato asked.

"Not for a while," the man replied. "The owner decided to stay here until Manari's killer is found."

"This is good," Rosa pointed out after she and Renato had left the circus's grounds. "We have time to find the girl and talk to her."

Renato asked, "How? We don't even know what she looks

like. What Giacomo said about her—black hair, long legs—could be true of all the dancers in this place."

Rosa gave him a cunning smile. "I know how to lie, remember? I'll figure something out."

The following day Rosa returned to the circus when the afternoon show was almost over. She approached the main tent and circled it with nonchalance until she found the side entrance. When she had attended the show with Renato, she had noticed the performers going in and out of that entrance at the beginning and end of their numbers. Three clowns left the tent through that entryway as Rosa arrived. "Excuse me," she said. "Where can I find Camila?"

The clowns gave her a stare. "Do we know you?"

"No," Rosa said.

"You're not supposed to be here if you don't work for the circus," one said.

"I'm an old friend of Camila's from out of town," Rosa explained.

A second clown said, "And?"

"Please tell me where she is. It's important that I talk to her. I heard what happened." She paused and spoke in a sad voice. "I was also a friend of Manari's."

The clowns looked at each other a moment, then one of them pushed aside the curtain that hung over the entryway. The show was in its final phases, with several groups of performers on the floor, moving to the rhythm of exotic music. "There," the clown said, pointing at a group of dancers with their faces covered by veils. "She's the last one on the right, with the white and gold dress." As the clowns walked away, Rosa heard one say, "He was a good man, that Manari."

She waited by the side entrance for the show to be over and the performers to begin exiting the tent and head for their homes. In the confusion, no one took notice of her. She recognized Camila by her dress and followed her through the ani-

mals' pens to the area where the caravans were. She approached
Camila as the girl was opening the door of her caravan, about to
go inside. "Camila?" she called.

Camila turned around. "Yes?"

"I'm a friend of Giacomo's," Rosa said softly. "He misses
you and sent me here to find you. Would you like to see him?"

Camila looked at Rosa with expressionless eyes. "I don't
care about Giacomo," she whispered as she stepped inside. "I
sleep with many different men in every town."

"What a fool I've been," Giacomo said when Rosa told him
what she had found out. "I'm in this mess now, and for ab-
solutely no reason."

"You couldn't have known," Renato said.

"At least we solved one of your problems," Isabel said. "The
worst one of all, in my opinion." She pointed at Giacomo's
heart. "You're no longer sick with love."

"What a pair you and I are," Giacomo told Renato later,
when the two of them were alone in the flower room. "Your
girl pretends to be someone else, my girl pretends to love me."

"Rosa had an excuse," Renato pointed out, "the stigma society puts on people. I was part of it. I judged her that day outside the Grifone, along with everybody else. Camila had no
reason to do what she did. I never met anyone that cruel."

Giacomo stared at the ceiling and sighed. "I never met anyone so beautiful."

For more than a week, Giacomo lived hidden in Isabel's
booth. During that time, as Isabel took care of his wound and
pampered him with her perfumed remedies from Costa Rica,
the two grew fond of each other.

"When I first saw you," Giacomo told her one day, "I
thought you were a creature from hell."

"Don't worry," Isabel said. "Happens with everybody." She
reflected a moment. "When I first saw you, bleeding in that dark
alley, I thought you were the ghost of Francesco Carravieri, re-

turned to Genoa to drag me with him to hell, where he certainly is."

"Who's Francesco Carravieri?" Giacomo asked.

Isabel's eyes fogged up for a moment. "Someone I wish I had never met."

While Giacomo recovered in the flower room, Rosa slept with Isabel in the distillery and during the day continued to sell oils on Piazza Banchi as usual. Renato returned to work and to his political demonstrations, after being questioned by the police numerous times about Giacomo's whereabouts. He and Rosa kept making love in the shack, because that was the place Rosa considered their home. They also took care of Giacomo's mother, who had gone into a panic at the news that her only son was wanted for brutally murdering a sword-swallower and fleeing the scene. "We can't tell her where Giacomo is," Renato had told Rosa as they were heading for her home. "Giacomo still lives with her and says she has the biggest mouth in the neighborhood. She can't keep a secret. We should reassure her that Giacomo will be all right, but not a word about Isabel, or the distillery, or Vico Usodimare."

The investigation into Giacomo's disappearance continued in full swing, until rumors began to circulate that maybe the circus people had killed him, that he had fled to Africa on a ship, that he had drowned himself because he couldn't live with his guilt. Renato, who continued to visit Giacomo's mother daily, implored her to ignore those rumors. "He hasn't been killed," he comforted her, "and you and I know all too well that he would never flee to Africa or drown himself. It's just gossip. Don't believe it." After that particular conversation, and in view of all the preceding ones, Giacomo's mother began to suspect that Renato knew more about Giacomo than he had told her, and, without specifically mentioning Renato, shared her thoughts about that matter with her neighbors. The grapevine came instantly alive, and before a day had gone by the theory spread that someone in the neighborhood was hiding Giacomo from the circus people. At that, both the police and the circus people began searching the buildings in the area where Giacomo's mother lived, which was only a few blocks away from Vico Usodimare.

"We have to get you out of here," Renato told Giacomo one night.

"How?" Giacomo asked.

Rosa made a worried face. "Even if he made it out of here unseen," she said, "where would we take him?"

"I have an idea," Renato said.

The family of Gabriele, the sailor who shared the apartment on Vico Cinque Lampadi with Marco and Renato, lived on a small farm in Vercelli, a town northeast of Turin. Renato had never been there, but Gabriele had invited him and Giacomo to visit numerous times, as a token of gratitude. A year earlier, he had gotten into a fight at the Grifone with some strangers, and Renato and Giacomo had gotten him out of the fight as the strangers had begun to pull out their knives. "Thank you," Gabriele had said, "for saving my life. You can count on me for anything anytime."

"We'll take him to Vercelli," Renato said, "to Gabriele's farmhouse. No one will ever look for him there."

"How would we travel?" Rosa asked.

"By train," Renato replied, "if we can get him to the station."

"We can't do that," Rosa said, alarmed. "He'll be recognized. His picture has been on the front page of every newspaper."

Isabel spoke in her serious face. "It's time that Rosa's black wig be used for a worthy cause."

Giacomo looked at her. "What do you mean?"

"She's right," Renato said. "No one will pay attention to a woman."

"You're joking," Giacomo said.

"Would you rather go to jail?" Isabel scolded him. "Or be lynched by the circus people?"

Several hours later, as the light of dawn began to settle on the rooftops, a woman peeked through the door of Isabel's booth. She looked to the left, then to the right, then to the left again before stepping gingerly outside. She was Giacomo. He was wearing the black wig and clothes Rosa had borrowed the night before from Maddalena: a long brown skirt, a long-sleeved matching shirt, and a light jacket. A hand-knitted shawl hid the bandages wrapped around his shoulder. Shortly, Renato, Rosa, and Isabel joined him in the deserted street.

"Take care of yourself," Isabel told Giacomo.

"I will," he replied. "Thank you for everything. I owe you my life. I'll never forget what you did for me."

"You don't owe me anything," Isabel said. "Just don't scare me like that ever again, or I'll be the one passing out. At my age," she smiled ruefully, "things don't get any easier."

"Rosa, or Tramonto, or whatever name you want me to call you," Giacomo said, hugging Rosa, "thanks for stopping by the alley that night. I'd still be behind that pile of furniture if it hadn't been for you."

"I'm so glad I found you," Rosa said, hugging him back.

"I'll be back in three days at the most," Renato told Rosa, taking her in his arms, "as soon as I drop Miss Gattamelata at his new home."

Giacomo elbowed him. "There's no need to rub it in," he said.

"Let me go with you," Rosa said. "Please."

Renato shook his head. "I don't want you to be involved in this escapade if we get caught."

"I'm already involved," Rosa begged, "and I can't be without you."

"When travelers see a man and two women," Renato said, "they wonder more. It's safer for us if Giacomo and I go alone."

Rosa sighed.

Renato kissed her on the lips. "I'll be back before you know it."

As Renato and Giacomo began walking down the street, Rosa took Isabel's hand and clasped with the other hand Renato's blue stone. She whispered, "I have a bad feeling."

Isabel caressed her head. "Your Renato is a wise man. He's doing what he has to do to help his friend. Be proud of him. You are a very lucky girl."

CHAPTER 9

The wait was unbearable. At the oil stall, the days passed with a slowness that made Rosa wonder if someone had by accident stopped time. Hour after hour she watched the Grifone and the longshoremen going in and out of it; she listened to the sounds of the harbor; she smelled the odors of Piazza Banchi, a mixture of food, saltwater, dampness, and spices that for months had been her daily, inseparable companion. Nothing felt good to Rosa anymore, not even the scent of her own oils. The Grifone and the longshoremen looked as if they belonged to another world; the sounds of the port were a cacophony of clanks and shrieks; and the neighborhood odors felt acrid and stale. Everything seemed to be missing Renato. And worse yet, there came the nights. Back in the flower room after Giacomo's departure, sleepless, Rosa broke into sweats and shivers all over again, as she had done when she had first seen Renato. In the middle of the second night, weary and restless, she got up and walked to the shack by the water. The docks were deserted, the silence deep. Inside the shack, Rosa lay on the bags where she had made love to Renato so many times, sinking in memories of the smell of him, feeling the warmth of his skin. For a moment she thought she heard his voice, talking to her about their life together and the children they would make and the house by the hill they would have. She stared at the dark water and the friendly rays of the lighthouse, wondering if it had all been a dream. The rest of the night, she became a vagabond, strolling aimlessly from one *caruggio* to another, avoiding all the streets she had walked with Renato. In the silence, she could hear the echo of her steps on the cobblestones, which sounded deafening to her even though it was a barely audible sound. At a certain point she found herself at the corner of Vico del Pepe and instinctively walked down the narrow street without entirely realizing where she was going. Ahead of her, the familiar silhouette of the building that hosted the Luna appeared like a ghost sprung from the past. It was four in the morning; all the windows were dark. In front of the Luna door Rosa stood still a while, staring at the aged stone walls. She sighed deeply as a wave of melancholy took hold of her, filling her bones. Slowly, she sat on the ground, back against the door, head leaning against the marble frame, hugging her bent knees, and stayed there immobile and thoughtless, blending with the shadows, almost invisible to the naked eye. She stood up when the neighborhood awoke, at the sounds of open shutters and sleepy voices.

At the end of the third day, when Renato didn't show up at the distillery as they had agreed, she went looking for him at his usual places. She knocked on the door of his apartment, but no one replied. She went to the cotton warehouse, but he wasn't there. Back at her stall on Piazza Banchi, out of sorts, she watched the Grifone across the street, imagining Renato coming out of it with his friends and walking with them toward the water. Several men went in and out of the café, but not Renato. At some point, Paolo Disarto, the bar owner, stepped outside, leaned against the external wall, lit a cigarette, and puffed smoke rings up toward the sky. Hastily, Rosa crossed the piazza as the man tossed his cigarette away and walked back inside. After a short hesitation, she pushed open the door of the Grifone. It was a busy time of day, with all the café tables occupied by men talking and drinking wine. A few were sipping espresso from minuscule white cups set on matching saucers. Timidly, Rosa stopped past the door threshold and listened to the buzz of the men's voices and the jingling sounds of glass and china. A few heads turned as she crossed the room, and curious eyes followed her as she approached the crowded counter. Paolo was behind the counter, a few meters away from Rosa, busy pouring wine from a carafe into a row of midsize glasses. He didn't notice Rosa until some of the customers began to murmur. He gave her a half smile. "White or red?" he asked in a mocking tone.

Rosa took a deep breath and spoke to the point. "Have you seen Renato today?"

Paolo put down the carafe. "You don't give up, do you," he said with a second half smile.

One of the customers elbowed Rosa. "Renato, Renato. What does he have that I don't?" Everyone laughed.

"Have you seen him or not?" Rosa burst out in anger.

"Haven't seen him these past days," Paolo Disarto replied in a more normal tone of voice. He turned to the customers. "You guys?"

There were several "No"s and heads shaken.

Without another word, Rosa turned around and headed outside, her heart heavy, her cheeks burning with shame.

Later, as dusk approached, in the booth, Rosa looked at Isabel with sad eyes. "I can't find him anywhere," she said in a raspy voice.

"It's exactly three days since he left," Isabel pointed out. "There's no reason for you to worry. He'll be here. Now you need to sleep, because you haven't for the past two nights. Your voice is a screech, and your eyes are red and tired. You're going to eat this soup," she said, pointing at a pot on the stove into which she had dropped a sprinkle of her white powder from the shaker, "and go to bed."

Contrary to her own expectation, Rosa slept peacefully

through the night and didn't wake up till noon. At that time, she came out of the flower room with eyes still dazed from the deep sleep. Isabel was seated on the rocking chair, watching the street through the open glass door. She spoke before Rosa asked. "He didn't come."

"Where is he?" Rosa asked in a broken voice.

"Maybe they had a hard time finding the farmhouse," Isabel said. "Maybe the weather was bad and they got delayed. You never know when you travel. Things can be out of one's control. Be patient. Wherever he is, he's thinking of you, I'm sure."

"I lost him," Rosa murmured. "I can feel it."

"No, you haven't. It's only the beginning of the fourth day."

The sun was shining and the streets were loud and crowded when Rosa went looking for Renato all over again. After checking out once more the Grifone and his house, she stood by the port entrance hour after hour, asking every longshoreman if he had seen Renato. The answer was a no every time. Then the last longshoreman left and the docks became quiet. That sudden silence screamed at Rosa. "He's gone," she whispered, staring at the sea. Nearby, on the deck of a fishing boat, two seagulls spread their wings and took off, circling the water. "I wish I were a bird," Rosa said, "so I could fly all over the earth till I'd find Renato." One seagull dove in a hurry, disappearing underwater. Shortly, its mate followed suit. Spellbound, Rosa watched the birds resurface and dive again, over and over, till darkness hid the cloudy sky. Only then did she leave the docks, slowly making her way back to the booth. Isabel shook her head the moment she saw Rosa arrive.

"It's because of my red hair," Rosa cried out. "Because it's short and ugly. And because he thinks I'm a prostitute. And because I don't understand what he says when he talks about his books and his politics. He must have found a beautiful girl with lush dark hair who went to school."

Isabel frowned. "And you think he would have left his job,

his house, his friends, his books, and all his personal belongings without saying anything to anyone?"

"Maybe he still thinks I'm a liar and he hates me."

"He doesn't think you're a liar. As for hating you, I saw how he held you the night we brought Giacomo here. And I heard what he said to you, that the only thing that matters is that you two are together. That's love, not hate."

"Then why?" Rosa shouted. "Why? Why? Why?"

"I don't know, Tramonto," Isabel said softly. "I know for a fact, though, that whatever is keeping Renato from coming back has nothing to do with you."

"Do you think that he and Giacomo were captured by the police?" Rosa asked.

"No, or we would have heard about it. The longshoremen would have told you."

Gingerly, Rosa took the blue stone out of her pocket. "This is all I've left of him," she said, entering the flower room. She spent a sleepless night, pacing the room, rushing to the door at every little noise that came from the street, murmuring to herself and sighing. Meanwhile Isabel sat on the rocking chair, eyes closed, humming occasionally one of her Spanish lullabies. She stood up around four in the morning, certain that she had heard sobbing sounds. In the flower room, Rosa was seated on her bed, cheeks flooded with tears. Isabel sat next to her and took her gently in her arms. She held her without talking, singing at times, slowly rocking her at others, until Rosa stopped sobbing and fell asleep.

Steam was beginning to fill the curly pipes when Rosa appeared in the distillery in the morning, carrying a bag and wearing a light coat. "I'm going to Vercelli," she said, "to look for Renato."

Without looking at her, Isabel placed two handfuls of eucalyptus leaves in boiling water.

"Did you hear me?" Rosa said loudly.

"Ice," Isabel ordered. "Pass it over."

Ignoring the order, Rosa walked out the door. She heard steps behind her as she began walking down the street. "Do you even know where Vercelli is?" It was Isabel's voice.

Rosa stopped in her tracks and turned around. "No," she admitted, "but I'll find it."

"How?" Isabel pointed out. "And what if he comes while you're gone? How would we find you?"

Rosa dropped the bag on the cobblestones. "I can't just stay here and do nothing!" She stuck her hand in her pocket and felt for the blue stone, freezing as she realized it wasn't there. Without a word, she ran back into the booth, to the flower room, where her eyes examined thoroughly and quickly the corner where her mattress lay. "I set my stone here last night," she said in an agitated voice, "next to my perfect oil. Where is it?"

Isabel joined her in the flower room. "Did you put it in the bag? Or in a different pocket?"

"No. The blue stone is always on the floor next to the perfect oil or in my right pocket," Rosa said, lifting the mattress, then shaking the sheet. "Where is it?" she screamed. "Where is it?"

"I have no idea," Isabel said, then she watched Rosa frantically push around the fruit boxes and the flower vases and every object she could find, silently but with fast movements and an icy look in her eyes that betrayed the depth of her fury. When there was nothing left to move, Rosa grabbed Isabel by the shoulders. "Where is it?" she screamed again. Isabel said nothing while Rosa kept holding on to her. Suddenly, the girl let Isabel go, ran to the distillery room, and started her feverish search there as well, inside the cooking pots and the distillation equipment, under Isabel's bed, and in every corner, until no space was left unexplored other than a large bag where Isabel had placed the discards of several days of distillation. The bag was full of a stinking, muddy mush of cooked, rotten leaves, into which Rosa dipped her arms to the elbows and began rummaging furiously like a starved animal, until she became certain, beyond any possible doubt, that the stone wasn't there, either. Then she pulled her forearms out of the mush and looked at Isabel with mean eyes. "Did you take it?" she grunted.

"I think you've lost your mind," Isabel said calmly.

Rosa grew more infuriated. "If you didn't take it, where is it?" she shouted.

"I don't know," Isabel said. "Wash your arms," she added, pointing at a pot full of clean water.

Isabel found the stone twenty minutes later, in a corner of the flower room, under a pile of clothes Rosa had shaken during her mad search several times. "When you look too hard, you don't see things that are under your nose," she said, handing Rosa the blue stone. In silence, Rosa took the stone and sat on her mattress, her lips closed tight to keep from crying.

"I'm going to the flower market," Isabel told her. "I'll be back in two hours."

When she returned, Rosa was lying in bed, cuddled into a ball, arms around her stomach, shaking. Her face was pale and swollen, and her eyes had turned gray. "Dear God," Isabel exclaimed when she saw her, "this can only be the sickness of love."

Rosa didn't get up for five nights and four days, during which Isabel heard no news of Renato. All along, Rosa remained motionless in her curled-up position on the bed, emitting on occasion barely audible moans. Soon, she refused food and water, and the only way Isabel could keep her hydrated was with a dropper placed at the corner of her mouth. Every hour, she dried Rosa's cold sweat and wet her dry lips with rags dipped in water. At the same time, she tried on her all her incantations: oils, leaves, massages, and Spanish lullabies. She recalled the time of her own youth when she had been sick with a fever and Azul had spent the night at her bedside, singing and burning oils, and she repeated faithfully Azul's healing routines for Rosa. Nothing worked, one of the reasons being that all those remedies reminded Rosa of Renato. One morning, out of options, Isabel placed the open flask of her perfect oil under Rosa's nose. Rosa let out screams so loud that Isabel's heart began to race. She sat on the floor and cupped her hands over her ears, praying for her heart to calm down. "I won't do that again, I promise," Isabel said later, after recovering from the scare, as she rubbed Rosa's back to calm her down.

Rosa got up briefly on the fifth day, only because the old mattress and the pillow stank from being soaked in her sweat and tears. She crawled out of bed and sat on the floor like a discarded rag while Isabel took the mattress and the pillow outside and threw buckets of water on them and then scrubbed them with one of her oils. The neighbors thought it was one of her witchcrafts and made the sign of the cross repeatedly as they walked by. When nine hours later the mattress and the pillow had dried, Isabel took them back to the flower room. Rosa, who in all that time hadn't said one word or moved from her position on the floor, murmured, "Take me to my bed. Please."

Isabel helped her up. As Rosa struggled toward the mattress, leaning on Isabel's arm, Isabel realized with horror that the girl had lost so much weight that she, an eighty-year-old woman, could have lifted her easily off the floor. The moment she was on the bed, Rosa curled up again and began to cry. Isabel crossed her hands on her heart. "Azul," she prayed, "please make Renato return safely, and until then, please see Rosa through her pain."

It was around midnight when one of the Luna girls heard knocks on the door. She was coming down the stairs from the second floor and deemed those knocks unusual, as the door wasn't locked and all the clients had to do was push it to come in from the street. There was business in the parlor that night. Three men were waiting for girls, one was talking to Margherita, and three more were relaxing in armchairs before going home. Behind the counter, Madam C was making conversation and keeping the financial matters straight. When the Luna girl opened the door, she looked curiously at an old woman with penetrating dark eyes and tangled white hair, wearing a black vest that covered her feet. "Can I help you?" she said.

"I need to see Maddalena," Isabel said.

"She's busy," the girl replied. "Who should I tell her came by?"

"Call her," Isabel ordered, looking the girl straight in the eyes. "Right now."

"But—"

"Call her, I said," Isabel groaned, pointing her hands toward the girl, "or I'll turn you into a toad before you know it."

Maddalena was at the door one minute later, her face the reflection of her surprise. "Isabel," she said. "What are you doing here?"

"I need help," Isabel said. "I'm afraid Rosa is dying."

"What?"

"Please come with me," Isabel begged, tugging at Maddalena's sleeve. "She's terribly sick, and I don't know how to help her anymore."

"Wait here." Maddalena crossed the parlor and took Margherita by the arm.

Margherita shook her off. "I'm working."

"It's Rosa," Maddalena explained. "She's sick. Go find Stella and come to the door."

"What's going on here?" Madam C demanded, arriving at the door as Margherita and Stella were coming down the stairs. She stared at Isabel, then turned to Maddalena. "What is *she* doing here?"

"Rosa's very sick," Maddalena said. "Isabel says that she may die."

"I wouldn't care if Rosa were already in hell," Madam C

said in her cold voice. "Everyone back to work," she added. "We've got clients."

Stella stepped in front of Madam C with eyes of fire. "How can you be so cruel?" she shouted. "She's not even seventeen and she's dying! Do something, for Christ's sake! She's your daughter!"

"She's not my daughter," Madam C stated. "And I feel sorry I spent so much time and energy raising her."

"Let's put it this way," Margherita said in a cold tone to match Madam C's. "You can either stop acting like a mean, jealous spinster and go with us to Isabel's booth, or we'll all quit working this instant. We'll shut down the Luna. What do you choose?"

"You wouldn't dare," Madam C said with a frown.

Maddalena stepped forward. "Try us."

The five women arrived at Isabel's booth ten minutes later. Madam C pinched her nose as she crossed the distillery and entered the flower room. In the penumbra, she squinted her eyes in the direction of a small bundle of clothes. To her dismay, she realized that what was inside those clothes was Rosa. She stared at the short, disheveled hair, the pale, gaunt cheeks, the gray eyes swollen with tears, and felt the first quiver of tenderness in almost a year. In an instant, she relived Rosa's birth and Angela's death, the trips to Mafalda down the street, the good-night kisses, the strolls to the port to see the ships, and the harshness of Rosa's life in school. She whispered, "I never thought . . ."

"She needs a doctor," Margherita suggested.

"I'll go find one," Maddalena said, then ran out of the booth.

Stella crouched next to Rosa. "Rosa?" she called, rubbing her hair. "Say something."

At that, Rosa stirred and turned her head toward the voice. Through tired eyes, she gazed at Stella, Isabel, Margherita, and finally Madam C. She turned away. "Why is she here?" she murmured.

"We are all here to help you," Stella said. "Including Madam C."

Rosa sank her face into the mattress. "Liar."

Madam C took a step back. "I should go."

"You're not going anywhere," Margherita said. "Remember? Shut down?"

Madam C took another step toward the door. "Isn't it obvious that Rosa doesn't want me here?"

"Maybe," Margherita rebutted. "But she needs you here. And you know it."

In the corner of the flower room, Isabel nodded. "She does."

"What is this?" Madam C said. "A conspiracy?"

Margherita and Stella smiled.

"All right," Madam C said through her teeth. "Rosa?" she called. "I'm here to help you. I promise."

"Did you hear that?" Stella whispered in Rosa's ear. "Madam C wants to help. Tell me, how are you feeling?"

Rosa lifted her face from the mattress. "Like I have no life in me . . ."

Shortly, Maddalena returned with Michele Merega, the doctor of the Luna girls for many years. The last time he had seen Rosa was on the night of her sixteenth-birthday party. When he saw her in the flower room so thin and pale, he rubbed his eyes in disbelief. He examined her carefully for half an hour. "Rosa has nothing wrong with her," he finally said, "other than her desire to die."

"We can't just let her die," Stella said.

Margherita turned to Isabel. "How did she get herself into this state?"

Over the next twenty minutes, Isabel told everyone Rosa's story. She told about Renato and the reason Rosa had cut her hair, and about Giacomo, the circus, the murder, Giacomo's disguise and escape from town, and the farmhouse in Vercelli where he was going to hide.

"Who would have thought that my black wig would have so much power?" Maddalena said at the end of the story.

"Renato was supposed to be back eight days ago," Isabel continued. "Rosa went looking for him all over town, then dropped on this bed, and here you see her. I'm afraid that the only person who can make her feel better is Renato, but I have no idea where he is."

"Do you think that he may have run away with a street girl or decided to stay in Vercelli with his friend?" Stella asked.

"No," Isabel said. "He's very much in love with Rosa, and in Genoa he has a job, friends, and a home. The only explanation for the fact that he hasn't returned yet is that something happened to him along the way." She paused. "Rosa had a premonition."

Madam C spoke with a tinge of disdain. "There are no such things as premonitions."

"Premonition or not," Margherita said, "we must find Renato."

"How?" Stella wondered. "We don't even know what he looks like."

"I know what he looks like," Isabel said with a clever smile, "but I'm a little too old to be chasing men."

"Then Rosa will have to go with us," Maddalena concluded. "There's no other choice." She squatted next to Rosa. "Rosa?" she called. "Try to get up. Lying here crying will do you no good. We'll help you find Renato, but we need you on your feet."

Rosa uncurled her body and stretched her legs.

"Good girl," Maddalena said.

Stella headed for the door. "I'll run to the Luna and bring back some food."

"How about you?" Margherita asked, looking straight into Madam C's eyes. "Are you going to help us or are you just going to stand there?"

"If you ask me," Madam C muttered between her teeth, "Rosa needs a long bath and a change of clothes." She bent her neck in Isabel's direction. "So does she."

The investigation began the following morning. Rosa, whom the girls had forced to sit up and swallow bits of food, had explained in a tremulous voice the exact location of Renato's apartment and the fact that the farmhouse in Vercelli belonged to the family of Gabriele, a sailor. At once, Margherita headed for Vico Cinque Lampadi. "I'm looking for Gabriele," she said when Marco opened the door.

"He's not here," Marco replied.

"When will he be back?" Margherita asked.

"In four months," Marco said. "His ship left three weeks ago for Rio de La Plata."

Margherita's disappointment was clear. "Do you know where in Vercelli is the farmhouse his family owns?" she asked.

"No."

"Do you know anything at all about his family or their place?"

Marco thought a moment. "The last name is Valle. And the only details Gabriele ever told me about that farmhouse are that it's next to a rice field, off a dirt road, and that when he was a kid he could always find his way home when he walked back from town because at the corner of that road there's a funny-looking tree. Its trunk is shaped like an amphora."

Meanwhile, Madam C, who had finally given in to everyone's insistence that she do something useful for Rosa, had gone to the Stazione Principe, Genoa's main train station. "A close friend," she said when she was seated in the office of Quasimodo Martelli, the stationmaster, "took a train one week ago from Genoa to Vercelli and is supposed to be back by now. I haven't heard from him, and I'm worried. Have there been any accidents along that line?"

"No, madam," Quasimodo Martelli replied. "No accidents." He proudly lifted his head. "And not a single delay."

On the way back to the *caruggi*, Madam C stopped at the main police station. "Have you found the man who killed the sword-swallower?" she asked a young policeman with a large nose. "I have a family, and I'm concerned about this murderer walking in our streets."

"Not yet," the policeman replied. "But we'll find him. We're looking mostly downtown, but also elsewhere. He can't hide forever."

"Thank you," Madam C said, then rushed back to the distillery to tell everyone the news.

Stella arrived a few moments later, having checked the Pammatone Hospital, the hospice for vagabonds, and once more the Grifone. "Nothing," she said. "Not a trace of someone by the name of Renato Corsi."

As for Rosa, once she understood completely that the girls and Madam C herself were willing to help her find Renato, she made a spectacular recovery in a very short time. She ate a large amount of Antonia's food, drank bottles of water and warm tea, and slept peacefully for several hours. All along, she and Madam C exchanged uneasy glances and silences, avoided all direct conversations, and made sure they were never alone with the other. Isabel watched them with her hawk eyes. "It's like a dam ready to give in to a sea of water," she told Margherita when Rosa and Madam C couldn't hear her.

Margherita nodded. "You have no idea how badly those two have hurt each other."

"I hope they'll find peace some day," Isabel said.

"Sometimes, when bigger problems arise, people can face their own issues in unexpected ways. I know that from my own experience with my father. He threw me out of the house for

no reason when I was very young. Accused me of having seduced a priest, can you imagine? I swore not to talk to him ever
again. A year ago I learned he was in a hospital, close to dying. I
went to see him, I don't even know why."

"Did he die?" Isabel asked.

"Yes. I'm glad I saw him before it happened. Perhaps Rosa's
problems will help her and Madam C reconcile."

"I'll have a word with Rosa," Isabel said. With a sarcastic
smile, she added, "Occasionally, she listens to what I say."

Meanwhile, the girl kept gaining strength. The day after
Margherita had spoken to Marco and Madam C's investigations
had established that Giacomo was likely to be safe at the farmhouse, Rosa was up and ready to go to Vercelli. "Or to the end
of the world," she said, "if that's where Renato is."

As for Madam C, she had by then clearly taken charge of the
situation. Three days after seeing Rosa sick in the flower room,
at six in the morning, she spoke to Margherita, Maddalena, and
Stella in the quiet parlor of the Luna. "I need one of you to
come with Rosa and me to Vercelli, and one of you to run the
Luna while I'm gone."

"I'll come," Margherita said.

"No way," Maddalena stated. "It's my black wig we're chasing. And I'm a Gypsy. I can follow trails like no one else can."

"All right," Margherita conceded. "You go to Vercelli. I'll
run the Luna."

"Fine by me," Stella said. "I don't travel on Tuesdays, and
running things is not my forte anyway."

Madam C turned to Margherita. "You're in charge. But . . .
easy with the poetry, please. I'd like to find all my customers
when I return."

Jokingly, Margherita bowed. "Everything will be in order,
my queen."

With a frown, Madam C turned to Maddalena. "Get ready.
We leave in two hours."

"I knew that Madam C would love to get involved in helping Rosa," Stella told Maddalena later, as Maddalena was packing on the second floor of the Luna. "All she needed was a little push."

"And a little arm twisting," Maddalena joked.

"Do you think you'll be able to find Renato?" Stella asked.

Maddalena shook her head. "It's a big world. He could be anywhere, doing anything. But this trip is good for Rosa. It's much too hard for her to sit and wait."

Two hours later, Maddalena, Rosa, and Madam C were at the Stazione Principe, boarding a train headed for Turin. Isabel had given Rosa a small velveteen bag containing one bottle of oil to cure motion sickness, another to keep away bad dreams, and a third to build up strength and body weight. To all that Rosa had added the flask of her perfect oil. In her right pocket she had, as usual, the blue stone. "Come back safe, Tramonto," Isabel had said, "and with Renato."

The first leg of the trip was long and uneventful, other than for the obvious awkwardness between Madam C and Rosa. As the train tackled a hill, Rosa stepped out of the compartment. "Stop looking at Rosa that way," Maddalena told Madam C. "Why don't you two talk about what happened and put it all behind you?"

Madam C said, "I'm waiting for her to say something."

"Why her?" Maddalena asked. "She's a young girl. You're a grown woman. Help her."

"I am helping her," Madam C said. "Isn't that why I'm on this train headed for God knows where?"

"I don't know. Maybe you are on this train because you enjoy leading this expedition."

"I resent your insinuations. I know why I'm here."

"Then talk to her. You two haven't exchanged a word since we boarded. How do you think she feels?"

Madam C shrugged and stared out the window as Rosa returned quietly to her seat.

"Are you liking your first train ride?" Maddalena asked, hoping to engage Rosa in some conversation.

Sadly, Rosa shook her head.

"Why, I thought you liked to travel," Maddalena said.

Rosa said nothing as she nervously changed positions on her seat. A moment later she stood up, then sat down, then stood up again. She asked, "Are we there yet?"

"You need to calm down, Rosa," Maddalena said. "We're not even close. If you keep moving around like this, you'll drive us crazy."

Rosa looked at her with helpless eyes. "I can't stay still. I feel as if time had stopped passing altogether. All I can think about is Vercelli and finding Renato. I wish I had a magic wand, to make me be in Vercelli right now."

Maddalena sighed. The train's slowness, she thought to herself, would make anyone edgy and impatient. There were long stops at little stations and stops for apparently no reason in the middle of the countryside. "I brought my tarot cards," she said at some point, thinking that the game might distract Rosa. "Let's see what the cards have to say." She slid her hand into her purse.

"Stop," Rosa said, grabbing Maddalena's wrist before she could take the cards out. "I'm scared of hearing bad news."

The train continued its way north, now crossing flat plains. Suddenly the countryside became populated by houses of all sizes, and the train slowed down as it entered an urban area and then finally a station. "Turin," Madam C said, taking her luggage off the shelf. "We have a much shorter trip ahead of us now."

Uncomforted, Rosa followed Maddalena and Madam C off the train, along the platform, to a ticket office, where Madam C inquired about the train to Vercelli. "Platform nine," a man in uniform said, pointing to his right. "In half an hour."

The day was almost over when Rosa, Maddalena, and Madam C arrived in the humid and foggy city of Vercelli, known to the rest of Italy for its rice fields, which were kept flooded year-round by the many bodies of water that surrounded the town, chiefly the Sesia, one of the northern tributaries of the Po River. Off the train, outside the station, Maddalena, Madam C, and Rosa found themselves at the edge of a piazza, wrapped in wet air that was so much heavier than the clear air near the sea. Maddalena removed her hat and wiped her forehead with the back of her hand. She said, "It's a steam bath."

"This is Vercelli?" asked a dismayed Rosa. "I can hardly breathe!"

"I'm afraid so," Madam C said as she turned to a group of coachmen standing by their horses. "Excuse me," she asked, "could one of you take us to Mr. Valle's farmhouse?"

"Valle who?" asked a young coachman with a pointy beard.

Maddalena shrugged. "They have a son named Gabriele."

The coachmen exchanged long looks. In a deep, hoarse voice, the oldest one in the group said out of his web of wrinkles, "Valle is a common name. Where is this farmhouse?"

"We know it's next to a rice field," Rosa said, "marked by a tree on the road that is shaped like an amphora."

All the coachmen laughed and shook their heads. The old coachman spit tobacco on the sidewalk. He said, "All there is around here is rice fields. And do you know how many trees we have?"

"Is there someone around here who could give us a list of all the farmhouses that belong to someone named Valle?" Maddalena asked.

"I don't know," the younger coachman said. "Maybe the police?"

Rosa looked at Maddalena with worry in her eyes.

Madam C addressed the older coachman. "You look like you have been in Vercelli a long time."

"All my life," the man said with pride.

"Then you must have some idea as to where this place could be. Drive us around the rice fields," Madam C continued in her usual peremptory tone, stepping into the carriage and signaling Rosa and Maddalena to step in as well.

Dumbfounded, the old coachman asked, "In which direction?"

Madam C gave him a look. "You decide."

Mumbling and shaking his head, the old coachman took the luggage and secured it with ropes in the very back of the coach. Then he cautiously took his seat in the front. "Ha!" he shouted, and the horse began to walk. "All my life I spent driving this coach," he muttered softly, popping another tobacco ball in his mouth, "and now I've got to escort three lost women to a rice field and a funny-looking tree." He stopped the horse and turned around. "I don't have time for this!" he said in an angry voice. Madam C took two bills out of her purse and placed them on the front seat. The coachman took the bills, spit dark saliva on the ground, and led the horse toward a side street.

Ten minutes later, they were at the outskirts of the town, surrounded by rice fields and farmhouses. "There," the coachman said in a scoffing tone. "Rice fields and trees. Just as you wanted."

The daylight was dimming as the sun made its way slowly below the horizon. The heat of the summer day was still strong, as was the buzz of the mosquitoes feasting on the horse. The whipping of the horse's tail kept the insects in motion. In their seats, Madam C, Maddalena, and Rosa kept blotting their foreheads with handkerchiefs and fanning their hands up and down their cheeks. Their discomfort didn't distract them from the task at hand: Madam C kept her eyes fixed on one side of the road,

Maddalena and Rosa on the other, hoping to spot the tree that would take them to Gabriele's farmhouse. They saw nothing that resembled an amphora in any way.

As the carriage came to a T in the road, Rosa looked right and left. "The land is so flat around here," she said. "Where's the sea?"

The coachman turned around, stared at her, and shook his head twice.

"There's no sea in Vercelli," Maddalena said, surprised. "We're deep inland, in farming country, as you can see."

Rosa's aquamarine eyes opened wide. "No sea?" she murmured.

"No," Madam C confirmed, amazed that Rosa could be so naive.

"Really?" Rosa asked.

Madam C pondered a moment. "Have you ever seen a map of Italy, Rosa?"

Rosa shook her head.

"Didn't they teach you geography in school?" Maddalena asked.

Rosa shook her head for the second time.

"Are you . . . convinced that there's the sea in every town?" Madam C asked, unable to hide her disbelief.

"There isn't?" Rosa said timidly.

"No, dear," Madam C said. "There are lots of towns on earth that don't have the sea nearby."

Rosa lowered her eyes, feeling the weight of the revelation. As the carriage continued its wobbly way along a street bordered by berry bushes and short trees, she wondered how life would be without looking at boats, listening to the sounds of the waves, watching the seagulls dive for food, and with no fishermen bringing fresh fish ashore. She looked at Madam C and Maddalena, realizing that there was still mockery in their eyes.

What's so funny, Rosa thought. "I can perhaps live without crossing the ocean," she said aloud, "but I could never live in a place where I can't look at water." Madam C and Maddalena exchanged a glance, as the coachman shook his head again and spit tobacco one more time.

"How much longer shall we keep this going?" he asked in his harsh voice. An hour had passed since they had left the station. The sun had set, and the streets and fields were by then a blur in the darkness and hard to see. Reluctantly, Madam C asked the coachman to take them to a place where they could spend the night. "Now we're talking," he mumbled as he sped up the horse.

One kilometer down the road, he pulled up in front of the Locanda Dell'Orso, a hostel set back from the street in a field that smelled of freshly cut hay. A red tile roof sat on walls of thick stone studded with small patches of green and brown moss.

"Wait here," Madam C said, getting out of the carriage, "while I make sure they're not sold out for the night."

The coachman mumbled something no one could hear. While he, Rosa, and Maddalena waited outside, Madam C entered the hostel lobby, a small, cozy room with an unlit fireplace carved in the stone wall and a few armchairs set around it in a half moon. The cool temperature inside was a pleasant surprise. In a corner was a desk, and behind the desk Madam C saw a middle-aged man with thick glasses busy turning pages. He lifted his head at the sound of Madam C's steps. "Need a room?" he asked.

"I need three," Madam C replied. "The best ones you have."

Yawning, the man opened a drawer. "All the rooms are the same," he slurred, handing Madam C three keys. "Second floor, to your right." He pointed to a closed door opposite to him. "Dinner will be served in an hour."

"They have rooms for us," Madam C said once she was back outside. She turned to the old coachman, who kept chewing tobacco without talking. "Be back here at dawn."

The coachman said, "No."

Without arguing, Madam C took more bills out of her purse. "Six o'clock," she said, pushing the bills into his hands, "and don't be late."

CHAPTER 10

The sleeping quarters were off a narrow hallway on the second floor, where the heat trapped below the roof overwhelmed the cooling effects of the thick stones. Madam C, Maddalena, and Rosa sweated copiously as they carried their luggage to their respective rooms. The furnishings in the three bedrooms were alike: a double bed with an embroidered red cotton bedspread, an armoire, two chairs, a portable basin for water, an enameled chamber pot centered between the legs of a nightstand, and a rustic rug set on the wooden floor. With her clothes on, Rosa lay on top of the bedspread and stared at the low ceiling for a long time. Meanwhile, Maddalena joined Madam C in her room. "Forgive my asking," she said as Madam C took a change of clothes out of her suitcase, "but what are we going to do next? We have no idea where this farmhouse is. No one does. It could be on the opposite side of town, many kilometers away, for all we know."

"We'll go to dinner," Madam C said, closing her suitcase, "and question the innkeeper."

The meal exceeded everyone's expectations. The innkeeper's wife served it on an elegant china set that seemed out of place in a hostel that looked so much like an old farmer's house. She served *antipasti*, *brasato di maiale*, *coniglio al forno*, and a sweet meringue pie, all accompanied by a full-bodied local red wine. At the elegantly set pine table, Madam C, Rosa, and Maddalena were joined by two male guests and the middle-aged man with the thick glasses, who, everyone soon found out, was the innkeeper. The conversation proceeded casually for some time: the weather, the rice business, the soccer games. Over the *antipasti*, Madam C introduced herself as a landowner from Genoa, who was in town looking for land to buy. The two guests introduced themselves as salesmen who often traveled the Vercelli countryside. At that, Madam C steered the chitchat her way. "Then you must know of a farmhouse owned by some Valles," she said in a casual tone of voice. "I was told it may be for sale."

The two salesmen looked at each other and shook their heads twice. Maddalena took the role of a skeptic. "There's no truth to it," she said, chewing on a piece of *coniglio*. She poured herself some wine. "Imagine, the person who told us about that farmhouse didn't even know where it was. All he knew was that it's by a tree shaped like an amphora. He must have been dreaming."

The innkeeper's wife, who had begun to make the rounds with the meringue pie, jumped into the conversation. "I think I know where it is," she said, putting down the dessert plate. Her husband nodded. "I do, too. It's not close by, but I can draw you a map from here to there. Then you'll be able to find out if the land is truly for sale."

Rosa could hardly contain her excitement. "Really?" she shouted. She turned to Madam C. "Can we go now?"

"What's the hurry, young lady?" asked the innkeeper.

Maddalena bumped Rosa's knee under the table.

"No hurry," Madam C said calmly. "She was joking. Of course we'll go tomorrow, in the daylight."

"Do you really want to let these people know that there's

something in this farmhouse that cannot wait till morning?" Madam C scolded Rosa later, when they were back upstairs.

"Like someone who's wanted by the police?" Maddalena echoed. "You know how much people gossip in little towns."

"I'm sorry. I got excited," Rosa admitted. "I won't do that again, I promise. Let me see the map, Maddalena, please."

Maddalena handed her the sheet of paper on which the innkeeper had drawn a confused maze of roads and country paths. "It's so hard to read," Rosa said, sounding discouraged like never before.

Madam C took the map from her hands. "Our coachman will figure it out."

The night passed very slowly for Rosa. The anxiety that had flustered her all day long hadn't subsided. Knowing that in a matter of hours she'd be headed with Madam C and Maddalena for the Valles' farmhouse made her even more frantic and unable to sleep. She paced the room for an hour, she lay on the bed and got up countless times, she stood by the open window staring at the shadows of the countryside. At a certain point, she left her room and knocked on Maddalena's door. "I can't sleep," she said when Maddalena appeared.

"Me neither," Maddalena whispered. "Come inside."

They sat on the bed next to each other. "Want to read me the cards?" Rosa asked after a moment.

"I thought you didn't want to know."

"I do now," Rosa said. "Please."

The tarot cards were on Maddalena's nightstand, inside a cardboard box tied with a blue silk string two centimeters wide. Deliberately, Maddalena untied the string, opened the box, and set the cards on the bedspread in front of Rosa. "Ready?" she asked.

Rosa nodded. With quick motions, Maddalena shuffled, cut the deck, and turned up four cards.

"It can't be," Rosa babbled, realizing that the four cards were the Lovers, the Ace of Cups, the World, and the Fool. "These are the same cards you turned up for me months ago, when you arrived at the Luna."

"They sure are," Maddalena said thoughtfully.

"You're tricking me," Rosa said, scrunching her nose.

"No," Maddalena said calmly. "This is your future."

"It can't be," Rosa insisted. "I remember you telling me that these cards mean that I will find love and I will go on a long trip."

Maddalena nodded.

"Well," Rosa said in a louder, screechy voice, "it's impossible! The love of my life has disappeared, and I'm not going anywhere without him. And even if I found him," she shouted, "I can't go on my trip across the ocean because he's afraid of boats!"

"He is?" Maddalena asked, surprised.

"Yes!" Rosa yelled. "So, you see? You must be cheating!"

"There's no cheating with tarot cards, my dear. You saw me turn up the cards. You'll find love, and you'll go on a long trip. That's that."

Angrily, Rosa lay down with her back to Maddalena. Maddalena replaced the tarot cards in the box, tied the blue string, and lay down quietly next to Rosa. They remained silent a while before Rosa spoke in a soft voice. "Are there really lots of places in the world that don't have the sea nearby?"

"Lots," Maddalena replied.

Rosa rolled over to face Maddalena. "I never thought it possible," she said. "All the books I read were about the sea. And all the people I know grew up by it. Even Isabel's village, which is so far away from Genoa, is on the water. She came to Genoa by water. And my father was a fisherman, Madam C told me, who made his living casting nets in the water." Her voice broke down. "How was I supposed to know?"

"It's all right, Rosa. You know now."

"It's not all right. I noticed how you two were making fun of me earlier today. Even the coachman was laughing. I saw him."

"We weren't making fun of you," Maddalena explained. "We were surprised."

Rosa sat up. "How do people travel to far places when there's no sea?" she asked.

"By train. And now by automobile. They say there'll be lots of automobiles in the streets very soon."

"Have you ever been on one?" Rosa asked.

"I have," Maddalena said. "One of my clients took me for a ride."

"Did you like it?"

"I was scared at first," Maddalena admitted, "because we were going so fast. Twenty kilometers an hour, my client told me. Then I got used to it, and I enjoyed it."

"Maybe Renato and I could have an automobile some day," Rosa said with dreamy eyes. "So we'll be able to go far without boating."

"That would be nice," a disconcerted Maddalena replied.

Quietly, Rosa lay down again, nestling her head on the pillow next to Maddalena's. "Do you think we'll find Renato at the farmhouse?"

Maddalena glanced at the open window. "We'll know very soon," she murmured. "Dawn is coming."

"Maybe he liked it in Vercelli," Rosa said sadly. "Maybe he found out, too, that there are places that are not on the sea, where he doesn't have to look at boats all the time and feel afraid." She paused. "Do you think I'll be able to convince him to come back to Genoa with me?"

"Rosa," Maddalena said in her sweetest voice. "We don't even know that he is here. I wouldn't worry about his fear of boats now."

"You're right," Rosa said disconsolately. "He may not be here. We may never find him. I may never see him again. Why?"

Maddalena patted her cheek. "See if you can sleep for a while."

At six in the morning, with a low fog hiding the hay and dewdrops shining on the grass blades, the hostel door opened with a squeak, and Madam C, Maddalena, and Rosa stepped outside. Behind them, the innkeeper and his wife set their luggage on the gravel. Maddalena thanked them, and the two went back inside. "Where's the coachman?" asked Rosa.

"Good question," Madam C said.

"Do you really believe he's going to show up?" asked Maddalena.

"I paid him," Madam C shrugged. "He seemed a bit of an ass, but not dishonest."

"He'd better show up," Maddalena mumbled, "or we'll be stranded in this place for the rest of our lives."

Time passed. Seated on her suitcase, Madam C grew more infuriated with every minute that went by. "I hate it when people don't do what they're supposed to do," she grinned, stomping a foot on the gravel. As for Rosa, she acted more like a caged tiger than a young lady waiting for her ride: she kept walking up to the main road and looking right and left, only to return to the hostel door and open her arms wide to signal that the coachman wasn't in sight. "He's not coming," she said despairingly. She tugged at Maddalena's sleeve. "What shall we do?"

"There's nothing we can do till eight," Madam C replied dryly. "That's when the innkeeper said we can get a different ride. If worst comes to worst, we'll be at the farmhouse a little later." She looked sternly at Rosa. "I suggest you calm down."

Rosa turned away. She mumbled, "All she can do is order people around."

"What did you say?" Madam C said with indignation.

Shrugging, Rosa walked back to the road. It was close to

seven when she heard the rhythmic thumps of horse's hooves. "There he is!" she shouted, pointing to her right.

"An hour late," Madam C spit out from between her teeth. "If he thinks he's getting more money from me, he's crazy."

In front of the hostel door, the coachman pulled on the reins. "Morning, ladies," he said with a mocking smile. "Ready for another wild-goose chase?"

Madam C took the innkeeper's drawing out of her purse and placed it under the coachman's nose. He gave it a distracted look. "What's that supposed to be?" he asked.

Madam C gave him her best victory smile. "A map to the amphora tree," she hissed. "Take our luggage and drive."

Soon everyone was aboard, and the foursome resumed the search for the farmhouse based on the innkeeper's map, following a maze of quiet country roads dipped in a misty, yellow fog. It was a little past eight when Maddalena screamed, "There it is!"

"That way," Madam C told the coachman, pointing at a small dirt road that cut into the fields next to the amphora tree.

"I'll be damned," the coachman said, smacking a hand on his forehead. "I thought this tree was a fantasy of three crazy women, but here it is."

He guided the horse to a right turn, and the carriage eased onto the dirt road. For some time they crossed only fields and occasional groves of aspens and weeping willows. Then the farmhouse appeared, set in a large, dry meadow studded with horse chestnut trees. An archway led the carriage into a graveled courtyard, around which stood the two-story house, the stable, the hayloft, and the chicken coops. In the middle of the courtyard, the horse came to a halt. Madam C, Maddalena, and Rosa stepped down. "We appreciate your help," Madam C told the coachman with a smile. She dipped her hand into her purse.

"You already paid me," the coachman said, grinning. From his post up on the carriage, he spit tobacco onto the gravel.

Then he clicked at the horse and soon became a shadow in the mist of the morning fog.

Shortly, a man came out of the house. Rosa spoke first. "Good morning," she said. "We're looking for Giacomo. Is he here?"

The man took a step back. He said, "I don't know anybody by that name."

"We are his friends," Rosa reassured him. "We know he came here with Renato."

The man became thoughtful, but didn't speak.

"Show Giacomo this," Rosa said, handing the man the blue stone. "He'll know who we are."

With ill-concealed interest, the man took the stone and went back inside. He returned with Giacomo two minutes later. "Rosa?" Giacomo said. "What are you doing here?" He pointed at Madam C and Maddalena. "Who are they?"

"Friends," Rosa explained, "who came here with me to help me find Renato. Is he with you?"

Giacomo seemed surprised. "No," he said. "He left over a week ago, as soon as we got here."

Rosa took Maddalena's hand. "I was hoping so much he'd be here . . ."

"We need to talk," Madam C said. "Can we come inside?"

The conversation between Rosa, Madam C, Maddalena, Giacomo, and Anna and Berto Valle, Gabriele's parents, took place in the kitchen, at a round oak table. Anna served strong, hot coffee, for which everyone was grateful.

"What's going on?" Giacomo asked. "All this time," he said, looking at Rosa, "I thought Renato was back in Genoa with you."

Rosa shook her head slowly.

"Is it possible that he decided to go somewhere else?" Madam C wondered.

"I doubt that very strongly," Giacomo said. "On the train he spoke only of Rosa and how much he missed her and how he couldn't wait to be with her. He even said"—he smiled—"that he could smell her odor even when she was far away."

"I insisted he spend the night here," said Anna, "but he was in a hurry to catch the night train, and I couldn't change his mind."

"How did he get back to the station?" Maddalena asked.

"With Geraldo Bassi, a neighbor who was here that evening and was headed that way," Berto explained.

"Could we talk to him?" Madam C asked. "At least we'll know if Renato made it back to the station."

"Sure," Berto said. "I'll hitch the horse to the wagon. The neighbor in question is only a short ride from here."

"Of course I dropped him at the station," Geraldo Bassi said when they found him cutting hay in the field behind his house. "Then I went my way."

"At least," Madam C pointed out as they all headed back to the Valles' farmhouse, "we know that whatever happened to Renato happened at the Vercelli station or on the train."

"But they told you there were no train accidents this past week," Rosa whined.

Giacomo said, "It's very strange."

"My brother works at the station," Anna said. "I'll ask him to talk to people there. Maybe someone will remember Renato."

Her husband added, "And I'll talk to the women who sell produce at the market. They know everything about everybody. If Renato didn't leave Vercelli, they may know where he is. And we should also check the hospital and the jail."

"You can all stay in our home as long as you want," Anna told Madam C. "We have space. We'll do anything we can to help you find Renato. He and this man"—she pointed at Giacomo—"saved our only son's life."

Thankful for the invitation, Madam C, Rosa, and Maddalena settled in two rooms on the top floor, a larger one

Madam C and Maddalena shared, and a smaller one for Rosa. "Rosa needs privacy," Maddalena had told Madam C earlier, when the two of them had discussed the logistic situation. "She's very upset, and it's hard to share space with others in that kind of state." She paused. "Have you two talked yet?"

"No."

"I can't believe it!" Maddalena blurted out, throwing her hands up in the air. "What are you waiting for?"

Madam C said nothing as she opened her suitcase.

Later that afternoon, while Maddalena was helping Anna with dinner and Giacomo and Berto were at the market asking questions about Renato, Madam C knocked on Rosa's door. There was no answer for a while, but the door finally opened as Madam C had begun to walk away. Barefooted, in a white vest that hardly covered her knees, Rosa stood in the doorway with dark, swollen eyes. "Did I wake you?" Madam C asked.

Rosa shook her head. She whispered, "I haven't been able to sleep in quite a while."

"Can I come in?"

Slowly, Rosa moved aside.

They stood in front of each other in the middle of the room. "How are you feeling?" Madam C asked.

Rosa shrugged.

"Look," Madam C said. "We'll be spending the next several days under the same roof, so I thought that perhaps we should stop beating around the bush."

For the first time, Rosa looked Madam C straight in the eyes. "You hurt me."

"And you hurt *me*."

"How?" Rosa asked. "You're the one who threw me out of my home."

"Rosa, I'm trying."

"What are you trying?"

"To help you. And to reach you."

Rosa spoke with a thread of voice. "What am I supposed to say?"

"I don't know," Madam C replied. "Is there something you'd like to say?"

Rosa straightened her slumping shoulders and spoke with defiance. "As a matter-of-fact, yes. There *is* something I'd like to say. I don't understand why you had to toss me and my things out the door. What got into you? I grew up thinking you loved me. Were you faking?"

Madam C took a step toward Rosa. "How dare you think that my love for you was fake," she said, giving Rosa an icy cold glare.

Rosa raised her voice. "Then what did I do that night that was so bad!"

"You still don't get it, do you?" Madam C said, raising her voice as well. "You"— she pointed a finger at Rosa—"took from me the only man I ever cared for. Do you know what that means?" She shouted, "Do you?" She stared into Rosa's eyes as her lips trembled. "I spent a lifetime giving my body to drunks, vagabonds, and rich men who not once looked past my buttocks and the size of my breasts. And then there was Cesare. He was different. And you took him!" She screamed, "You ruined everything!"

Rosa looked at Madam C in silence. She spoke after a long moment. "They say that mothers are supposed to love their children no matter what. It's one thing to get angry; it's another thing to throw your daughter in the street."

Madam C took a deep breath. "I realize I hurt you," she said in a calmer voice, "and it breaks my heart because, trust me, you are the last person on earth I would want to see in pain. But I couldn't help it. If I could go back, I know I would do the same thing all over again."

"Why?" Rosa asked.

Slowly, Madam C said, "You obviously care for Renato a

lot. How would you feel if the person you love more than anything in the world took him from you?" Her voice broke down. "What would you do?"

Rosa's eyes softened. "I had no idea you loved Cesare so much."

"Now you know," Madam C whispered as she turned around and headed for the bedroom door.

"Does he feel the same way?" Rosa asked in a soft whisper.

Madam C froze in her tracks. She stood still a long moment, then walked on, slamming the door behind her.

After dinner, Giacomo found Rosa on the back porch, staring at the fields. In the distance, invisible crickets sang their night melodies to the moon. "Are you all right?" he asked.

Rosa turned to him. "Why is everything so difficult?"

"I don't know," Giacomo replied. "But I believe there's a reason things happen the way they do."

"I can see no reason for how my life has turned out in the past months."

"Years from now," Giacomo said, "you'll look back and understand what today seems absurd."

They stood quietly next to each other as a light breeze brought aromas of fruit trees and hay to them. "Tell me," Rosa said, breaking the silence, "how's your wound?"

Giacomo opened his shirt. "It healed, but I have this ugly red swollen mark on my shoulder."

"It'll get better," Rosa said. "Isabel said so."

Giacomo smiled. "How is she?"

"Fine."

"I miss her, you know. I find myself thinking of her for some reason."

"She's special," Rosa said. "In more than one way."

Giacomo nodded. "Anna and Berto have been wonderful to me," he said, "but I can't stay here much longer. I miss Genoa—

the water, the longshoremen, my job at the warehouse. And I'm sick of fog and mosquitoes and steaming heat. I was thinking today that after we find Renato I want to go back to Genoa with you all."

"They will arrest you!" said Rosa.

"It's like I'm already in jail here. Now that some time has gone by, I can explain to the police what happened. I was defending myself from that crazy sword-swallower."

"And I know for a fact that Camila is no innocent girl," Rosa added.

"Is the circus still in Genoa?" Giacomo asked.

"I'm not sure. I haven't been paying much attention to anything in the past days."

"We'll find Renato, I promise," Giacomo said. "He can't have vanished from the face of the earth."

"Did he ever say anything to you about wanting to live in a different place?" Rosa asked.

"No."

"He never mentioned wanting to be . . . away from the water?"

"Rosa? What in the world are you talking about?"

"I don't know," Rosa sobbed. "What if. . . ."

"What?" Giacomo asked.

Rosa spoke in a whisper, "What if he's dead?"

"Don't even think about it. Renato is a tough guy. It'd take ten sword-swallowers to take him down."

Rosa said, "I don't know what to think anymore."

"Get some sleep," Giacomo said. "Tomorrow is another day."

"Angela," Rosa prayed that night by her bed, head on the scented sheets, "if Renato is in heaven with you, please let me know. But it would be even better if you could send him back here, because he belongs in Genoa with me and Giacomo and the longshoremen and all the other port people." She kept her hands crossed as she lay down and closed her eyes, falling inadvertently into a shallow sleep.

There hadn't been ten sword-swallowers to take down Renato, only a couple of bandits along the road. He had boarded Geraldo Bassi's wagon late that night, after parting from Giacomo and the Valles at the farmhouse. The wagon had gone swiftly down the dirt path, headed for the intersection with the main road that would take it eventually to town. The road and the fields were dark, the only light far above that of the moon and the stars. At a certain point, in that dimness, Renato thought he saw something ahead lying in the middle of the path. Geraldo Bassi stopped the horse, and Renato got out. "It's a man," he said, approaching the figure and bending down. "He seems unconscious."

Geraldo Bassi joined him on the road. "We should call for help," he said.

"Strange," Renato murmured. "He has a sock on his face."

At that very moment, a masked man came out of the bushes behind them and hit Renato on the head with a bat. At the same time, the man who was lying on the road stood up and punched Geraldo Bassi in the face. Renato dropped facedown on the dirt while Geraldo Bassi fell backward screaming. "Shut up," one of the men said, "and give us your wallet!"

Hands shaking, Geraldo Bassi did as he was told. The man snatched the wallet from his hands while his accomplice searched Renato. When the accomplice found what he was looking for, he dragged Renato to the side of the road and kicked him into a ditch. "As for you," the first bandit told Geraldo Bassi, "we won't kill you tonight. But one word about what happened and we'll come for you and your family. We know where you live, so don't even think of betraying us. Get on your wagon, and don't look back."

Terrified, Geraldo Bassi obeyed. Once the wagon was no

longer in sight, the bandits stepped into the ditch. One of them lifted Renato's arm and let it go; the arm dropped in the mud with a squishing sound. Then he lifted Renato's eyelid. "He's dead," he said. "Let's go."

Renato regained consciousness five hours later, in the dead of the night, smelling the wet earth at the bottom of the ditch and tasting the blood in his mouth. Ten minutes passed before his arms and legs could move. Slowly, he came to a seated position. At once, dizziness overcame him, and his head hurt so badly he thought it was split in two. He tried to open his eyes, but all he could see were black stains. One bone at a time, he lay down at the bottom of the ditch again, where he fell instantly asleep.

He awoke again before day dawned, with the same splitting headache and an unbearable burning in his chest. With fatigue, he pushed himself to his knees and after taking several deep breaths, he stood up and walked unsteadily toward a tree. He leaned against it for a while, looking around. There was fog, and he had no idea where he was and why. In the dim light of dawn, he began to walk, stumbling and leaning occasionally against poles and trees. Feet in the water, he made a beeline across a rice field and kept walking straight in the same direction without a clue as to where he was going.

A group of *mondine*, women who worked in the rice fields, spotted him as he approached them slowly from the east. They were all wearing the customary wide-brimmed hats and light pants rolled up above their knees. The water was up to their calves, their backs were bent forward, and their hands worked swiftly underwater to collect the grains. One of them lifted her head at the sound of steps splashing in the field. She pointed in Renato's direction, and all the *mondine* stood up and began to whisper to each other. As Renato moved closer, they retreated, frightened by his appearance: he had blood and dirt all over his head and face, and his clothes were filthy and wet, as if they hadn't been changed in years. He passed the *mondine* and continued on, without even taking notice of their presence. Later, as he emerged from the wet field onto a road, two farmers approached him and asked him if he was sick. Renato nodded.

"Can we take you somewhere?" one farmer asked.

"Where do you live?" the other added.

Renato stared at them without talking.

"What's your name?" the first farmer asked.

Again, Renato stood silent.

"If you ask me," the second farmer said, "this fellow escaped from prison. Let's call the police."

"Don't bother," the first farmer said. "He's probably just a bum who had a large dose of booze last night."

With weary steps, Renato resumed his aimless walk along the road.

"Stick your head in the water, pal," the second farmer yelled after him. "You'll scare the shit out of everybody looking like that."

That's what Renato did as soon as he saw water. It was a small pond on the side of the road which its owners used to quench the thirst of the cows. The water stank of manure and was covered with mosquitoes and dragonflies. Nevertheless, Renato washed off his face and hands, then removed his shirt, rinsed the dirt off it, and set it on the grass to dry. The morning fog had lifted by that time. In a daze, Renato sat next to the shirt at the edge of the pond, face in the sun, breathing the warm air. That was when he realized that he hadn't answered the two farmers' questions because he didn't know who he was. In his aching, muddy head there were only two things he was aware of: the scent of Rosa's oil and the sound of the sea waves.

He stood up as soon as his shirt had dried. The sound of the waves rang in his ears and Rosa's scent tingled in his nose. He had no clue what either one was. There was, however, one thing he remembered about the odor: he knew that he had smelled it the first time while a breeze was blowing into his face. So he walked against the breeze, looking for the source of the odor. He walked all day long, slowly but constantly, stopping only on two occasions to eat grapes from a vine and drink water from a fountain he encountered behind a farmhouse. When darkness arrived, he lay in a meadow looking at the sky. At dawn, he stood up. His headache had partially subsided. The breeze had changed direction, so he changed the direction of his walk. He zigzagged through the fields for days, stopping occasionally for water and fruit, always walking into the breeze. When there was no breeze, he imagined one. All along, he looked desperately for the source of that spicy-sweet odor.

CHAPTER 11

The news that there were strangers at Berto Valle's farmhouse who were looking for a friend who had disappeared spread quickly through the countryside. The market women and the *mondine* took it upon themselves to establish if the Genoese man had ever left town. They passed on information from stall to stall and from one rice field to the next, until soon people were knocking on Berto Valle's door with all kinds of tales about strange individuals who had been spotted in various locations throughout the plains. Over the next few days, Maddalena, Rosa, Giacomo, and Madam C obstinately followed every single lead: they chased down a vagabond without an eye, a businessman who was in town looking for land, the rider of a limping sorrel horse, and a French merchant who had set a tent in front of the Church of Sant'Andrea and sold hot stones that made one see the saint when held in a hand for one hour. All was in vain. Meanwhile, Madam C had sent a telegram to the Luna, asking Margherita to check with Isabel if Renato had by any chance shown up at her door. Margherita's reply was a no. As for the Valles, they checked the hospital and the jail, and heard back from Anna's brother that no one at the station remembered a man who matched Renato's description in any way. The *mon-*

dine who had recoiled at the sight of the wounded Renato reported having seen the devil crossing on foot one of the rice fields and then spreading his black wings and vanishing in the fog without a sound. "There's no way," Rosa stated with firmness, "that anyone could mistake Renato for the devil." On that note, the talk of the *mondine* was dismissed as superstition.

That evening, when everyone convened for dinner around the oak table, Rosa saw only long faces. Madam C was the first to speak.

"What options do we have left," she asked, "other than involve the police?"

There was a long silence in the room.

"I hate to give up," Maddalena said after a moment, looking sadly at Rosa, "but I must agree with Madam C that the police is all we've got left."

"So much for your tarot cards," Rosa grumbled, "which said twice that I'll find love."

Maddalena said firmly, "The tarot cards said what they had to say."

"If we call the police," Anna hinted with worry in her eyes, "we must send Giacomo elsewhere."

At one end of the table, Giacomo slumped his shoulders. "I don't understand," he said. "There must be a reasonable explanation."

No one said anything else for quite a while. Eyes on her plate, Rosa kept stirring her minestrone with a spoon. The silence was broken by knocks on the door just as Anna had begun to collect the dirty dishes. Berto stood up. "I hope it's not another crazy story about the devil," he mumbled, exiting the kitchen with a tired gait. He returned a moment later accompanied by a man in his sixties. Berto said, "I think you should all listen to what this man has to say."

At the kitchen table, over a glass of red wine, the man introduced himself as Daniele Marzio and explained that he was a gardener, with a weekly job on the grounds of the Benedettini. "The monks," he said, "are taking care of a man who wandered to their monastery. Apparently this man was hurt and in a lot of distress when they found him."

"Did you see him?" Rosa asked.

"Yes," Daniele Marzio replied. "This morning. I was helping the monks groom one of their gardens, and he was seated on a bench. Quiet man. Didn't speak or move the whole time I was there."

"What does he look like?" Giacomo asked.

"I'm not sure I can describe him. I didn't pay much attention, because I wasn't aware that you were looking for a man who disappeared. This evening my wife told me about your search, and that's why I came here. I can take you to the monastery if you want. It'll have to be tomorrow, though, because the monks don't let anyone in at night."

Madam C, Maddalena, and Rosa looked into each other's eyes. "As strange as this story may sound," Maddalena said, "it sure seems more reasonable than all the tales we've heard so far."

"Very well, then," Madam C said, raising her glass. "We'll go to the monastery first thing in the morning."

Giacomo whispered in Madam C's ear, "I hope this is not another popular invention. For Rosa's sake."

The monastery was ten kilometers northeast of the Valles' farmhouse, at the top of a small elevation. It was enclosed on three sides by a tall stone wall and accessible through a wrought-iron gate. Maddalena and Madam C entered the compound on Daniele Marzio's wagon, followed by a second wagon carrying Anna, Berto, Giacomo, and Rosa. Inside, the wagons followed an aspen-lined path, soon reaching a three-story building with a cross and an inscription in Latin over the front door. The door opened, and a monk watched the group get off the wagons. "I'm Brother Nunzio," he said as he approached them. "How can I help you?"

"I brought these people," Daniele said, "because they may know the man you found in the fields."

"I hope you do, because we have no idea who he is. Please follow me," Brother Nunzio said, pointing at the monastery door. "I'm the one who found him," he continued, "in our vegetable garden, seated by the tomato vines. He was dirty and scared. He wouldn't talk or move. All he did was sniff the air. I called for help, and two of my brothers joined me outside."

"Was he hurt?" Rosa asked, as they all stepped inside. She sneezed as wafts of burnt incense filled her nostrils.

"We weren't sure at first," Brother Nunzio said. "He sure looked sick. That's why we kept trying to convince him to go inside with us. When we tried to help him up, he kicked us, but we kept trying. I think his body gave in, and that's how we managed to bring him to one of our rooms. It took all three of us to do that." He was leading the group through a long corridor with floors of polished white marble. "He had a wound on his head, we found out. We cleaned the wound, bathed him, fed him, and he has been sitting in our garden ever since, without talking, continuing to sniff the air. I think he likes the smell of our flowers."

"Doesn't sound like Renato at all," Rosa said.

"I agree," Giacomo nodded. "Renato would never kick anybody—or sit by a tomato vine."

"We came all the way here," Madam C said. "We should at least meet this poor man. I'm intrigued."

At the end of the corridor, Brother Nunzio opened a door that led to a flower garden with benches set around a small fountain. "There he is," he said, pointing to a man seated on one of the benches.

"Renato!" Rosa screamed, running toward him.

Renato looked at her with spent eyes.

"Renato?" Giacomo called. "It's me."

Without talking, Renato kept looking at the people around him with bewilderment but not the least hint of curiosity or fear.

"What happened to you?" Rosa cried out. Then her eyes widened. "You don't know who I am?"

Renato didn't reply.

Rosa turned to Giacomo. "What's going on?"

"Looks like he doesn't recognize anybody," Madam C said. "How long has he been here?" she asked the monk.

"Four days," Brother Nunzio replied. He paused. "Who is he?"

"Renato Corsi," Giacomo said. "He lives in Genoa, with us."

"We need to call a doctor," Maddalena said.

"Brother Costante is a doctor," Brother Nunzio explained. "He visited him several times. Obviously the hit this man took on the head affected his memory, and in a very bad way."

"We would like to take him with us, if you don't mind," Madam C said. "Maybe we'll be able to help him."

"Sure," the monk agreed. "I'm glad you came. It's better for him to be with people he knows, or, at least, he knew at one time."

Giacomo placed his hand on Renato's arm. "Let's go home," he said. "Remember? Genoa. The port."

Renato didn't reply. Giacomo pulled on his arm, and Renato recoiled, letting out a short scream.

"Renato," Rosa begged, "look at me. How can you not remember who I am? Remember this?" she said, showing him the blue stone.

Quietly, Renato took the stone, turned it in his fingers, and gave it back to Rosa.

"And this?" Rosa asked, taking the flask of her perfect oil out of the velveteen bag. She opened it and set it under his nose.

The moment Renato smelled the oil, his lips stretched in a happy smile. "I have been looking for this odor all along," he said. "What is it?"

"My perfect oil," Rosa replied with an equally happy smile. "It's lavender, basil, apple blossoms, and Azul's oil. Azul is Isabel's grandmother. Remember Isabel? With the black vest?"

Empty-eyed, Renato kept staring at Rosa.

"You don't remember anything, do you?" Rosa said in a disconsolate voice.

Renato shook his head.

"Come with us, "Giacomo said. "We'll help you figure out what happened. And we'll take you home."

Renato nodded, then pointed at Rosa's flask. "Can you open it again, please?"

They spent the rest of the day and that night at the farmhouse, where Renato rested and everyone else tried to figure out what had happened to him either at the station or on the way to it. Too afraid, Geraldo Bassi never told anyone what he knew, even though he was questioned many times. To his credit, he had returned to the ditch early in the morning after the fact, looking for Renato, but when he hadn't seen him anywhere, he had concluded that either the bandits had kidnapped him or he had found his way to the station. In either case, he had figured, there was nothing for him do at that point in time. As for Renato, he had stood up from the garden bench holding tight in his hand the flask of Rosa's oil and docilely followed the group to the monastery door. He had taken his place on the wagon with surprised eyes. As the wagon had hobbled its way to the main road along the aspen-lined path, he had handed the flask back to Rosa. He had said, "It's good that I don't have to walk anymore."

A doctor came to the farmhouse and examined Renato carefully from head to toe. "He was obviously hit on the head with a hard object," the doctor said, "and that's why he can't remember anything. There's nothing else wrong with him as far as I can tell. The monks took good care of his wound. All he needs is rest and time. And caring people who can help him through this difficult moment. Talk to him," he told Rosa, Giacomo, and the Valles, "about things he did and knew. The more he hears familiar voices and sees familiar places, the better his chances to start remembering."

"Can he travel by train?" Giacomo asked.

"Yes," the doctor said. "Traveling will not be a problem."

That evening, in Rosa's room, Renato lay on Rosa's bed as Rosa and Giacomo sat next to him and told him about his life. They told him about Genoa, his job at the warehouse, the political demonstrations, the Grifone, Isabel, and the story of the sword-swallower, Camila, and Giacomo's disguise. Renato listened to their tales with marveled eyes. "It all sounds made up, you know," he said.

"It's not," Rosa said. "And there's more." She spoke slowly. "Behind the warehouse there's a shack by the water where you and I used to make love every night."

He looked at her with his deep blue eyes. "I must be crazy not to remember that."

"What do you remember about this past week?" Giacomo asked.

"Not much," Renato said, "other than waking up in a ditch with a splitting headache and walking about the fields." He thought a moment. "There's something strange about you two. I don't know you, but I know you. You feel like . . . family."

Rosa whispered, "We are." Gently, she took Renato's hand and held it a while. Renato took a deep breath and closed his eyes.

"Let's go," Giacomo whispered in Rosa's ear after a moment. "He's asleep now."

"He's so peaceful," she said, noticing Renato's calm breathing. She untangled her hand from his, stood up, and laid a light blanket on his body. "What in the world happened to you?" she sighed.

Giacomo tiptoed to the hallway and waited for Rosa. She came out of the room shortly with an anxious look in her eyes. She said, "What can we do to help him?"

"One thing at a time," Giacomo replied. "Up till this morning we had no idea where he was. We found him, and he's alive. Come," he added, taking the stairs down. "Let's talk outside."

They took a walk in the fields, following a dirt path that cut through the darkness and wound away from the farmhouse. "Get ready to be patient, Rosa," Giacomo said. "It may take a long time. I'm no doctor, but I read somewhere that memory losses are one of the hardest illnesses to cure."

"Patience is not one of my virtues, I'm afraid," Rosa replied. She added, "I wish I knew what to do."

"He thinks we're family," Giacomo pointed out. "It's a start."

Rosa nodded.

"Talking about family," Giacomo asked, "what's with you and Madam C?"

"Why?" Rosa asked.

"I noticed that you never talk directly to each other."

Rosa stopped, bent down, and picked a pink wildflower. "It's something that happened in the past."

"She obviously cares about you," Giacomo said, waiting for Rosa to resume walking. "She accompanied you all the way here to help you find Renato."

"We have issues," Rosa explained. "And a hard time talking about them." She paused. "I used to live with her. At the Luna."

"How was it?" Giacomo asked.

"Great," Rosa replied. "Madam C raised me and protected me, and all along told me how much she loved me. It all changed on the night of my sixteenth birthday. I did something, we shouted bad things at each other, and then she threw me out of the Luna. That's why I went to live with Isabel."

"Do you miss living at the Luna?" Giacomo asked.

"Yes."

Giacomo said, "Maybe Madam C misses having you there."

"I'm not sure that Madam C and I will ever be able to put the past behind us," Rosa murmured.

"I had phenomenal fights with my mother," Giacomo said. "They were so bad that after every one of them I felt I'd never be able to speak another word to her."

"How did you manage?" Rosa asked.

"A happy occasion, a gesture, a little smile, and we'd get along again. Till the next fight."

"Renato told me you still live with her. Why?"

Giacomo nodded. "I'm all she has. And I guess we love each other in our own ways."

The air had cooled slightly when they returned to the farmhouse. The Valles, Madam C, and Maddalena were in the living room, seated around a coffee table.

"How's Renato?" Madam C asked, when Rosa and Giacomo came in.

"Shaken. Tired," Rosa replied, fiddling with the wildflower. "But he managed to fall asleep in my room."

"We'd better go to sleep, too," Madam C said, standing up. "We have a train to catch early in the morning." She began walking toward the stairs, followed by everyone else in the room.

"Can I talk to you for a moment?" Rosa asked.

Madam C stopped and waited till the two of them were alone. "Yes?"

Rosa cleared her throat. "I wanted to say thank you for all you did," she said in a soft voice.

"I'm so happy we found him. He seems like a wonderful man."

"He is," Rosa said. "I hope you'll get to know him."

Madam C smiled. "I'd love to. And I'd love to get to know you as well. You've changed."

Rosa swallowed twice. "I'm sorry I slept with the mayor. And I'm sorry for the things I yelled at you. I guess I couldn't help it, either."

"I'm sorry I reacted the way I did. I shouldn't have." There was a long silence, then Madam C spoke in a gentle voice, "Maybe when we get back to Genoa you could spend time at the Luna, like in the old days. It'd be nice to have you back."

Rosa nodded, then handed Madam C the wildflower. "I picked it tonight," she said. "Reminds me of our trip to the hills."

Madam C swallowed visibly as she took the flower. "It's beautiful," she murmured. She brought it to her face. "Its petals still smell of the meadows. That was a great trip we had." She was still a moment. "Well," she continued, regaining her confident tone of voice, "time for bed. See you at breakfast, dear. Be on time."

In the morning, at the train station, the good-byes took a long time. "Are you sure you want to go back to Genoa? You'll be in danger," Anna Valle said, hugging Giacomo for the third time.

He nodded. "Don't worry. I know that what I'm doing is right."

"Take good care of him," Anna said, smiling, to Rosa. "And I guess I don't need to tell you to take care of Renato."

"I'll do all I can," Rosa said, "you can be sure. Thank you for all you've done," she pointed at Maddalena and Madam C, "for all of us. And for Renato."

"Your train leaves in ten minutes," Berto said. "I hate to see you go, but you should rush to your platform before it's too late."

"Good-bye!" Madam C shouted, heading down the underpass stairs.

Maddalena and Giacomo rushed along, followed by Rosa and Renato. Near the ticket counter, hand in hand, Anna and Berto kept waving good-bye. "Come back to see us!" Anna shouted.

"They can't hear you," her husband whispered in her ear. "They're too far."

As the couple headed for the exit door, Anna said, "Giacomo looks so much like our Gabriele. Don't you think?"

Berto smiled at her. "If you say so, dear."

On the train, in the compartment, Renato sat quietly between Giacomo and Rosa. "I don't know what was wrong with me," he said as the train slowed down near a station, "holding a woman's perfume bottle like it was gold."

"There's nothing wrong with holding perfume bottles," Rosa said. "And for your information, you are the only person on earth I would allow to hold my perfect oil."

"Am I that special?" Renato asked, surprised.

"You have no idea," Rosa replied.

Later, as the train made its way toward the Turin station, Giacomo opened his suitcase. "I believe this is yours," he told Maddalena, pulling the black wig out from under his clothes. "You can have it. I don't think I'll be needing it again any time soon."

"Let me see how it fits you," Maddalena said, placing the wig on Giacomo's head. "Hmm, you *are* cute."

Seeing Giacomo in the black wig, Renato laughed for the first time. "You're too funny," he said.

Giacomo took off the wig. "Let me remind you," he told Renato, "that you traveled a whole day with me dressed like a woman and pretending to be your wife."

Renato said humorously, "That is something I'm glad I don't remember."

"There's something else you should know about this wig," Giacomo went on. There was an ill-concealed irony in his voice. "Rosa will tell you all about it."

Unseen by Renato, Rosa shook her head and gave Giacomo a mean stare.

Renato turned around. "What about it, Rosa?" he asked.

"It's nothing," Rosa said. "Giacomo has a strange sense of humor."

They switched trains in Turin and soon were headed south, crossing at moderate speed the lower Piedmont countryside. Quietly, Renato kept looking at the people around him and out the window at the passing fields. At a certain point, he noticed a mirror hanging above Madam C's head, across from him. He looked at it for a while, then stood up during a long stop at a station and stared at the image in the mirror for a long time.

"Do you remember your face?" Rosa asked.

"No." he said. "I don't mind it, I must say." He turned his head right and left to examine his profile. "Although for some reason, I thought I'd be younger. How old am I?"

"Twenty-seven," Giacomo said. He whispered, "You look older right now than you normally do."

"It's the emptiness I feel inside," Renato said sadly, sitting down.

"We'll help you learn everything about your past," Rosa said. "Then the emptiness will leave you."

They arrived in Genoa at six in the afternoon—right on time. Immediately, Giacomo turned himself in at the police station. He was arrested, waiting to be arraigned, and within a day the labor union had hired for him the best criminal lawyer they could find. The circus had left town, and public opinion was no longer inflamed. No one was thinking about the reward anymore. Rosa told Giacomo's lawyer about her encounter with

Camila and the girl's cold words, and a number of longshoremen lined up to attest to Giacomo's integrity as a worker and as
one of their political leaders. In tears, Giacomo's mother begged
the lawyer over and over to do all he could to save the only love
of her life. "My life would end," she sobbed at the visibly an-
noyed lawyer, "should my Giacomo end up in jail."

One week later, at the arraignment, the judge asked Giacomo, "What do you have to say?"

"I was defending myself from Manari's attack," Giacomo
explained. "He was trying to stab me. He fell on the blade when
I hit him on the head with the stone."

"The fact remains," the judge said, "that you fled like a
guilty man would."

"I didn't flee because I was afraid of justice," Giacomo explained. "I fled because I was afraid of the circus people and of
the reward they had placed on my head."

Then Giacomo's lawyer spoke to the judge. "My client
turned himself in and is clearly a good person who was in the
wrong place at the wrong time. And the girl, if you'll allow me,
is obviously a slut without a conscience. But, most important,
the circus people are no longer here to press charges. They even
took Manari's body along when they left town. In view of all
this, I ask that you dismiss the case."

After pondering for a moment, the judge said, "Everyone
knows that the circus people are a bad sort. Case dismissed.
But"—he looked Giacomo in the eyes—"don't get yourself in
any other trouble, young man, or I'll come after you with the
wrath of a sea storm."

Meanwhile, as soon as they had gotten off the train, Rosa
had taken Renato straight to Vico Usodimare. They arrived as
Isabel was placing bags filled with distillation discards outside.
"Good God!" she screamed when she saw them down the
street. She walked up to them and hugged Rosa tight. "I prayed
so hard for you," she said, "you have no idea." Then she turned

to Renato. "I feel like I want to hug you, too," she said, placing a hand on Renato's cheek.

Renato took a step back.

"Don't be afraid," Rosa reassured him. "This is Isabel. I told you all about her, remember?"

Dumbfounded, Isabel looked at Rosa.

"He doesn't remember you," Rosa explained disheartenedly, "or anyone else." She gazed at Renato. "Not even me," she added in a sad voice.

It took Isabel a moment to say, "Come inside."

In the distillery room, she pointed at the rocking chair, "Here," she told Renato. "Have a seat."

Without arguing, Renato obeyed. Isabel turned to Rosa. "You mean to tell me that he doesn't remember having been here before?"

Rosa shook her head.

"Start from the beginning," Isabel said. "From your train ride."

Over the next ten minutes, Rosa described to Isabel the main events in her trip, as Renato stared around at the stove, the equipment, and Isabel's face.

"Let me tell you something, young man," Isabel said, interrupting Rosa. "I'm getting tired of people looking at me and being afraid. I'm not going to bite you. Would you please stop staring at me that way?" She smiled. "You used to like me, if you can believe it. Sorry, Rosa. Go ahead with your story. I'm all ears."

"I'm not scared of you," Renato hummed so softly no one could hear him. "I'm scared of myself and of everything I can't explain."

"I knew it!" Isabel said at the end of Rosa's story. "I knew that something bad had happened to Renato." She turned to him. "Don't you worry," she said. "I have what you need." She disappeared into the flower room for several minutes. When she returned, she was carrying a bottle, which she handed promptly to Renato. "Rub this on your temples three times a day. Azul used to say that this oil brings back the good memories and kills the bad ones. I hope it will bring back your love for Rosa."

Renato sniffed the bottle. "I'll have to start using it right away," he said. "I can't stand not remembering being in love."

Rosa and Renato made many more stops that day. After leaving Isabel's booth, they headed for the port and the warehouses. It was the end of the evening shift, and the longshoremen who were leaving work spotted Renato immediately as he arrived. "Where have you been?" one asked.

"We thought something happened to you," another said.

"Something did happen to Renato," Rosa explained, "and he has no memory of the past."

"No memory at all?"

"None," Renato confirmed in a bit of dismay. "I don't remember any of you."

The men looked at each other in disbelief. Patiently, Rosa gave a brief account of the incident and the miraculous way in which she and her friends had been able to find Renato.

"You're safe," a longshoreman said, patting Renato's shoulder, "and that's all that matters."

"Yes," someone agreed, then suggested, "Let's celebrate Renato's return tonight at the Grifone." To Renato, he said, "A bottle of wine will help you remember, you'll see."

The Grifone was packed that night. In the middle of the bar, seated on a high stool, Renato tried his best to come to terms with the crowd. His closest friends stood by him the whole time, recounting his speeches from the podium and explaining to him the current political situation. "We need you and Giacomo back," one of them said. "Since you two left, the shipowners refuse to listen to our complaints."

"They know you're not around," another man added, "and they feel safe."

Renato shook his head. "I don't remember anything," he said, "so I can't help you. But Giacomo will be back soon."

"If his mother will ever let him out of her sight," someone said. The whole group laughed.

As for Rosa, she sat on a stool by the bar counter the whole time, keeping a vigilant eye on Renato. "I'm sorry I scoffed at you," Paolo Disarto told her as the party was winding down. He shook her hand. "I had no idea you were Renato's girlfriend. You can pour this on my head," he added, lifting a pitcher full of white wine. "That will teach me not to be an ass to pretty girls."

It was late when the party broke up. "You must be exhausted," Rosa told the confused Renato.

He nodded.

She said, "Let me take you to your home."

At the apartment on Vico Cinque Lampadi, Marco, who had heard the news about Renato's return and his loss of memory no one could explain, was excited to greet him and show him the place. Renato, of course, didn't recognize him. "You and I have lived together in these rooms for the past three years," Marco said. "All this time you complained about the stench of my clothes and whined that I should wash them twice as often. Does that sound familiar?"

Renato looked at him with lost eyes. "No." He was silent a moment, then said, "But I can tell you smell bad now."

In his room, Renato walked up to his bookshelf and looked at every volume on it for a long time. There were books of philosophy, politics, history, and current affairs. Among the authors were the French utopists Saint-Simon and Proudhon, as well as Diderot, Leibniz, Hegel, Engels, and Karl Marx. "Are these mine?" he asked.

"Yes," Marco said.

"Have I read them?"

Marco nodded. "Several times."

In silence, Renato began turning the books' pages. "I don't remember any of these books," he said, "but I have an urgency I can't explain to read them all." He paused. "I know I will."

"I'll leave you now," Rosa said softly. "I can tell you're about to fall asleep."

The following day, under the warm sun of the early afternoon, Rosa and Renato went to the belvedere. "It's strange," he told Rosa as they stood near the edge, looking at the city and the water. "I don't remember anything, and yet everything I'm learning about my life, I like. My job, the longshoremen, Isabel, Giacomo, Madam C, Maddalena, and all the people I met in the past days. And I'm moonstruck by this town, its smells, its streets, the water, the hills. I feel as if I had been here all my life."

"You have," Rosa said.

"I got lost this morning," Renato confessed, "in the maze of downtown."

Rosa looked at him with alarm. "What were you doing walking around by yourself? Marco was supposed to be with you."

"I needed to be by myself to see this city through my own eyes. I must have walked in circles for close to an hour. Do you know how I found my bearings?"

"How?"

"I closed my eyes at a certain point, and for some reason, with my eyes closed, I could tell in which direction the sea was. So I walked in that direction and saw the port, and from there I was able to return home. I can't explain it."

"I think it's a sign that some things are coming back to you," Rosa said.

He looked her in the eyes. "I think I'm falling in love with you," he whispered, "even though I'm not even sure what that means."

"Kiss me," she said. "It'll become clear."

They went to the shack that same night, Rosa leading the

way along the pier, Renato following docilely like a curious child. "This is it," Rosa said, pointing at the sacks. "The place where you and I used to make love."

Silently, Renato gazed about.

"Feel familiar?" Rosa asked.

"No," Renato said, sitting down. He looked at Rosa. "Help me."

She sat by him, put her arms around his neck. The rays of the lighthouse kissed them as they kissed each other. Then Rosa lay back on the sacks and drew Renato close, and in that motion she detected a slight resistance in his body. Surprised, she felt him lie on her almost inquisitively, cautiously tracing the contour of her neck with his fingers. Her gaze captured his face, and she saw in his blue eyes an unmistakable shadow of doubt. She noticed the wariness in his movements, the clumsiness of his limbs, and the controlled restraint with which he touched her. It never occurred to Rosa, who remembered vividly every moment of their tumultuous passion, that Renato's tentative, passionless conduct was to be attributed to his inability to remember her as well as the experience of loving a woman. He was groping through ancestral instincts, but Rosa gave it a whole different interpretation. As her lips timidly grazed his chest, she realized that she had never considered the possibility that Renato might not fall in love with her again, or might not be physically attracted to her. There, entangled with him on the sacks, the fear of this possibility came to her in a hurry. She became as cautious as he was, as the prospect of losing him suddenly loomed. She loosened her hug and distanced herself from her beloved ever so slightly to have a better look at him, to read his expressions and the movements of his body. She began studying intently the look in his eyes, the shape of his mouth, the trajectories of his hands, looking for hints of rejection. She became an anguished observer with no spontaneity or warmth. Correspondingly, Renato's insecurity grew, and she noticed it.

Her stomach twisted. Her throat closed up. With her mind's eye she saw herself living a life without Renato, fathoming at the same time the irrationality of her own thoughts and that by acting the way she was acting she was the one who pushed Renato away. She desperately tried not to stare at him, not to analyze him, not to judge him. She attempted a smile, realizing she was grimacing instead. She hugged him tightly, knowing the hug wasn't tight at all. She was aware of being more awkward than she had been the first time they had made love and that the more awkwardly she acted, the more wary he became. *I've lost him*, she cried to herself, longing desperately for the old Renato, the one who had kissed her softly the first time on the pier, chased her all over town, held her tenderly during their carriage ride. She breathed deeply, trying to calm down; the deeper she breathed, the more anxious she became. Her lips quivered as she tried to speak, but no sound came out of her mouth. She tried to say his name; all she did instead was gurgle an indecipherable sound. Out of sorts, she erupted into sobs as a bewildered Renato unwove himself from her and came to a seated position. He looked at Rosa, still sunken into the sacks and shaking from her sobs. "Come here," he said.

In tears, Rosa pushed herself up and sat next to him.

"I have no idea what it is we're doing or what's in your mind or what's in mine," he went on, "but I can see that you're very agitated. Please tell me why."

Rosa didn't speak.

He lifted his arm, placed it around her shoulders. Gently, Rosa laid her head on his chest. They stayed there in perfect silence, facing the sea, and in that silence Rosa heard the strong, deep thumps of Renato's heart. Her muscles started to relax, her throat to open. In Renato's tender yet firm embrace, listening to the rhythmic throbs of his heart, she felt a soothing calm swelling inside her. In an instant, she grasped the extraordinary strength of her love for him and realized with clarity that she didn't need the certainty of his love for her and that her fear of losing him was only the fruit of her imagination. Suddenly, nothing mattered to her anymore beyond the indisputable fact that she loved him. She lifted her head from his chest and kissed him deeply. He returned the kiss without restraint, and they fell on the sacks again. They made love with a slow buildup of passion, no longer watchful of each other, moving in unison as they always had, with Rosa lost in Renato's embraces, not for a single moment aware that she was helping him and leading him as he had led her the first time they had been together.

They stopped much later, worn out and sweaty. Renato spoke first. "The scent of your skin," he whispered in her ear, "is the most maddening odor I've ever smelled."

Rosa sat up, pushing herself to the edge of the sacks. "I believe I have heard this before," she said slyly.

He joined her. "Am I dreaming," he asked, "or at the monastery, while I was seated on the bench, did you tell me that one of your oil's ingredients came from Isabel's grandmother?"

"You're not dreaming. She and Isabel picked the herbs on a hill in Costa Rica, when Isabel was a child. I'm sure that's the ingredient that drives people crazy."

"In Vercelli," Renato said, "your scent was the one thing that gave me the strength to keep going when my body wanted to drop to the ground. It was a strange feeling," he continued. "I was exhausted from walking through those rice fields, and yet I needed to find the source of that odor. That's why I couldn't stop."

"But you stopped at the monastery."

"Only to rest. The monks took me by force, and then, when I was in their garden, I was confused as to which way to go, because I could smell your scent everywhere. So I sat on the bench and stayed there."

"What would you have done if we hadn't come to the monastery?" Rosa asked.

He thought a moment. "I would have gotten up," he murmured, "and walked the earth until I found you."

Slowly, a large transatlantic steamer made its way toward a pier. Renato said, "We could go on a boat ride sometime."

Rosa stared at him with her large aquamarine eyes. "You mean it?"

"Yes," he said. "I keep looking at these ships, and I'm fascinated. Have you ever been on a boat?"

"N-no," Rosa stuttered, amazed at what he had said. "I'd love to do that with you."

"Next week maybe," Renato said. He gazed around him. "I deal with so many new things every day, so many emotions."

Rosa was radiant when she walked through the distillery door that night. "He forgot!" she shouted at Isabel, who was dozing off on the rocking chair.

Startled, Isabel woke up. "Who forgot what?"

"Renato! He forgot he's afraid of boats!"

"How lucky. And I bet you didn't remind him."

"Is it wrong? I mean, it's not like I'm lying to him. It's not my fault if he doesn't remember."

Isabel thought a moment. "I guess not, but I thought you were helping him remember his life."

"I am."

"Do you realize how much power you have over him?" Isabel asked. "You can't decide what he should or shouldn't remember. I thought you learned a lesson about truth and lies. I heard what you told Renato in this very room the night Giacomo was bleeding. You said, 'I promise I'll always tell the truth, no matter how difficult, no matter how painful.' Remember?"

"Certain things are more important to remember than others," Rosa argued.

"That's your personal judgment," Isabel said. "Let me see if I can get this straight. You are helping him remember his love for you, but not his fear of boats. A little self-serving, don't you think?"

"Should I tell him?"

"Of course you should. But for now, let's go to sleep. I feel tired"—Isabel closed her eyes—"like I've never felt before."

Madam C, in the meantime, had again taken charge of the Luna. "Thank you," she had told Margherita on the day she had arrived. "The place looks great. And guess who's coming to lunch on Thursday."

"Who?"

"Rosa. With Renato."

Margherita smiled. "Back to normal. I'm so glad." She turned to Stella. "Is Thursday a good day for a reconciliation?"

"As a matter-of-fact, yes," Stella said. "Thursdays are good for relationships, and on this coming one the wind will be blowing from the south. Southern winds bring warmth. Everything will be all right."

It was indeed a warm day when Rosa and Renato arrived at the Luna on Thursday around noon. "Have I been here before?" Renato asked as Rosa knocked on the door.

"No," Rosa said. "You were never too fond of prostitutes. You'll see now how nice they all are."

Stella came to the door. "So this is the famous Renato," she said as she moved aside to let them in. "Let's see," she continued, taking Renato's hand and turning it palm up. "Deep, long lines. Few crossings."

"Is that good or bad?" Renato asked, smiling.

"It's all good," Stella said, "or I wouldn't let you anywhere close to Rosa. Come in, dear. Meet the rest of the family."

In the parlor, Rosa and Madam C introduced Renato to the girls, who after only a few moments of awkwardness warmed up to him and treated him as if they had known him all their lives. Next, they introduced him to Antonia, who had prepared a sumptuous banquet for the occasion. Before sitting down to lunch, Rosa gave Renato a grand tour. First, she brought him to her bedroom behind the kitchen. The wrought-iron bed was still there, as were the batiste sheets and the white bedspread filled with goose feathers. It was the first time Rosa had set foot in that room since she and Madam C had had their big fight. The memories of her sixteenth-birthday party overwhelmed her, and for a moment she thought she saw the silhouette of Cesare Cortimiglia's naked body curled up on her sheets. "I slept here from the day I was born," she told Renato in a soft voice. "Something happened in this room that changed my life. One day I'll tell you the story."

"I'm glad you decided to bring me here," Renato said. "Seeing this room, where you slept and lived, is like peeking into the past. It's a treat, given that in my condition the word *past* has no meaning."

"Let's go see the rest of the Luna," Rosa said, chasing away the vision of the naked mayor. "There's history there, too."

They climbed the stairs to the second floor and walked the girls' corridor as Renato looked right and left with some uneasiness. "It's all right," Rosa said. "I used to play in these rooms every day when I was little. I loved to hide in the closets. And upstairs are Madam C's rooms. Things happened there as well."

Quietly, Renato followed Rosa from room to room and then up the stairs to Madam C's quarters. He stood in front of the unlit fireplace and gazed about, looking hesitant, almost afraid to walk through Madam C's bedroom door. Behind him, Rosa thought of him in the monastery garden, seated on the bench, lost in his thoughts, looking scared, so unlike the magnetic Renato who could stand tall at a podium and readily bewitch a crowd. And yet, that day at the monastery, she had instantly loved the new Renato as well, perhaps more than she had loved the unharmed Renato. She took his hand and squeezed it, pointed at the half-open door of Madam C's bedroom, which revealed the edge of the bed and part of the yellow curtains. "I never felt comfortable going in there, either," she said. "I guess a mother is . . . a special matter." She paused. "They're waiting for us downstairs."

Everyone was at the kitchen table when Renato and Rosa returned to the first floor. They sat down, and as they all savored the first of Antonia's specialties of that day, *stoccafisso in umido con patate,* the girls began telling Renato the stories of Rosa's childhood: the games on the second floor, the evenings in the kitchen, the school adventures. They were stories they had heard from their predecessors, so they felt free to embellish them for the occasion. Madam C, who knew exactly where the line was between fantasy and truth, said nothing to undermine the girls' efforts. Renato was in awe of everyone, especially of Rosa. "I feel like I know you now," he said once the lunch was over. He, Rosa, and Madam C were seated in the parlor. "I don't think I'll ever forget this day."

Madam C turned to Rosa. "Your room is still your room, as you noticed," she said. "Everything in it is exactly as you left it. Why don't come live here while you and Renato sort out your lives?"

"My home is in Isabel's booth now," Rosa replied. "I want to stay with her. She doesn't look good these days. She's always tired. I haven't seen her distill a single oil since we came back to town."

"Take care of her," Madam C said. "As for me, there's someone I need to take care of right now."

A few hours after Rosa and Renato had left the Luna, Madam C was knocking on Cesare Cortimiglia's door. Roberto Passalacqua let her in.

"How is he?" she asked.

"See for yourself," he replied. "He's in the living room."

She found Cesare seated on the floor surrounded by books.

His beard was down to his chest, and his eyes were red and dry from having spilled all their tears. In one hand, he was holding Rosa's handkerchief, which had by then lost its odor. On his lap he had an open book and was reading it aloud. "What are you reading?" Madam C asked, picking up one book from a pile and examining it front and back a few times.

"Poetry," Cesare Cortimiglia replied.

"Mother of God!" Madam C exclaimed. "You *are* out of your mind!"

"This poetry," he said in a ranting voice, "and this"—he waved Rosa's handkerchief—"are what are keeping me alive."

"I have a better idea for keeping you alive," Madam C said, helping him off the floor. "Come live at the Luna." She paused. "I have your briar pipe."

The former mayor looked at her with his weary eyes. "Why would you want me to live at the Luna? I thought you hated me."

Madam C became thoughtful for a moment. "Life is a circle," she said. "Your adult life started in a brothel, and it's only fitting that it should end in one. Does this answer your question, dear?"

CHAPTER 12

The evening shadows were lengthening all over downtown when Isabel, who was arranging bottles on the shelf, stopped her hands in midair.

"What's the matter?" Rosa asked. She was by the stove, dropping tea leaves into a pot of boiling water.

Wearily, Isabel shuffled to her rocking chair. "You don't need me anymore, Tramonto," she said, sitting down. The chair rocked gently back and forth, squeaking. "I'm ready to leave."

"What are you talking about?" Rosa asked in a worried voice.

"I've been dreaming of Azul and the hill every night. I think they're calling me. And I want to go there."

"I'll take you there. We'll buy tickets with the money I made selling your oils. Remember? My dream has always been to cross the ocean."

"There's no time," Isabel said. "And it doesn't matter. Where I'll die is only a geographical detail. I'll always be on that hill. I've always been."

"You're not going to die," Rosa said.

"Oh yes, I will," Isabel said. "You will, too, one hundred years from now."

"Then you'll have to stay alive another one hundred years."

"I would if I could," Isabel sighed. "But I haven't been feeling well these days."

"I noticed. Let me take care of you my way."

Upon Rosa's request, Michele Merega came to the distillery the next day. "I don't like to be touched by strangers," Isabel grumbled as soon as the doctor stepped in and approached her. "And I don't like doctors at all. Go away."

Michele Merega, who for many years had treated prostitutes, thugs, and various other members of the Genoese underworld, was not the shy type. "I'll go after I visit you," he replied firmly. "I suggest we do this the easy way, madam. My hard way is something you'll never want to see." Isabel gave him a very hard stare.

The examination was far from easy with Isabel fencing the doctor away and mumbling and tossing and turning, but in the end he was able to come to a conclusion. "She's weak, but not truly ill," he told Rosa. "Give her these," he added, holding out a bottle. "These pills should help her gain strength. And for sure she could use a breath of fresh air. This place stinks."

Isabel made her position clear after the doctor had left. "I never took medicines, not once in my life, and I'm not going to start now."

"You *will* take these medicines," Rosa said firmly. "I'll force them down your throat if I have to. And I'll find you a different place to stay."

"You may be able to force these pills down my throat," Isabel stated, "but you'll never be able to make me leave these rooms."

"We'll see," Rosa said. "I'll be back in five minutes."

She followed the doctor down the street. "Can Isabel take a trip on a boat across the ocean?" she asked him.

"Old people react to changes in unpredictable ways," he said. "For sure the air of the sea would be better for her than the air of that booth. But being on a ship for a long time may be hard on her body. Which would be better, I can't tell you."

"If I brought her with me on a trip to Costa Rica, do you think I would be killing her?" Rosa asked.

"Like I told you, she's not sick. If she should die here some-time soon, it would be because of her old age. And if you took her across the ocean, I don't know which would be stronger, the stress of the trip or the benefits of the sea air."

"I can't make this decision by myself," Rosa told Madam C later that day. They had met for lunch at the Corona, a homey *trattoria* two blocks from the Luna, busy as usual and brimming with the unmistakable odors of *pesto* and *farinata*.

"What does Isabel say?" Madam C asked, pouring white wine.

Rosa thought for a moment. "I think that part of her would like to go, part of her doesn't care. She has said it's irrelevant where she will die."

"False," Madam C stated, putting her glass down. "I think it *is* important where one dies, even more so than where one comes into the world. I wouldn't want to die anywhere other than on the third floor of the Luna. You know why?"

Rosa shook her head.

"Because it's the only place where I feel at home. Find out where home is to Isabel, and make sure she gets there."

"I know where Isabel's home is," Rosa said. "I have no doubt."

"Costa Rica?" Madam C guessed.

Rosa nodded.

"Then you know what to do, dear. In my opinion, dying on the way home is better than dying in a foreign place." She turned and waved her hand. "Waiter? One more serving of *fari-nata*, please."

That evening Rosa went to Vico Cinque Lampadi, where

Renato was staying. She found him in his room, reading the first chapter of *Il Capitale*.

"Do you like your books?" she asked.

"I do. The more I read them, the more familiar they seem."

"It's a good sign." she said, kissing him on the cheek. "There's something I came to ask you. Something . . . unusual."

"Tell me."

"It's about boats and dreams. You don't remember," she said, "but the very first time you and I made love at the shack you told me that wherever I'll go, you'll go." She paused. "Would you go with me on a ship across the ocean? To take Isabel home? She wants to die there and be buried next to her grandmother, on their hill, where my oil's magic ingredient was made."

"Costa Rica?" Renato wondered. "I'm not quite sure where it is, but it sounds like a long way."

Rosa nodded.

Renato pondered a moment. "You're right. I don't remember anything I said to you before my accident. But I can see myself saying to you that wherever you'll go, I'll go." He smiled. "And I don't want to get a reputation as someone who doesn't keep promises," he said jokingly. Then he spoke with a graver voice. "If you want to cross the ocean, that's what we'll do. I'm glad to be helping Isabel. She helped you when you were in trouble. It's our turn to do something for her. Will she make it all the way home?"

"I don't know," Rosa said. "Dr. Merega doesn't know, either. He says that the only way to know is to try."

"Then we'll try," said Renato.

Rosa fidgeted with her hands, then spoke with her eyes cast down. "There's a small . . . detail I need to talk to you about."

"What?" Renato asked.

She cleared her throat. "Before your accident, you were afraid of going on boats."

"Really?"

"Really. I mean, very afraid. You told me the best you could do was be on a moored boat when there were no waves. You also said you felt sick at the mere thought of being on water." She examined him with curious eyes. "Are you feeling sick now? Thinking of the boat ride?"

"No."

Rosa smiled. "Good." She hesitated a moment, then spoke in a whisper. "Maybe we should go on a small boat before boarding a ship," she suggested, "to make sure you're all right."

"Why didn't you tell me about my fears at the shack, when I said I wanted to go on a boat ride?" Renato asked.

Rosa took a deep breath. "Crossing the ocean on a ship has been my dream since I was a child. When I fell in love with you, I thought my dream would never come true. So I was happy that you couldn't remember your fear. Then Isabel helped me realize I can't decide which things you should remember and which things you should forget. So I'm telling you the truth now." She breathed deeply. "And there's another thing you should know. You said you never wanted to leave Genoa and the longshoremen because your political battles are what gives meaning to your life."

"I don't remember anything about my political battles," Renato said after a moment of reflection. "Right now, I'm reading these books and learning. I'm not concerned about leaving the longshoremen because I know it'll be a long time before I can be helpful to them in any way. Giacomo, I hear, is doing great." He paused. "As for my fear of being on water, we should experiment and find out."

Rosa took his hand. "I'll ask Giuseppe, a fisherman who buys many of my oils. He'll let us aboard his sailboat."

Renato nodded. "Let's go fishing for my fears."

Rosa didn't waste time setting up the test. Early the next morning, shortly before dawn, she went looking for Giuseppe at the beach where he kept his fishing boat ashore on a row of dark logs. She found him by the boat in the company of other fishermen and conferred with him briefly before handing him two candles scented with Paradise Oil. He took the candles, nodded, and shook hands with Rosa. The following afternoon, after Giuseppe had returned from his daily fishing trip, Rosa and Renato met him at the beach. It was a windy day, and there were waves crashing ashore. As Giuseppe and two other fishermen held the vessel at the shoreline, Rosa jumped aboard with a radiant smile. It was her first time on a boat after thinking about it for so many years, and her joy was obvious in the sparkle of her aquamarine eyes. Renato, on the other hand, boarded cautiously, unsure as to what to expect from the experience. "Sit at the stern, next to me," Giuseppe told him, jumping in. "You won't feel the effect of the waves as much." Then the two fishermen pushed the boat away from the beach, into the deep water, and Giuseppe rowed for a few minutes before lifting the sail. Off the boat went toward the more open sea as Rosa's eyes shimmered and Renato looked curiously about. Aware of the reason for their trip, Giuseppe did the best he could with the tiller to minimize the pitching and rolling of the boat, but the choppy waves, with their crests whitened by wind, shook the hull right and left without respite. Seated at the bow, Rosa looked intently at Renato the whole time, trying to spot signs of discomfort, such as seasickness and fear.

"Are you afraid I'm afraid?" Renato asked jokingly at a certain point.

She didn't answer.

"I'm fine," he said. "Enjoy the ride."

They followed the coastline east of the harbor for an hour before Giuseppe turned the boat around. "My boat is no ship," he told Renato, "and it's hard to tell for sure how you will feel when you'll board a large transatlantic steamer, but it seems to me that you have no fears. With this sea, if you had any you'd be screaming by now."

They disembarked safely on a pier. "You're not afraid!" Rosa rejoiced, jumping up and down as soon as she set foot ashore. She hugged Renato tightly. "Our trip to Costa Rica will be the best trip ever."

"I had no idea one could get so excited over a boat ride," Renato said, hugging her back.

"I told you it's the dream of my life," Rosa said. "I hope you'll be happy with it. It wouldn't be such a good dream after all if you had to be hurt by it somehow."

"Doesn't look like that will happen," Renato said. He added, "I'm glad you told me that I used to be afraid. I know more and more about myself every day."

They headed for the distillery hand in hand. Inside, they found Madam C, Maddalena, and Stella in the process of trying to convince Isabel to leave the booth. "You need a place to stay while you get ready for this trip," Madam C was saying.

"My distillery is fine," Isabel said in a determined voice.

"No," Madam C said. "We should sell this place for you before you leave. Let's go."

"I said no."

Madam C exchanged looks with Maddalena and Stella, then the three of them lifted Isabel off the floor and took her outside. "You'll live at the Luna for a couple of weeks," Madam C said in her peremptory tone, "and that's that."

"I decide where I live," Isabel disagreed. "I hardly know you. I can't live with strangers."

"I'm Rosa's mother," Madam C said. "Isn't that enough for you?"

"No."

"You'll have to make do, sweetheart," Maddalena said. "Madam C doesn't take no for an answer."

No one could argue with that. As Isabel's resistance wound down, Maddalena and Stella crossed their arms and grabbed each other's wrists. They lowered their forearms below Isabel's buttocks and, gently, Madam C pushed Isabel onto the improvised seat. Before Isabel realized what was happening, Maddalena and Stella lifted her and began to walk.

Isabel was mute with stupefaction. As the group, headed by Madam C, turned the street corner and headed for the Luna, the neighbors crossed themselves at the sight of the witch being carried away in the arms of the prostitutes.

"What kind of witchcraft is this?" one said.

"Everyone look away, or you'll turn to dust," another hollered.

Despite her protests, Isabel found herself inside the Luna around six in the evening, as Antonia was leaving for the day. "Men, old women. What's with this place," Antonia mumbled as she closed the Luna door behind her.

Madam C settled Isabel in Rosa's room. "It's quiet, it's cozy, it's close to the kitchen," she said once she and Isabel were there alone. "This bed has been Rosa's since the day she was born."

Isabel gave her a look of mistrust.

"Try it," Madam C said.

Isabel pushed on the mattress with her right hand. "For today only," she said, then laid her frail body on the white sheets. Madam C left the room without talking. When she returned ten minutes later, Isabel was sound asleep, her face softened by a peaceful smile.

Over the next days, the girls pampered Isabel, as their predecessors had once pampered little Rosa. They helped her take a warm bath in the lacquered tub on the third floor and washed the jungle of her hair twice with jasmine-perfumed soap. They were surprised to find no lice at all. "So you know, I never had lice once in my life," Isabel scolded them when they asked, "not even when I was two months on Francesco's miserable boat."

Combing her hair was another story. After ten minutes of pulling and fighting years-old knots, Stella said aloud what all the girls thought all along: "I give up. This is a job for Madam C."

Madam C took out of her drawer the wide-tooth comb she had used for years on Rosa's red curls. "It's a curse," she said, dipping the comb into Isabel's stubborn locks. "I must have done something bad in my previous life and now have been condemned to untangle crazy hair till the day I die."

Stella gave her a naughty smile. "Oh, stop it," she said. "We all know that you love taking care of people."

An hour later, Isabel's hair was untangled and, neatly combed, looked like a summer cloud. Gently, Madam C gathered it at the base of Isabel's head in a round chignon. With her new hairdo and dressed in one of Madam C's light chamber vests, Isabel, everyone agreed, looked ten years younger. "I don't know about this," Isabel mumbled, looking at herself in Madam C's mirror. "I think I'd like to have my black vest back."

Margherita coughed. "I have bad news," she said. "We washed it at the fountain with our clothes, using the soap we always use for our wash, and it lost most of its color. Right now, it looks more like a stained rag than anything anyone would want to wear."

"I knew I shouldn't have taken it off," Isabel moaned.

"Must be a magic thing," Stella whispered.

"We'll get you a black vest, Isabel," Maddalena reassured her. "I promise."

To console her, Stella took Isabel to her room, where she showed her all her amulets and talked about her witchcraft, which she had learned as a child from her mother, a woman from Africa almost two meters tall. "What about you, Isabel?" she asked. "Where did you learn your witchcraft?"

"Perfumes are not witchcraft," Isabel explained calmly. "They're an art. Do you know the difference between witchcraft and art?"

Stella shook her head.

"Witchcraft is made up of rituals that come from popular beliefs. Lots of people can perform the same rituals. Art," she said, placing a hand on her chest, "comes from your heart. No one can imitate it or take it from you."

"I don't know about that," Stella argued with a friendly smile. "But," she added, "I know for sure that no one will ever be able to imitate *you*, my dear."

Because of the proximity of Rosa's room to the kitchen, Isabel ended up spending time with Antonia during the afternoon. Despite her initial mistrust, Antonia grew fond of Isabel in a very short time, helped by the fact that Isabel volunteered to share with her the recipes of her soups, which Antonia gradually included in the Luna menu, gaining the approval of all the Luna people. Isabel never told Antonia, or anyone else for that matter, about the white powder she had twice sprinkled on Rosa's soup and, in a few instances, on her own. It was opium. She had bought a handful of it years earlier from the Spanish sailors who brought her the eucalyptus leaves, and used it following Azul's teachings about the prodigious healing qualities of poppy seeds and their by-products when used sparingly and on the right occasions. In gratitude for the shared recipes, Antonia cooked for Isabel her best vegetarian dishes: *farinata, torta pasqualina*, and *torta di bietole*. Overall, Isabel blended into the Luna's life gracefully.

"With Isabel in the kitchen, it's like having Rosa here all over again," commented Margherita.

"The difference is," Madam C said, "we don't need to watch for her to stay out of the parlor."

"She knows better." Stella giggled.

"Do you think that Isabel understands completely what's going on here?" Maddalena asked. "She seems so out of this world."

"Isabel," Madam C said in a grave tone, "knows a lot more about life than you and I can ever imagine."

"But she hasn't left her distillery in sixty years," Margherita said doubtfully.

Madam C nodded and smiled. "That's the beauty of it, my dear."

The only accident involving Isabel and the Luna clients happened on a stormy night, while the parlor was packed and the clients particularly loud. Isabel stepped into the parlor from the kitchen around midnight, shoeless and in a dark gown. She looked right and left at the girls and the clients; then, with no hesitation, crossed the room under everyone's stunned eyes. From across the counter, she tugged at Madam C's sleeve twice. "The wind may have broken a window back there," she said, then walked away before Madam C could recover from the surprise. All the men in the room gaped at Isabel as she passed by. "Good Lord," one of them grimaced.

"Is she a ghost?" said another.

Stella took Isabel's arm. "Don't be bothered by what they say," she told her as she pushed her back in the kitchen. "I know what ghosts look like. Nothing like you, dear. Keep this door closed now, and go to sleep."

In the parlor, the men wouldn't stop talking. "What was that, Madam C?" a sailor asked, rubbing a hand on Margherita's hips. "Someone you save for a special treat?"

Madam C gave him one of her icy glares. "She's my mother," she said. "Don't you dare make fun of her, *capito*?"

There was an exception to Isabel's idyllic relationship with the Luna people: Cesare Cortimiglia. "I don't like him," Isabel told Antonia one day. "He smokes like a chimney and never looks you in the eyes."

Cesare Cortimiglia never looked Isabel in the eyes because he was afraid of her. He had heard the shopkeepers talking about her many times during his days of sitting on Piazza Banchi, and despite his attempt to convince himself that there were no such things as witches, he was never capable of overcoming his fear. He had arrived at the Luna a few days ahead of Isabel, in the company of Madam C, carrying one suitcase and, with his long beard and red-rimmed eyes, looking like a creature from another world. "Girls," Madam C had said after summoning everyone in the parlor, "I believe you all know my friend Cesare. He'll live at the Luna, in my quarters, as of today." She turned around and smiled at the still disoriented former mayor. "Please make him feel at home."

He climbed the stairs with weary steps. As he put down his suitcase in Madam C's bedroom, he looked at the bed with melancholy eyes. "So many memories . . ." he whispered, then smiled as he saw himself lying naked on those sheets, surrounded by a flock of young girls, celebrating his farewell to the brothels. He blinked as he noticed, on the nightstand, his beloved briar pipe. All caught up in the fever of his love for Rosa, and later in his dementia with the poetry and the handkerchief, he had forgotten all about it, until Madam C had mentioned it in his living room earlier that week. Ever since the mishap on Rosa's birthday, he hadn't had a single smoke. He took the pipe gingerly, as if it were a jewel. "Here," Madam C said, handing him a box of extra-long matches. "I took good care of your pipe, because I knew you'd be coming someday to reclaim it. There's Cuban tobacco in it, ready to be smoked." He took the matches and with a flick of his wrist struck one of them and dipped the flame in the bowl of the pipe. As he began to puff, a look of contentment filled his face. Madam C, who hadn't allowed anyone to smoke in her rooms since the end of the mayor's farewell marathon, watched him and said nothing at all. His only chore later that day was to cut his chest-long, matted beard and shave.

"Now I can recognize you," Madam C said as they both looked in a mirror at his hairless face. "You haven't changed much on the outside."

He thought a moment. "I had a battle going on inside. I don't know myself anymore."

"We'll figure you out, mayor," Madam C said, taking his hand in hers. "What else have we left to do?"

He asked, "May I call you Clotilde?"

"Why?" she said, surprised.

"I like it better than Madam C."

"You told me you liked Madam C. I remember your exact words. You said, 'I like it. It's exotic. I'm already turned on.'"

"I lied," he said. "May I call you Clotilde?"

Madam C took a step back. "What else did you lie about?"

"May I?"

She pursed her lips then, spoke in a serious voice. "Only in private. Don't you ever call me that in front of the girls."

Cesare nodded and took a seat by Madam C's fireplace.

She stood in front of him. "Tell me, Cesare, are you happy to be here? Or are you here only because I dragged you out of your house?"

He waited a while. "I'm not sure that I know how to define happiness," he said gravely, staring at the *graniglia* floor. "I know I feel like I woke up from a bad dream, and I have this certainty I can't explain that the bad dream will not return." He looked her in the eyes. "And when I look at you, I'm at peace. Is this happiness?"

Madam C lowered herself into a chair next to him. "I guess so, Cesare. I guess so."

As life at the Luna settled into new routines with new people, Rosa and Renato took care of the distillery and the flower room, both badly in need of sprucing up after Isabel had occupied them uninterruptedly for sixty-one years. The idea was to make the space usable as a store and sell it before Isabel's departure for Costa Rica. First, Rosa and Renato boxed all the oil bottles and brought them to the Luna, together with Isabel's old rocking chair. Then they scrubbed the floors, washed the walls, threw away the old mattresses and the worn-out sheets, cleaned and disinfected the stove, and left the windows and the glass door open day and night to get rid of the stubborn odors. They enlisted the help of Santina, who scrubbed the place once more with a mixture of water, alcohol, and Marseille soap. Finally, following Isabel's advice, they lit five bergamot candles and vaporized pine oil. The neighbors watched the cleaning operations vigilantly, taking due notice of Isabel's absence as well as of the absence of the steam. Their conclusion was unanimous and was passed on from house to house in whispers and loud shouts: "The witch is dead." Infuriated by the gossip and exasperated by the curious looks, Rosa hung a sign on the booth wall: *Isabel is not a witch*, the sign said, *and she's not dead either.* The neighbors shrugged. "She's dead," they went on saying, "with prostitutes at her bedside."

One week after the cleaning process had been completed, a merchant offered to buy the booth for little more than half its market value. "It's my last offer," he told Giacomo, who was handling the sale on Isabel's behalf. "No one in his right mind would pay a higher price for a space known to have hosted a stinking sorceress for more than half a century. Take it or leave it." After a group consultation in the Luna parlor, the unanimous decision was to accept the offer and sell. Isabel drew a cross at the bottom of the papers with a shaky hand and let out a long, heavy-hearted sigh.

"Well," Madam C said with a rare relaxed smile, "now that we took care of business and Isabel is a rich woman, there's only one thing left to do before she, Renato, and Rosa leave us." She paused a moment and looked at the eight people—Maddalena,

Margherita, Stella, Rosa, Renato, Giacomo, Isabel, and Cesare—standing around her. "Party."

There was an awkward silence. "You can't be serious," Margherita said, squinting her eyes.

Maddalena gazed at the people in the room. "I don't know about you," she said with a long face, "but I've had enough of partying at the Luna."

"Oh, come on," Madam C urged. "Would someone please be happy around here? Let's not call it a party. Let's call it a . . . family dinner." She waited for a response. "What do you say?"

The party/family dinner was set for the upcoming Wednesday, a day everyone had agreed on because it was three days before the ship departure and would work well with Stella's fear of Fridays. "And there will be no *libeccio* blowing," Margherita said, "so hopefully nothing will go wrong this time."

On that Wednesday, the only outsiders at the party were Giacomo, who had returned to work and to leading the longshoremen's political battles; Renato, still struggling with his lack of memory but better able to come to terms with it, mostly thanks to Rosa; Marco, in brand-new, clean clothes; and Roberto Passalacqua, paler and shyer than ever. Everyone else at the gathering lived or, in Rosa's case, had lived at the Luna. When Rosa arrived that day and stepped into the parlor, she saw Cesare Cortimiglia for the first time since the day he had left Piazza Banchi. He was standing by the counter, talking to Maddalena. She looked at him from a distance, unable to identify that deeply wrinkled, red-eyed old man with the man who had taken off his clothes and fallen asleep in her bed on the night of her sixteenth birthday. As for Cesare, he gave Rosa a quick glance, then turned away from her and poured Madam C a glass of Barbera. Isabel, in a brand-new black vest purchased for her by the Luna girls, was seated on her rocking chair in the middle of the room.

"See?" Rosa told her. "You can go to parties after all."

"I guess," Isabel said. She paused a moment. "I can't believe I'm doing this."

"What?" Madam C asked.

"Going again on a ship across the ocean."

"I can't believe I walked into your booth a year ago," Rosa said. "I was so afraid."

"Attention, everybody," Margherita shouted. "I'd like to read a poem for Renato and Rosa."

"Oh no," Cesare moaned, cupping his hands over his ears.

"I thought you had come to like poetry," Madam C said, amused.

"Only because I was miserable and alone," he replied. "Now that I have you," he added, taking her hand, "the hell with poetry and poets."

Despite Cesare's protest, Margherita read one of Petrarca's most famous poems:

> " 'Si traviato e'l folle mio desio
> a seguitar costei che 'n fuga e' volta
> e de' lacci d'Amor leggiera e sciolta
> vola dinnanzi al lento correr mio;
> che quando richiamando pur l'envio
> per la secura strada men m'ascolta:
> ne' mi vale spronarlo o dargli volta;
> ch'Amor per sua natura il fa restio.' "

At the end, as everyone applauded, there were knocks on the door. "I have a surprise," Madam C said. She let in a small man with a limp and a young boy who was carrying two heavy bags. "This man," she said, "is a photographer, and I asked him to come here to take pictures of us."

The photographer and his helper took some time to set up their gear. Then the photographer asked everyone to stand by the counter. "Don't breathe," he said, disappearing behind a black cloth. A second later, a flash blinded everyone's eyes.

"Take more," Madam C told the photographer, then whispered in Cesare's ear, "In case this is the last time we'll all be together."

"I want you to have this," Maddalena told Rosa when the photography session was over. She handed her the black wig.

"I miss it already," Giacomo chuckled behind Maddalena's back, "but you can have it."

"Thank you," Rosa said, hugging Maddalena. "There are so many memories with it."

"I envy you, you know," Maddalena said. "For a Gypsy like me, five years in the same town is a long stretch."

"Why don't you come with us?" Renato asked.

Maddalena shook her head. "And leave the Luna, Madam C's tantrums, Stella's prophecies, and Margherita's poems? You must be joking."

Meanwhile, in a corner of the crowded parlor, Roberto Passalacqua was not handling the attention of the Luna girls too well. Margherita, intrigued by his pallor and shyness since the first time he had set foot in the brothel to announce Cesare Cortimiglia's acceptance to attend Rosa's party, was trying all sorts of tricks to loosen him up and make him smile: drinks, furtive caresses, jokes. The more she tried, the more withdrawn Roberto became. Stella joined her in the game. "How old are you?" she asked at a certain point.

"Thirty-one," he replied in a whisper.

"You look and act like a child," Margherita said. "When is the last time you were with a woman?"

Nearby, Cesare overheard the question. "As far as I know," he said, "he's never been with one."

Stella turned around. "You mean to tell me he's a virgin?"

Cesare nodded as Roberto blushed all the way to the tips of his spiky hair.

"How's that possible?" Margherita asked.

"I haven't been too successful with women," Roberto murmured. "My stomach twists whenever I see a woman I like. My legs become heavy, and I can't speak. I open and close my mouth like a fish."

"You need professional help in a hurry," Margherita said, taking him by the arm and pulling him toward the stairs. "Let's go."

Roberto pulled back, trying to disentangle himself from Margherita's hands. "Thank you, but no," he babbled.

"What do you mean, 'no'?" Cesare said. "Go for it, my boy. Trust me, there's nothing better than losing your virginity to a master of the art of love."

"Make it two masters," Stella said, pushing Roberto toward Margherita.

Caught between two fires, the young man stopped arguing and let Margherita and Stella lead him up the stairs. Everyone in the parlor whistled and applauded. "The bill is on me," Cesare shouted, raising his glass.

As the threesome reached the top of the stairs and disappeared down the hallway, Madam C spoke into Cesare's ear. "Remember?"

He turned to her. "As if it were yesterday."

The celebration in the parlor went on a while longer. Finally, Renato took Rosa and Giacomo aside. Rosa was still holding the black wig. "Remember what Giacomo said on the train?" Renato asked Rosa. "That you had a story to tell about this wig?"

Rosa opened her eyes wide as Giacomo and Renato exchanged a glance of complicity.

"Just so you know," Renato said, "Giacomo told me everything."

Rosa blushed, then stared at Giacomo. "Traitor."

Renato chuckled. "It was clever, I must say. Would you put it on for me? So I can see whom I fell in love with the first time?"

"No," Rosa said.

"Please," begged Renato.

Slowly, Rosa put the black wig on her head. "You are not mad?" she asked in a shaky voice.

"My dear Tramonto," Renato said, sliding an arm around Rosa's shoulders. "I have decided that I will not worry about what I can't remember. Giacomo vows that at the time I left Genoa, when I had all my memories with me, I was madly in love with you. I wasn't upset about the black wig or anything else. That and the way I feel now are all that matter. I love you, on or off the water, black or red hair. I loved you before the accident, and I love you now, even though I can't remember I loved you before. I can't imagine ever falling out of love with you. All I'm asking of you is that you love me forever."

Madam C arrived as Rosa was wiping her tears. "Rosa?" she called. "Would you remove that silly wig and come with me to the third floor? There's something I want to tell you. Excuse us, please," she told Renato. "She'll be back in a moment."

In the sitting room, Madam C opened a pouch and took out of it a roll of banknotes. "For you," she said, handing them to Rosa. "You will need them. But this is not the main reason I asked you to come up here."

Rosa looked at her inquisitively.

"Sit down," Madam C said. "Do you know what cremation is?"

Rosa shook her head.

"It's a process that turns a body into ashes," Madam C explained. "The law forbids it." She took a deep breath. "When Angela understood that she wouldn't survive, she asked me not to bury her. She was afraid of darkness and tight spaces. She told me she wanted to stay at the Luna, as close as possible to where her child would grow up. There's a blacksmith who lives two blocks from here and who, unknown to the authorities, cremates bodies. He does it only to help the people of the *caruggi* who are poor and don't have the means to pay for a plot at the cemetery or provide for a funeral and a burial. He did it for me because he was a client." She walked to the fireplace and picked up the vase with the lid. "In this vase are your mother's ashes. Now you know why I got so upset when you threatened to break it."

Gently, Rosa took the vase from Madam C's hands and said, "Now I know why it felt so heavy when I picked it up." She looked at Madam C. "Can I open it?"

"Sure."

Gingerly, Rosa looked inside. She whispered, "This must be the reason I always felt that Angela was near me."

"I never told you about these ashes," Madam C said, "because it's hard to explain the aftermath of death to a child. You're no longer a child, and you'll leave us soon, so I thought"—she dried her tears—"that you should take Angela with you."

Rosa said, "Can we put the ashes in two vases?"

Madam C nodded, then smiled. "You have no idea how much I still miss her."

"I miss her, too," Rosa said, caressing the rim of the vase.

The following morning, two days before Rosa's departure, Antonia arrived early at the Luna, carrying the largest grocery bags the girls had ever seen. In the kitchen, she took out dishes, pots, and pans and began cooking whatever food she thought Rosa should have with her on her way to Costa Rica. With her hawk eyes, Madam C supervised the preparation. "After this," Antonia said, placing a torte in the oven, "I'm retiring. This place is not the same."

"Don't even think about it," Madam C scolded her. "I'm already losing a daughter. I'd like to keep my cook, if you don't mind."

THE SCENT OF ROSA'S OIL 259

"A man living in a brothel is bad luck," Antonia grunted.

"Cesare living here is a blessing," Stella said, coming in with Margherita from the parlor. She pointed at Madam C. "Look at her. She's never looked better in her life."

"And, most important," Margherita added, "she doesn't act crazy anymore. That alone is a success."

Madam C looked them in the eyes. "I never acted crazy in my life. I had my reasons for what I did, and they were good ones."

"We could argue over this for a long time," Stella pointed out. "Why don't we just do what's left to do before Rosa leaves us?"

Madam C lifted her chin and placed her hands on her hips. "Antonia and I are working, as you can see. What about you two? Is there anything you'd like to do other than waste our time?"

Stella placed a hand on Margherita's shoulder and laughed. "I guess love can cure bitter souls only to an extent. The essence remains."

"Get out of my kitchen," Madam C growled, brandishing a bread knife.

EPILOGUE

The ship, half-cargo, half-passenger, would head for the Colombian port of Cartagena after one stop in Morocco and one in Portugal. On the deck, by the rail, gazing down at the pier, stood Rosa, Renato, and Isabel. Next to them were three suitcases and a cloth bag filled with packages of Antonia's food. At the edge of the pier, among a small crowd, Madam C, Maddalena, Stella, Margherita, Antonia, Cesare, Giacomo, Marco, and Roberto stared at the ship's deck, waving. "Do you have everything you need?" Madam C shouted.

Rosa nodded. In her suitcase, besides clothes, she had one of the photographs taken at the Luna, the black wig, a box with half her mother's ashes, the books Madam C had bought for her when she had stopped going to school, the dried blossom Isabel had given her, the dried petals of Renato's rose, Angela's earrings, and the little that was left of her perfect oil. Around her neck was a leather string with a pendant—Renato's blue stone. Renato had packed all his books; Isabel, only her discolored black vest and a few bottles of oil. She had left most of the bottles and her rocking chair at the Luna, for the girls to use. From the pier, Maddalena, Margherita, and Stella blew kisses, crying. At some point, Maddalena waved the cardboard box with the tarot cards inside. On the deck, Rosa muttered unheard, "Yes, Maddalena, your cards were right."

Giacomo mouthed the words, "Write to me." Renato nodded in silence.

Then the siren rose above the sounds of the port, and the ship slowly detached itself from the pier like an elephant struggling to set its body in motion. Rosa held Isabel's hand and slid her other arm around Renato. As the ship began crossing the port toward the exit, she was struck by the thought that the world was so immense and yet so small. All her world was there, in her suitcase, in the nine people who stood silently on the pier, and in the two she was holding at that moment. While she breathed the biting odor of the saltwater, she felt in her nostrils all the perfumes and stenches she had smelled in Isabel's booth, the odors of the Luna kitchen, those of the parlor, and the fragrances of the flowers she had picked on the hills with Madam C when she was still a child. "Thank you, Angela," she whispered, "for giving me my dream."

"I'm scared," Isabel said. "This was a crazy idea."

"Crazy ideas are what make the world turn, Isabel," Renato said. "Aren't you glad to be going home?"

"Yes," she admitted. "And I'm also glad because you two are together and I get to be with you a while longer. Rosa, the day you walked into my booth was the best day I had since leaving Costa Rica sixty-one years ago. And you, Renato, are a very special man. In all my life, I never met or heard of anyone who fell in love with the same woman three times." She took a deep breath. "I must go inside now. It's much too difficult for me to be looking at Genoa from the water." She began to walk away, then stopped and turned around. "My perfect oil," she said, looking intently at Rosa, "is hyssop and sandalwood with hints of tangerine." She opened her eyes wide. "I can tell my life is over," she murmured to herself. "I gave all my secrets away."

Quietly, Renato and Rosa watched Isabel open a cabin door and step inside.

"How are you feeling?" Rosa asked once the two of them were alone on the deck.

"Fine," Renato said.

"Your stomach doesn't hurt?"

"No."

"And you're not shaking?"

"No."

"I'm glad," After a moment, she said softly. "We wouldn't be on this boat had it not been for your accident, you know."

"Tell me again how we met," Renato said. "I love that story."

"I dipped my handkerchief in my perfect oil and dropped it. You picked it up"—she stretched her lips in a naughty smile—"and instantly fell in love."

"And then?"

"We have time. I'll tell you everything that happened between us."

"Without holding back?"

Rosa nodded. "Promise."

"Did you really wear that black wig and call yourself Tramonto to get my attention?" he asked.

"You were very judgmental at the time."

"I was stupid," he said. "I'm so happy now. Are you happy?"

"Very." She paused. "It's strange. I'm leaving the city where I grew up and the people who raised me, and I'm standing on moving water, going toward the unknown, but for the first time ever I feel like I found my place in the world. How do you explain it?"

Renato said, "That's what happens when your dreams come true. I found my place in the world when you came to rescue me at the monastery." He raised his index finger. "Actually, let me rephrase. I found my place in the world the moment I smelled your oil at the monastery."

Rosa fidgeted gently with the blue stone. She thought of the Valles' farmhouse with its horse chestnut trees; the hostel where she, Maddalena, and Madam C had spent the night; Giacomo behind the broken furniture, wounded and in pain; Renato's mildly surprised face when he had rushed to meet her in her red hair at his apartment door. She smiled as with her mind's eye she saw Tramonto running stealthily through the night to lose her suitor. As the ship turned and headed for the open sea and Genoa's steep hills and calm port waters became an image in Rosa's memory and no longer real, she wondered when exactly Renato had understood that the odor he had smelled on Tramonto's skin and followed like a hound in the *caruggi* had been instead the scent of Rosa's oil.